"Sharply drawn, intricate, and interesting, Coleman's *Fighting for Bread and Roses* is a delight."

> —ALTON GANSKY
> Author of *The Incumbent*

"A page-turner. Coleman blends the past with the present into a spellbinding plot."

> —DIANN MILLS
> Inspirational writer and speaker

"Lynn Coleman's newest work is a well researched, fast-paced read that hooked me from the first page to the last. . . . *Fighting for Bread and Roses* is a winning combination; engrossing, enjoyable, and educational."

> —CARMEN LEAL
> Author of *The Twenty-Third Psalm for Caregivers* and
> *The Twenty-Third Psalm for Those Who Grieve*

"While I have savored her previous works, *Fighting for Bread and Roses* moves Lynn into a whole new strata! The history and story line weave together seamlessly, making it a fascinating read—educating and stimulating."

> —MARITA LITTAUER
> President, CLASServices, Inc.

FIGHTING *for*
BREAD & ROSES

FIGHTING *for* BREAD & ROSES

A Novel

LYNN A. COLEMAN

Kregel
Publications

Fighting for Bread & Roses: A Novel

© 2005 by Lynn A. Coleman

Published by Kregel Publications, a division of Kregel, Inc., P.O. Box 2607, Grand Rapids, MI 49501.

The persons and events portrayed in this work are the creations of the author, and any resemblance to persons living or dead is purely coincidental.

Scripture quotations are from the *Holy Bible, New International Version®*. Copyright © 1973, 1978, 1984 by International Bible Society. Used by permission of Zondervan Publishing House. All rights reserved.

Published in association with the literary agency of Janet Kobobel Grant, Books and Such, 4788 Carissa Ave., Santa Rosa, CA 95405.

Library of Congress Cataloging-in-Publication Data
Coleman, Lynn A.
Fighting for bread and roses: a novel / by Lynn A. Coleman.
    p. cm.
    1. Detective and mystery stories—Authorship—Fiction.
2. Women textile workers—Crimes against—Fiction.
3. Lawrence Strike, 1912—Fiction. 4. Strikes and lockouts—
Fiction. 5. Lawrence (Mass.)—Fiction. 6. Women
novelists—Fiction. I. Title.
PS3603.O4353F54   2005
813'.54—dc22   2005013164

ISBN 0-8254-2409-7

Printed in the United States of America

05 06 07 08 09 / 5 4 3 2

FIGHTING *for*
BREAD & ROSES

Prologue

Anna Lopizzo pushed her way through the surging crowd. Her heart pumped with frustration as she edged toward the center of the gathering. All around her the striking workers shouted slogans and shook their fists. Anna shouldered her way past a gray-haired woman who was screaming in Italian, *"Pan é rose! Pan é rose!"*

Bread and roses.

"Get back to work!" A pencil-thin man stepped from the police line, waved his rifle with its gleaming bayonet, and yelled at the strikers.

Anna drew back. The cold wind bit her nose and cheeks. *The mill owners had no right to cut our pay,* she reminded herself. *And those machines are dangerous.* Sylvia Giovanni, her best friend, had already lost a finger. Anna knew it wouldn't be long before she'd lose one too, if she could not keep her mind focused on the job. They had to strike. But how long could she hold out with no money and no food?

"Anna!" Sylvia waved.

Anna threaded her way through the crowd toward her friend.

"Stay close," Sylvia cautioned, looping her arm around Anna's. "The militia has stabbed a few of the men already."

Anna nodded. They stood their ground, shouting with the others and waving their arms to demand better pay and safer working conditions. The restless crowd on the street corner spilled over the curb, inching closer to the line of militia and special police.

Anna followed Sylvia's gaze. She was staring at a young, curly blond-haired militiaman standing to their left. Sylvia shivered. "I can't believe they have knives on the ends of their guns."

"It seems terribly unfair," Anna added above the din of protests, roiling forth in a sea of languages. She waved her hands and shouted in her native tongue, *"Pan é rose!"*

She needed the bread, and she wouldn't mind a rose every now and again. But year after year of twelve-hour days had washed so many dreams down the gutter.

"Did you eat tonight?" Anna whispered to Sylvia.

"Bread and molasses." Sylvia shook her fist in the air. "No pay, no work," she chanted.

Anna chimed in with the same chant.

"What about you?"

The swell of the crowd pushed them back toward the street. "I had some leftover beans, but my cupboard is nearly empty."

"Mine too. We'll get through. This strike has to be costing the owners a lot of money."

The freezing wind cut through Anna's thin coat. She clutched it tighter, losing her hold on Sylvia. "Yes, but their pockets are deep."

Anna stepped toward the street. She needed more space. The sound of a gunshot pierced the air. At the same instant, a hot iron burned in her heart. Gasping for breath, she fell to the ground. The crowd went silent.

The cold cobblestones under her seemed to soften. She gulped for air.

People were looking down at her, mouths agape. What were they saying?

"Anna?" She heard Sylvia scream.

She opened her mouth for one more breath . . .

Chapter One

Lindsey blinked at the newspaper story displayed on the library microfilm monitor. Three lines—only three lines. But in her mind's eye she could see the incident as if she were watching a television screen. Blood trickled from Anna Lopizzo's chest . . .

Lindsey's mind shifted to another time, another city, another book she'd been researching. Fear spiraled down to the pit of her stomach and lodged there. Her hand froze on the control knob of the microfilm machine and cold sweat beaded on her forehead.

Squeezing her eyes shut, she pushed the memory away. *Not now, not here.*

Taking in a deep breath, she let it out slowly and released the knob, forcing herself to concentrate on the here and now. Two years had passed since she had witnessed that murder in New Orleans. One year since . . . Lindsey held back the memory. Before leaving Miami, she and her husband, Marc, had talked about the very real possibility that her research would bring back the recurring nightmares.

Lindsey thought back on the transcripts she'd found on the Internet regarding the Bread and Roses strike. She needed to stay focused.

"Anna Lopizzo," she whispered. "Who killed you?"

"May I help you?" A thin woman in a fitted wool suit interrupted Lindsey's musing. She hadn't seen this librarian the other day when she'd asked about microfilm copies of the old newspapers from the time of the strike.

"I'm researching the Bread and Roses strike of 1912. Do you have any additional resources here?" Lindsey asked.

"You've pulled up the newspapers from the time, I see. Have you looked at some of the books in the resource library?"

Lindsey smiled. "Planning on that next."

The librarian pointed to the waist-high bookshelves in the far left-hand corner of the room. "I work with the reference material. If there's anything I can help you with, I'll be glad to. You look familiar. Are you from here?"

"No, I grew up in Maine."

"Sorry. I'm pretty good with faces. I thought maybe you were here for the high school reunion."

"Nope." Lindsey smiled. "I'll finish up here and head over to the resource stacks. Thank you for the help."

"You're welcome." The woman nodded and walked away, straightening a few books and picking up some magazines left on a table.

Looking at the screen, Lindsey forced her mind back to the brief newspaper account. The sooner she got her research done, the sooner she'd be able to return to Marc in Miami. It had taken six months after her New Orleans research trip before she and Marc were comfortable with her going anywhere alone. He supported her passion for writing, and traveling was easier now with both the boys away at college.

Anna Lopizzo was the first to die during the textile workers' strike. Nine strikers claimed that Officer Oscar Benoit had killed her. The police said that one of the strikers shot her. A couple of days later, the men who had come up from New York to help organize the mill workers were charged with being accessories to murder.

Lindsey drummed her fingers on the Formica countertop. There was a story here. She could smell it.

Thirty minutes and a couple dozen printed pages later, Lindsey worked her way over to the resource section of the library. In the past, researching a novel had always been fun, a source of excitement. Today, she struggled to remain objective.

She scanned the shelves.

"Ms. Marc?" Lindsey jumped. The slender librarian stood beside her. A smile creased her friendly face. "I thought it was you."

Lindsey cleared her throat. Her most recent novel, *City Streets,* had hit the best-seller list. And she'd seen the book featured on the display shelves as she entered the library. Of course she'd be recognized. "How can I help you?"

"Nothing," the librarian stammered. "I—I came over to see if I could lend you a hand. I didn't mean to startle you."

Lindsey chided herself for being so edgy. "No problem."

"I've put some books on the Bread and Roses strike in the resource room. Would you like me to let you in?"

"Yes, thanks."

The librarian took a key from her waistband pocket and unlocked the door. "Here ya go. I'll note the time I let you in on the sign-up sheet, but you'll need to sign out when you finish."

"Thank you."

Lindsey had used special collections housed in climate-controlled rooms like this one in many small libraries around the country. Here, she found a few books written after the strike, some others about the organizing of the unions, and a few chapters and sections in other books that referred to the Lawrence strike.

Two hours later, she placed her laptop computer back in her briefcase and carried the books to the reference desk.

"Were they helpful?" the librarian asked.

"Yes, thank you."

"Please sign here." The woman pointed to the notebook schedule for the resource room.

Lindsey picked up the pen and signed.

"I'm supposed to ask to see your driver's license, but . . ." Her eyes glanced down at the book.

She noticed the librarian's questioning look and pulled out her Florida driver's license. Although the public knew her by her pen name, a combination of her own and her husband's first names, her real name was Lindsey Taylor.

"I'm a fan, Ms. Marc."

Interesting, she didn't call me by my real name. Lindsey's eyes were drawn from the woman toward a male librarian standing on the other side of the room behind another counter.

"I was wondering if you'll be coming back again?" the woman whispered. "Possibly tomorrow? I'd love for you to sign my books. Your books . . . I mean, if you'd sign my copies of your books."

Lindsey reached over and placed a reassuring hand on the woman's forearm. "I'd love to. I'll be back sometime tomorrow."

The librarian smiled. "Is there anything I could look up for you between now and then? I'm happy to help. May I research and assemble some book notations referencing the strike?"

Lindsey liked to do her own research, but considering how poor her concentration was today, she accepted. "I found precious little on John Rami. If you could find something on him, I'd appreciate it."

"How do you spell that?" The librarian lifted a yellow pencil and scribbled down Lindsey's response.

Lindsey glanced at her watch. Marc was due out of court, and Lindsey wanted to call him before going to an appointment with a local reporter. She hurried out into the nippy spring air, cinching her jacket tighter. *Twenty years in South Florida does thin one's blood.*

> ← ←

Straightening up from under the hood of a midnight blue Chevy sedan, he took a deep pull on his cigarette. What can a person do in a library for five hours? He grabbed his cell phone and auto-dialed.

"Hey, man, it's me. You'll never guess who I saw in town . . ."

Three minutes later, a middle-aged blonde woman carrying a brown briefcase exited the library.

"I gotta go," the man said as he watched the woman fumbling for her keys next to a white Toyota. He clicked off the phone and stuck it back on his belt.

Opening the car door, he leaned inside and tested the engine. He knew full well it functioned fine, but he smiled for any possible onlookers and exited the driver's side to close the hood. The woman pulled out of the parking lot, talking on her cell phone.

Some jobs are just too easy, he thought. Putting the car in drive, he slipped into traffic. The small red indicator light on his tracking device blinked to the right. He could follow five miles behind with this thing. *Yup, this job is a piece of cake.*

He flicked his cigarette out the window and checked the rear-view mirror.

JANUARY 30, 1912 - LAWRENCE, MASS.

With unwavering steps, Sylvia walked closer to the spot where Anna had been killed. Grief threatened to swallow her up, but determination coursed through her veins like fire through a furnace. The police had killed Anna, but the mill owners were the root of the problem. The police were just their puppets.

But why Anna? *They probably thought her death would cause us all to run in fear.*

Bile rose in her stomach as she joined the picket line along the sidewalk. She would not work—not today or any day—until the issues with the mill owners were resolved. Anna's death had to count for something. Sylvia couldn't give in now.

"Sylvia?" James Donovan hailed her from across the street.

Sylvia waved back. His handsome face, with that thick, curly black hair and blue eyes as rich as a summer sky, awakened her. Sylvia shook off her meandering thoughts. This was a time to fight. She had no time for romance—not that an Italian girl could marry an Irish boy anyway.

"How are you faring?" James asked as he approached, sidestepping three teenage boys who were sauntering down the street as if nothing was happening around them. Sylvia thought one of them looked like John Rami, a young Syrian who worked at the mill.

She tightened her worn woolen coat against a blast of winter air. "I'll go hungry a hundred nights before I let these"—she broke off in frustrated emotion—"these animals kill another one of us."

"I heard about Anna. 'Tis a shame to be sure." James placed a caring hand upon her shoulder. "Me prayers are with you."

The sound of the militia approaching on horseback drummed down the street.

"Pan é rose," Sylvia yelled as the bayonet-toting soldiers came into view.

"This can't be good," James whispered.

"Killers!" The crowd roared their protests. "Murderers!"

Fists rose in the air. The soldiers marched on. A dark-haired sentry's face reddened as he yelled at the boys to get off the street. James wrapped his arm around Sylvia and held her close. Another soldier joined the sentry, jabbing his bayonet at the boys.

The crowd gasped as young John Rami fell to the street.

"Killers!" a young man in the crowd called out.

James and Sylvia's cries were silenced.

"Dear God in heaven," Sylvia gasped. "What's happening here?" Tears burned icy trails down her cheeks.

Chapter Two

Lindsey drove through the narrow city streets and crossed the bridge, heading back toward the interstate and her hotel. The houses along the way were typical New England clapboards with multiple stories. Not like Miami at all. She rolled down her window to inhale the fresh scent of lilacs, rekindling childhood memories of grandmother's spring picnics.

As she drove, she retrieved a voice-mail message from Jeff, her oldest son, about wedding arrangements. After she returned Jeff's call, she auto-dialed Marc's cell phone.

"Hi, honey. How's it going?" he answered.

"Wonderful."

"Uh-oh, I've heard that response before. How long will you be away this time?"

"A week, maybe less. There has to be more to Anna Lopizzo's murder." She was disappointed with how little had been written about the woman's death. "It appears to have been seriously underreported."

Marc chuckled.

"How was court today?" she asked.

"Great. I think I've made the jury question the circumstantial evidence."

"Well, if anyone can get him off, it's you," she said. For years, she had worked side by side with Marc, doing research and proofreading his briefs. After several high-profile cases, some of their friends had wondered aloud how a Christian could defend such criminals, but Lindsey respected her husband and his decisions about whom he would represent.

"Thanks. Hey, Lins, what do you think of my flying up there and joining you for the weekend? Maybe take a trip up to Maine and visit with your folks, or"—he lowered his voice—"we could go to Rockport, just the two of us."

A flutter of excitement traveled through her. "That would be wonderful."

Lindsey glanced into the rearview mirror. A dark sedan pulled up behind her. The little hairs on the back of her neck rose.

"All right, babe. Before you go, I need to tell you that I had a brief episode in the library today. It was really brief, but the old nightmare flashed before me after I visualized Anna's death."

"I'm sorry. Are you okay?"

"I'm fine."

"If you need me to stay an extra day to help you wrap up your work, I can try and clear my calendar," he offered.

"I'm okay, I promise. I just wanted you to know, as agreed." They had been worried about her taking off to do research alone so soon after the trial in New Orleans. "One more thing. Jeff and Lisa would like a lobster bake for their rehearsal dinner."

"What? Maine lobsters, I suppose."

Lindsey laughed. "Are there any others?" She braked for a red light.

"No lobsters that matter," he chuckled. "What did you tell the kids?"

"I said I'd talk with you and Dad."

"What we don't do for our kids," he quipped. "Call your father. Tell him we'll need the seaweed too, and I'll spring for the expense of shipping it all down here."

Lindsey smiled.

She checked the rearview mirror.

"Lins, I've got to run. Love ya."

"Love you, too," she mumbled, pulling into the hotel parking lot. The driver of the dark sedan passed without glancing at her. It was a standard four-door with dark blue paint. *There must be a million of them on the streets,* she reminded herself. *I'm just nervous because I pictured the murder in New Orleans again.*

Lindsey entered the hotel lobby of the Lawrence Inn, mentally preparing herself for the session with a local reporter. She turned left and approached the main desk to ask for messages.

"Excuse me, Ms. Marc?"

Lindsey turned toward the voice. A flash of light caused her to blink and stop. She squeezed her eyes shut, but a huge dot of light continued in her sights.

"Where would you like to do the interview?" the reporter pressed.

Lindsey smiled. Sincerely, she hoped. "What did you say your name was? Refresh my memory. Who did you say you worked for?"

"I'm a freelancer. I'm hoping to sell the piece to the *Eagle Tribune,* but I'd like to sell it more than once. What was it like to be a witness for the prosecution in New Orleans? How did your husband feel? He's a defense attorney, isn't he?"

She couldn't fault the young man and his eager spirit. Eyeing the lobby, she noticed a couple of chairs beside a round mahogany table with a marble top. "Please, take a seat over there, and I'll be right with you."

She checked her messages at the desk and then joined the enthusiastic reporter. How he had learned she was in Lawrence still eluded her.

"Are you researching a new book in our area?" the young man asked. His shirt seemed too large for his frame. His pants were pulled down around his hips with little to keep them up except for a thin leather belt. The trim cut of his brown hair seemed fitting to his style in an odd way.

"I'm doing some research, yes." Lindsey took in her surroundings. The colonial colors blended with the contemporary design. Everything seemed normal. She relaxed a fraction.

"May I inquire what kind of book and where?" His thumb manipulated the recorder in his hand.

Lindsey's mind worked over the answers she'd practiced. She had learned the hard way that preparing for interviews was a must. "Be yourself, guarded, but relaxed. Take control of the interview," her instructor's words came back.

"What did you say your name was?" she pressed once again.

"Derrick Hutchinson."

"Hutchinson, now that's an old New England name. Have you done any research on your family history?"

He sat back in the stuffed, winged-back chair. "I can't imagine growing up in this area and not having some knowledge of your ancestors."

Lindsey chuckled. "So very true. My ancestors were some of the first to settle in the Boston area. What about yours?"

"Same, and I have a few from the Cape as well. Are you here researching your family history?"

Ah, he's keeping focused. Good man. "Actually, I love doing my family genealogy. I research it every time I'm in the New England area."

"So, this is a personal trip?" He leaned forward, kitty-corner to the table.

"Both." Lindsey fiddled with her rings.

He scanned the room and lowered his voice. "What's your newest novel going to be about?"

The contract was signed and a release date set. It couldn't hurt to start the buzz about the novel. "I'm looking into the death of Anna Lopizzo and the Bread and Roses strike of 1912."

"Who is Anna Lopizzo, and why is her death important?"

Lindsey sat back in her chair and fingered the smooth, polished wood of the arm. *Good question.* Lindsey summarized what she knew about the strike. "Plus, I've always loved a good mystery," she continued. "And I have no idea whether or not I can solve this one, but it's fun trying. Don't you agree?"

Derrick chuckled. "I don't write fiction—"

"—just the facts," Lindsey finished the sentence for him. She scanned the lobby once again, but nothing seemed out of place. Still, it felt like she was being watched. *This is ridiculous,* she chided herself. *I'm just edgy because of the earlier incident in the library.*

"Right. Did you start off as a reporter?"

"No, but I wrote some freelance articles for the historical society."

When Lindsey finished the interview, she went up to her room and showered. An hour later, the phone rang while she was reviewing her notes.

"Hello?" she answered absentmindedly.

"Mrs. Taylor, there's a gentleman on the phone who would like to speak with you. He asked for Lindsey Marc. Shall I forward the call?"

Lindsey sighed. "Sure."

A couple of clicks echoed in the phone and then she heard the connection. "Hello?" Lindsey brightened her voice.

"Ms. Marc, you don't know me, but I just discovered that you are staying in our fair city. I'm having a small dinner party in my home this coming Tuesday. If you're still in town, I'd love to have you as my guest."

"Excuse me?"

"I'm sorry. I didn't introduce myself." He stumbled over his words. "My name is Edgar Archer. My family and I are fairly well known in the city, and have been throughout its history. You can ask your hotel manager for my credentials. I read your first novel *City Streets* and enjoyed it immensely. We don't have too many celebrities who come to our city and, well, it would be an honor to have you at our small gathering."

If he or his guests were related to the mill owner families, it could provide an interesting angle for the other side of the strike, she speculated.

"Thank you for your kind invitation. I'd love to come," she accepted.

Edgar recited the instructions to his house and a list of the who's who in Lawrence who would be attending the dinner party.

News certainly travels fast in this area, Lindsey thought as she hung up.

She downloaded the images from her digital camera and uploaded a video clip into her computer. She'd taken the video the day before at the Lawrence museum across Canal Street. Various businesses and offices now occupied one of the refurbished mills. She had even managed to get down by the canal and click a few images. No one was around. The water had seemed cold, dark, foreboding. Only a couple of cars were parked in the lot near the old bridge. It was a lonely place—so different from the busy days when the mills were in full operation.

As she viewed the uploaded video, a dark, four-door sedan passed on the street. A few minutes later, another passed in the opposite direction. She eased out a pent-up breath. *It must be a common car in the area.*

Lindsey closed her eyes and pictured the long halls that made up the factory building. She visualized the old photographs of loom after loom, row after row, and tried to imagine Anna and other workers there.

DECEMBER 1, 1911 ~ LAWRENCE, MASS.

The heavy machinery hummed as the giant looms worked—except for Jenna Waverly's. She stomped over to the foreman and voiced her complaint once again. As a weaver, she lost money if the loom jammed, and it seemed her loom went down every day. She couldn't afford less than the measly pay of seven dollars a week. Rumors of a strike and no income brought fear to her heart. Sylvia and Anna had assured her that everything would be all right. In the end, they would have better pay and a safer working environment.

Billy wiggled between the looms. Jenna hated to see the children working in the factories. It didn't seem right. The mill owners treated the workers' children as if they were their personal property. A worker had little or no right to say her child would not work, without risking her job.

"My loom is down again, Mr. Vincent." Jenna placed her hands on her hips, hoping the act would show her frustration.

Buddy Vincent was in his mid-forties and as thin as woolen thread. His clothes were neat but hardly new. Jenna could see where his wife had mended his shirt and trousers a time or two. He blew into the whistle he kept hung around his neck and signaled for James Donovan.

James hoisted a leather bag filled with tools and headed straight for Jenna's loom. His thick, curly black hair bounced with his confident gait. She'd offered to cut his hair for him, but he would always thank her and refuse.

"What be yer problem today, Jenna?" he asked.

"The bobbin and feeder have too much tension, and the yarn is breaking."

"Aye, I'll adjust it as quick as I can."

"Thank you, James."

"You're welcome, lass."

Jenna wondered if James, or any other man, would see her as a woman soon. She'd been working in the mills for three years. At eighteen she felt old enough to find a husband and settle down. She looked away from James and the loom and out through the tall windows. Her heart felt as empty as the gray sky.

Her aunt had promised that leaving England and coming to America would fulfill all her dreams. Working in a factory for three years had not fulfilled even one. Of course, it might have been different if her aunt hadn't fallen sick and died before Jenna arrived. With no family and no one to take her in, the only jobs available to her were in the textile mills. If she'd had the money, she would have returned to England, to her family. Instead, she wrote them once a month, assuring them she was fine, making a good living, and happy. Why did she lie? *Why do I stay?*

"Jenna? Jenna?" James's voice grew louder.

"Sorry, what did you say?"

"It's fixed. Try not forcing it to work as fast as you do." He winked.

Jenna gnawed her inner cheek and fought off a curt reply. She wasn't mad at James. She wasn't mad at anyone in particular. She just wasn't content with anything these days. It would have been better to stay in England and work the farm.

"Thank you, James. I'll be more careful." The clean, thick odor of oil wafted past her nostrils.

He nodded his shaggy head, lifted his bag of tools, and headed toward the machine repair corner. As she watched him go, she noticed a handsome young man standing behind the paned-glass windows of the office area. He sported a crop of auburn hair. He smiled.

Jenna returned the smile. She fought the urge to look over her shoulder as she went back to work. *Who is he?* She'd never seen him before. Whoever he was, he was above her class. A well-trimmed suit, a fresh white shirt with a vest and upturned collars back-dropped a handsome necktie with a pin that glistened. *Probably silver or a diamond,* she thought.

Sylvia came up beside her. "The other girls say he's Mr. Wood's nephew."

"Who?"

Sylvia snorted, "That man you were gawking at. Mind your place, and stay away from fancy-pants men."

Jenna fed the loom, then managed another glimpse of the handsome man in the office. She sighed. There was something about his eyes . . .

Chapter Three

Lindsey stretched in the wooden chair at the library table as she read from an investigator's report dated February 10, 1912. "At present a reign of terror has the entire city of Lawrence in its grip. Fourteen hundred soldiers have converted the streets into an armed camp."

"No kidding," she quipped. The report went on to say that the protesters still gathered later that day, which was almost two weeks after Anna's death. Approximately twelve thousand strikers held off the militia, which was there to disband the strikers' meeting.

Today, forensic science would be able to tell from which angle the bullet had struck Anna Lopizzo. Back then, there was little hard evidence.

Lindsey tapped her pencil on the desk. *Unless someone were to exhume the body and see if the bullet hit any of her bones. Nah, what would it prove? And who would pay for it?* Besides, that tidbit of information was not something she needed for her novel.

"Excuse me." The middle-aged librarian from the day before was standing at Lindsey's elbow, her arms loaded with half a dozen books.

Goodness, she is a fan.

"Ms. Marc, I don't mean to interrupt . . ."

"Have a seat." Lindsey pulled her briefcase off the chair to her left. "What's your name?"

"Abigail Adams."

Lindsey raised her eyebrows. "I'm pleased to meet you . . . Abigail."

The woman flushed. "I know. I get it all the time. It doesn't help that my husband is a descendant of *the* Abigail Adams. I seriously considered not marrying him for fear of the reactions I'd get over the years." She looked down at her lap. "But marrying Hugh was a good choice." She glanced back at Lindsey. "You know what I mean?"

"Yeah, I think I do." Lindsey reached over to the small stack of books. On top was *City Streets*.

"I read that one three times." Abigail leaned closer and lowered her voice. "Was it scary in New Orleans?"

Lindsey absent-mindedly rubbed the scar above her left breast. In an instant her mind replayed the attack.

The stranger grabbed her just before she reached the glass doors. As he slung his right arm around her chest, the tip of a knife blade cut into her flesh.

The elevator doors chimed.

"Go home." His hot breath crawled down her body.

Lindsey swallowed the remembered fear. As if witnessing a murder hadn't been horrible enough, everything the killer's associates had done to keep her from testifying only embedded the terror deeper in her heart.

"Yes, I was terrified. I don't ever want to go through a situation like that again." She opened the cover of *City Streets* and poised her pen over the blank page. "Do you write?"

"Oh, no. I love research. Which is why I took the job at the library. But no, I could never write. I get all tongue-tied."

Lindsey addressed the book to "the other" Abigail Adams and autographed it. "Research, huh?"

"Yes, I love it. I've spent days tracking down information for a patron. Of course, there are some times I've not been able to locate anything at all. In those cases, I keep a list in hopes of one day coming across something. Oh goodness, look at the time," Abigail exclaimed. "Can I help with anything else?"

"No, I can't think of a thing. Wait. Do you know of an Edgar Archer?"

"Sure. He's a local politician. His family has been involved with the town for ages. In fact, I think his grandfather worked for William Wood, the owner of the American Woolen Company."

"Ah, thank you."

"You're welcome. By the way, I heard through the grapevine that a reporter is hoping to do a piece on you."

Lindsey chuckled. "Too late, already happened. Along with a dinner invitation by Edgar Archer."

"Ah," Abigail acknowledged with a brief nod of the head. "I really must go. Thank you again for taking the time to sign the books."

"My pleasure. And thanks again for your help."

Lindsey glanced back at her laptop and typed in a few remaining notes from the article she'd read prior to Abigail's visit. One more book remained before she finished her research at the library. She cracked it open. The yellowed pages crinkled and released a musty smell.

Lindsey studied the first page and typed into her computer, "A high moral standard was expected from the girls who rented a room or part of a room in the tenant houses."

➢ ➢

Pulling a sports magazine from the rack, he made his way to a secluded chair, the perfect angle to view his target. He noticed the computer and counted ten books opened on the table around her. *No wonder she spent five hours in here . . . take that long to read the first one.* He opened the magazine and thumbed through the swimsuit section. He grinned. *No sense wasting time out in the car.* Scantily-clad babes prancing on tropical beaches held more appeal than counting cars in the parking lot or watching a middle-aged bookworm.

He glanced again at his target. *Actually, not bad for a middle-aged bookworm. Blonde hair . . . pretty well put together . . .* His personal tastes ran a lot younger, but if he had to watch this woman, it didn't hurt that she was easy on the eyes. Besides, she was going to help him reach his goals.

As she closed the lid of her computer, he jumped up and exited the building before her. Clicking the remote locks on his cherry-red Corvette, he slipped inside. *Much more suitable than that boxy rental car.* He adjusted his sunglasses, the mirror, his seat—anything to delay his departure. Finally, the woman came out and went to her white Toyota.

"Stay focused," he reminded himself. "She'll be worth a small fortune."

DECEMBER 3, 1911 ~ LAWRENCE, MASS.

"Jenna," an unfamiliar male voice called as she exited the factory.

She turned and spotted the handsome, auburn-haired man she'd seen at the factory. "Yes, sir?"

He smiled and her heart fluttered. "I asked your name. I hope you don't mind."

Mind? How could she mind? Her heart raced. Jenna smiled, "Not at all."

"Would you care to join me for a hearty meal at the pub? You're welcome to bring along a friend." He looked down at his feet. "Your honor is safe with me."

A good hot meal would be a wonderful gift, far more than she could provide for herself. She asked cautiously, "Would you be payin'?"

"A gentleman would never ask a lady if he had no intention of satisfying her every wish." He extended his arm. She tentatively placed her hand in the crook of his elbow and followed his lead.

"It's a fine evening." Jenna tried to make conversation, to ease the voice in her head telling her she shouldn't be alone with the mill owner's nephew.

He placed his hand on hers and whispered, "It's a fine evening, indeed. I thank you for the company. I've met only my uncle's family and his friends. A man can get quickly bored with that crowd. All they talk about is how to turn a larger profit."

"We talk about better wages."

He nodded. "My father is the poor man in the family; he followed his heart to a modest life of leisure on Martha's Vineyard. He found it more compelling than turning a profit. My uncle says it's time for me to learn the art of high finance and be encouraged back into the family business. So, that is why I am here. What about you? What brought you to America?"

"My aunt . . ." Jenna explained how her aunt had sent for her. How her life would have been different if her aunt had lived. How she wouldn't have been forced to work in the mills.

"Your refinement is evident. Perhaps I should speak with my uncle and find you a place in the office. You can read, I presume?"

"Yes. I miss spending time with books. When I leave every night, I'm exhausted, and little is available in the house."

He tilted his head and paused. "This is the place." He reached for the door and opened it for her. The savory scent of roast beef mingled with the aroma of rosemary, onions, and vegetables. Jenna hadn't smelled such rich fare in years. The host scanned her clothing, then looked back at her escort.

"A table for two," the young man said as he reached over and shook the host's hand.

Jenna watched the host place his hand in his pocket. Did he pay for the man's silence about her clothes? Or was it a way of getting what you wanted quickly? Jenna wondered.

"Very well, sir, follow me."

He led them toward a back room off to the left. The stale smell of beer filled Jenna's nostrils, and cigar smoke circled the dim lights. Jenna cleared her throat. The smells of the factory were better than this.

The young man held out the chair for her to sit. She placed the cloth napkin on her lap and tried to remember every ounce of knowledge her mother had taught her about how a lady should behave. Mother would never approve of her having dinner alone with a man—a man whose name she didn't even know.

"You're a vision of loveliness." He bent down and kissed the top of her hand. "Thank you for joining me."

Mother didn't know America. Things were different here. She was different here. And he was more charming than any man had been to her since she left the ship. Yes, things were different in America. A girl could be a lady and enjoy a man's company without an escort. Perhaps he'd even give her fresh flowers once in a while. "Thank you, sir. If I may be so bold, what is your name?"

"You may call me Brad. All my friends do." He sat down beside her. "Order anything you like."

Chapter Four

Friday morning, Lindsey found herself fidgety. The minutes couldn't tick away any more slowly. Unable to concentrate, she'd driven into Boston hours before Marc's arrival and spent the day walking the historic Freedom Trail, revisiting some of the key locations of the Revolutionary War. She even managed a brief shopping trip through Faneuil Hall.

Two hours later, she was waiting in the outer terminal at Logan Airport, glancing at the flight monitor every so often. When the display finally confirmed the plane's arrival, she began scanning the terminal, sizing up the groups of people emerging from the security area. *Do they look like they flew in from Miami?*

When Lindsey spotted Marc, her heart soared. She waved.

Marc beamed.

"Hi," they said in unison.

He dropped his suitcase and pulled her into a loving embrace. "It's good to see you. I've missed you."

"I've missed you too."

Marc was a handsome man, tall and trim, with a healthy patch of gray at the temples. The dimple in the cleft of his chin made him downright huggable. He reached down and picked up his bag. "Shall we?"

Lindsey looped her arm around his waist, and they traipsed out of the airport toward the parking garage. "How was your flight?"

"Fine. How productive was your research today?"

"Lousy. I couldn't stop thinking about you. I'm having trouble deciding who to center this story around. I mean, I know some if not most of the characters, but I don't really know them yet. They aren't real to me."

"Hmm, sounds like we'll need to talk this out." He leaned over and kissed the top of her head.

Warmth and comfort flooded her. "If you don't mind."

"Never. You put up with far more over the years, helping me pass the bar and work through tough cases. You deserve my listening ear."

"Thanks." Lindsey spotted the Toyota and pushed the button on the remote to pop open the trunk and unlock the doors.

When they had paid the attendant and were on their way, Marc said, "OK, tell me what you've found." They talked the entire trip from Boston to Lawrence, hashing over the holes and limits of her research.

→ ←

As Marc dozed peacefully, Lindsey kissed him and slipped out of bed, unable to sleep the afternoon away. He was here now, and her mind was buzzing with all the work she should have done this morning. She scanned the hotel dresser covered with her pages of notes. Pulling a bottle of water out of the small refrigerator, she stepped between the loveseat and the coffee table and sat down. Her laptop sat open on the table.

She tapped the stack of historical newspaper accounts she had printed out. There was little there. They reflected the sentiment of the times—the strikers were trying to ruin the American way of life. The largest group supporting the strikers were socialists. She scanned the top report in her hand: "Thousands of strikers blocked the entrance to the American Woolen Mill, chanting, singing, and locked arm in arm. No one tried to pass by these women."

There were other passages she'd highlighted, which delved into the disappearance of workers' children.

One thing was certain, the mill owners thought little of the immigrants' needs. They were paid almost nothing, forced to live in overcrowded conditions, and had little or no hope for a future.

Lindsey jumped up and sorted through another stack of papers. "Where was that quote?" she whispered to herself. Something along the lines of "working in the mills for twelve hours each day brought gray hair and no husbands."

Pinching the bridge of her nose with her thumb and forefinger, she closed her eyes. *I understand why they went out on strike. I think I have a pretty good grasp of the times and all the corruption. But the brutality of the police . . . I just don't get it.* In one case, a woman had been beaten and arrested for simply walking on the sidewalk. In another case, a couple of boys were beaten for playing in the street. On and on it went.

Lindsey reorganized the reports chronologically, starting with the twelfth of January. She skimmed over the early days of the strike and moved on to Anna Lopizzo's murder. Giovannitti and Ettor, the union organizers who came from New York and who were charged with conspiring to murder Anna, were jailed for nearly a year before they were released and the charges were dropped. Two private detectives had given testimony that led to the arrest of the two organizers.

Reaching for her yellow sticky pad, Lindsey scribbled a note to herself to check on whether these were some of the Pinkerton detectives that had been sent to Lawrence because of the strike. She thumbed through the next two accounts. A woman's body was found in the river on February 10. Apparent cause of death, drowning.

Sitting back down on the sofa, Lindsey clicked a couple keys, bringing up the computer slide show she'd put together with various pictures of Lawrence. A click of the mouse and the show started its repetitive cycle.

She continued to go through the papers. Not much there . . . some minor outbreaks of people being arrested for disturbing the police. "Peace," she corrected herself.

Scenes of the river and the dam flicked on her computer screen. "Wait a minute." She stopped the slide show and backed it up a slide or two. A wintry black and white picture of the dam, dated 1918, glowed on the screen. She thumbed through the stack again and stopped at the drowning of the woman. "Gotcha," she said out loud.

Marc yawned and poked his head up from under the covers. "What?"

"Sorry, didn't mean to wake you. But I think I just figured out what's been bothering me about this research."

Marc pushed himself up and leaned on one elbow.

"There's a report about a woman who drowned in the river."

"Sorry, Lins, I'm half asleep here. You'll need to give me more details."

Lindsey came over to the bed and sat down beside him. "The river freezes every winter. All the reports of the weather at that time said it was a very harsh winter."

"I'm still not following." Marc sat up, plumped the pillow, and leaned it on the headboard behind him.

She pointed to the laptop on the table. "That's a picture of the river, specifically the dam, a few years later. I have no doubt the river was in much the same condition in 1912."

"And?"

"Don't you see? The river is frozen solid. How could anyone fall through and drown?"

Marc laced his fingers behind his head and smiled. "How did the mills get their power?"

"The river." Lindsey sat back. "Ah, but look at all that ice." She turned toward Marc.

"It's amazing," he said, "and no doubt the mills had to shut down if they couldn't get the water flowing for a day or two. But more than likely, there was a way to chop up the ice and keep the water moving."

Marc had a point. "But don't you think it's odd that during the strike someone just happened to fall into the river?"

"Possibly. But what are the facts? Was this woman even a worker at the mills?"

"Don't know. There's no name attached to the report."

Marc chuckled. "Sounds like something right up your alley." He stretched. "I'm starved. Are you up for going out for dinner? Or do you want to order room service?" He glanced over to the table and dresser. "On second thought, dinner out sounds better. I don't want to be up half the night trying to put your papers back in order."

She swatted him with the report she held in her hand. "Be grateful I'm leaving them here while we go to Rockport for the weekend."

"Good, because I left mine at home." He winked and headed into the shower.

Lindsey restacked the historical newspaper reports and straightened a few other piles. Marc padded back into the room, wrapped in a towel. Muttering to herself about the drowned woman, she jotted down notes on a legal pad.

"One mystery lady who managed to drown in the ice," she said. "The plot thickens."

"Oh," Marc groaned. "Bad pun."

DECEMBER 4, 1911 ~ LAWRENCE, MASS.

Jenna stretched her back as the loom ratcheted back and forth. A full belly and memories of a pleasant evening made her more relaxed than she'd been in years. She found Brad easy to talk with, almost like she'd known him all her life.

"Miss Waverly, come to the supervisor's office," the foreman shouted from across the factory floor.

Startled, Jenna placed her hand on top of a spool.

"Jenna!" Anna screamed.

Jenna jumped. The spinning of the spool could have cut off her finger. "Thank you." She straightened her apron and headed toward the back office. The supervisor's office lined the back wall of the factory with huge observation windows. Gnawing on her inner cheek, Jenna wondered if Brad had managed to get her reassigned into clerical work. Her heart quickened along with her feet.

"Be careful," Sylvia warned, going the other way with a basket full of wool-laden spools of multiple colors.

Reaching the office door, Jenna cleared her throat and knocked.

"Come in," the plump manager called out without looking upward. "Are you Jenna Waverly?"

"Yes, sir," she replied.

Mr. Billings appraised her over the rim of his glasses. "Says here you can read and write, is that true?

"Yes, sir." She surveyed the sparsely furnished office. A couple of filing cabinets, a waste can, the desk, and two chairs. That was it.

He tossed her a piece of paper. "Read this."

Jenna held down her anger. She didn't like it when people questioned her honesty. She picked up the piece of paper from his wooden desk and began to read.

"Fine, fine." His eyes trailed up and down her body as if she were a choice piece of meat. Jenna held her poise beneath his lecherous gaze.

She scanned the figures on the paper he'd given her. "Are you aware that these figures are incorrect?"

He pulled the paper from her hands.

"The sum in the first column is off by twenty-five dollars and nineteen cents. The percentage in the last column has been figured incorrectly as well, overpaying the supplier by at least thirty dollars." *That ought to stop the beast in his tracks.* Jenna held back a smirk. She had learned long ago that no one liked to be outsmarted.

"Yes, I was aware."

He lied. She held her tongue.

"It was part of the test. I believe we have a place for you in book-keeping. You'll have a desk and work with Mrs. Polly Reed. You'll need to wear your finest clothes since you may be called upon to deal with the public. Do you have a dress in better shape than the one you're wearing?"

"Yes, sir." *Not much better, but a wee bit.*

"Good. Be dressed in it tomorrow morning and report back to me. Mr. Wood needs people who can work the numbers quickly and accurately." He waved his hand toward the door. "Dismissed."

Jenna found her legs and walked out with her head held high. She would no longer be working with the looms but at a desk instead. *Could life get any better than this?*

Chapter Five

Lindsey rubbed the back of her neck. After two hours of research at the historical society, it was apparent that precious little about the strike was written by the strikers themselves. She had searched for diaries or journals from some of the women, but to no avail. That personal one-on-one connection from the strikers' own pens seemed to be missing. She studied a photograph of a little girl not tall enough to reach the upper level of bobbins. She would've had to climb the spinning frame in order to mend broken threads or change the bobbins.

"Children went to work at the age of eight and up, some even younger," Lindsey read. Another picture showed barefoot children working the huge looms. The children weren't of legal age to work, even for that time. They gathered the lint from underneath the weavers. If they wore shoes, they could cause a spark and start a fire.

Her heart went out to them. *These children never had time to play like mine did.*

She thought of the strikers and whispered a prayer of thanks. "Thank you, Lord, for these people who went before us and helped shape our world." Her mind strayed to some of the missionary stories she'd heard over the years. The fact remained that people in this world still lived and worked in conditions very similar to those of the strikers of 1912—or worse.

"Enough." She dusted off her hands, put the pages back in the cardboard file box and reached for another. The square table in the center of the room allowed for eight people to work at the station at one time; that is, if there wasn't someone like her with box after box of information to go through. Finding gems of history in historical archives was tedious work, but the texture of the people's lives, the events, and their environment added a dimension that her readers appreciated. Still, tedious was hard after a restful weekend with her husband.

She opened the next box and riffled through the various manila envelopes. She put aside a couple of loose pages, an article about the fish of the Merrimack River. Finally, she found the article she was looking for, a small clipping from a newspaper:

A female body was discovered this morning under the ice. No identification could be found. If anyone can identify this woman, please come to the county morgue.

The article was dated February 10, 1912. Lindsey reached in and pulled out another clipping. On February 12, the body had been identified as that of Jenna Waverly. Lindsey leaned back in the old oak chair and checked through her notes on the legal pad. *It seems odd that no one had reported Jenna missing. Didn't she have relatives or family around? Hadn't anyone realized she was gone? When had it happened? That morning? Or was she under the ice for days?*

Lindsey scribbled "Jenna Waverly?" on a yellow sticky note, placed the files back in the storage box, and returned them to the curator of the historical society. Taking a moment to collect all her thoughts and notes on her laptop, she quickly assembled her belongings and headed for the Merrimack River before the sun set for the day.

Exactly where did they find Jenna's body? she wondered, as she slid into the driver's seat and shoved the key into the ignition.

➤ ◄

"What's she all in a hurry about?"

He pulled out his wallet and dropped a twenty on the table, then took one final swig of his draft beer.

The woman pulled out of the gravel parking lot behind the historical society building. He watched from the darkened doorway of the pub until he saw the car head west on the small street.

By the time he reached his car, she had turned right onto Canal Street. He flicked on the tracking device. He wouldn't lose the bookworm, but he didn't want to fall too far behind, in case she finally did something interesting. Her trip to Rockport with her husband had proved to be a boring exercise in following the speed limit. The trip into Boston had been equally mind-numbing. In fact, the entire weekend had been a waste of his time. He'd debated even bothering to watch them while they were off romping around like two lovesick kids.

His stomach soured. *No one can be that happily married at their age.* If she weren't his target, he might go after her husband and watch him for a while, find something to blackmail the man with. *There isn't a lawyer living who's honest. Easy target.* A crooked smile rose on his cheek.

"Stay focused," he reminded himself. He glanced at the red indicator light. Lindsey Marc was straight ahead about a mile down the road. Yes, he needed to stay focused. She was his future.

DECEMBER 6, 1911 ~ LAWRENCE, MASS.

"Jenna?" Brad tapped the doorframe to her small office.

Her heart skipped a beat. "Come in, Brad. Thank you so much for this new position."

"You're welcome, but you earned it yourself." He positioned himself in the open doorway, his shoulders squared, looking dapper in his three-piece business suit, starched white shirt, and collar pin that dulled in comparison to the handsome set of his face.

Jenna looked down at her desk to catch her breath. *How can he affect me so? I barely know him.* "No, if it wasn't for you, I'm certain I would not be sitting at this fine oak desk."

He reached out to lift her chin. "Jenna." His voice softened. "Trust me. Franklin Billings would not have put you in this job if he didn't believe you could handle it. I merely suggested a clerical job for you. Apparently you have quite a head for numbers and can figure them quickly. It takes a bit to impress someone like Billings, but you did. Not that I'm surprised. You're a rare jewel in this factory."

He leaned closer as if to kiss her. Did she want him to? Did she want to kiss him? She closed her eyes in anticipation. Instead of his warm lips upon hers, she felt a cool breeze as he pulled back. *The perfect gentleman,* she sighed inwardly.

"May I take you to dinner again this evening?" He stood erect, more professional, keeping the distance that should have been there in the first place.

The problem for Jenna was she didn't want the distance; she wanted to be close to him. Too close. Mother would never approve of such behavior. "I'd like that very much," she replied.

"I'll come by at five, unless you prefer to go home first and change."

She glanced down at her dress; it was the best one she owned. Would he be embarrassed to be seen in public with such shabby attire? Who was she kidding? She wasn't from his world and never would be. She should end the relationship before it began.

As if reading her mind, he interrupted her thoughts. "You look lovely, Jenna."

Her countenance rose a notch, and she returned his smile. "I'm afraid it's my best dress."

"Hush. You're beautiful. Anything you wore would pale in comparison to your beauty."

She knew he exaggerated. A man only says such things to flatter a girl. His charms captivated her. As a moth goes to the flame, she accepted the compliment. "Thank you."

The rest of the day, Jenna worked hard trying to understand the fancy bookwork, double-checking the information she had entered in the ledgers. This job paid better than a weaver's wage, and she aimed to keep it.

It was six o'clock before she realized the time. *Where's Brad?* Should she wait a bit longer?

She set her files back in their proper places, cleared her desk, and grabbed her winter coat.

"Miss Waverly," Polly Reed called out. Polly was a middle-aged woman who kept her hair pinned back. She wore a wool skirt with matching jacket—simple, but elegant business attire. Nothing like Jenna's best. Mrs. Reed glanced up and down the hallway, furled her right finger back and forth, and whispered. "Mr. Billings asked me to give you this before you leave." She pulled a brown paper package tied with white string from under the countertop.

"What is it?"

Polly leaned closer and whispered, "Material to make yourself a business outfit."

"Oh dear, will he take it from my pay?"

"I can't imagine he'd do that. The material didn't come from our factory."

Jenna looked down at the package and back at Miss Reed. "I don't understand."

She pointed to a marking in red on the paper. "Appears that Mr. Billings had someone purchase this for you."

Jenna made a mental note to write a thank-you note to Mr. Billings. Had she read him all wrong? Was he actually a kindhearted man? Or did he want her to feel obligated to him because he'd been so generous? "I don't know if I can take this. It doesn't seem right, somehow."

"Nonsense, this is a business office. This is where the customers come to order our material for their factories. He merely wants the office to reflect the type of business this is. Customers never see the factory floor or the poor souls that work them." Polly quelled her words. "I'm sorry. I didn't mean . . ."

"I understand." Jenna took the package from Polly's arms. She'd be up half the night sewing her new outfit if she was to have it ready by morning. Hopefully, Anna and Sylvia would lend her a hand.

By six-thirty, Brad still had not arrived. Jenna's stomach rumbled as she walked to the boardinghouse. She froze in the winter and sweated in the summer in the corner attic room. It wasn't the best place to live, but it was the cheapest. She hoped one day to get a room on a lower floor, but there was solace in the attic, a place where she could retreat and write in her journal.

She ran down Canal Street and up Jackson. Just as she rounded the corner and grabbed the iron rail of the stairway, she spotted Brad walking toward her.

"Good evening, Jenna. I'm sorry I was so late."

Jenna's heart filled with excitement just hearing his voice. "Where did you come from?"

"I've been waiting for you. I probably should have returned to the office, but it was already well past the hour. I figured you would have been home sooner." Brad shivered.

"How long have you been standing in the cold?"

"An hour, perhaps a bit less."

She wrapped her arm around his and led him to the stairs. "Come inside, and I'll make a cup of tea for you."

"No, thank you. It wouldn't be proper. I'll wait right here."

"Nonsense, you can come in and warm your bones. The girls will take care of my virtue."

"Jenna," he whispered. "I can't. Please put your package in your room quickly, and I'll wait for you over there." He pointed to a fancy black automobile sitting across the street, a Cadillac Roadster, if she wasn't mistaken.

Why doesn't he want to be seen by my friends? she wondered. Then she knew. As much as he said that he didn't care about their diverse social classes, he was concerned. Would he take her to another darkened restaurant where they wouldn't be recognized?

"It's late, Brad. Go home. We can have dinner another night." She slipped her hand from his. The day had been perfect. Now she felt as heavy as the giant looms in the factory.

"Please, Jenna, try and understand. It's not me; it's my uncle. If he were to know I was seeing one of the girls from the factory floor, he'd ship me home to my parents. It doesn't matter to me, but I have to be careful. I couldn't give you that package directly. I had to arrange for it to appear to come from Billings. Don't you see? If we're to have a liaison, it must be done in secret. If I were to come into your home, the other girls would talk. They'd tell their friends, who would in turn tell their friends. I can't risk it. Please try and understand."

She wanted to believe him. The sincerity in his deep blue eyes drew her closer. He had purchased the material for her to have a new outfit. He'd concocted a story about appropriate attire for the office. *Well, perhaps that wasn't completely a lie. There was a certain dress that all the men and women in the office wore.* "I'll have to think on this."

"All right." He stepped back. "I purchased a fine steak and was going to cook it on an outside fireplace for us."

Meat. Temptation comes in all forms, she mused. "Steak is hard to say no to but, honestly, I don't have time tonight if I'm to make a business suit for work in the morning."

"Very well, my precious rose, I'll give you the time you seek." He leaned over and kissed her hand. "Good night."

Chapter Six

Organizing the new digital images of the riverfront and the dam took longer than Lindsey had anticipated. At midnight, she finally gave in to her weary body. She slept until nine.

During her morning devotions, she read Psalm 56:4: "In God, whose word I praise, in God I trust; I will not be afraid. What can mortal man do to me?" She needed that reminder to trust the Lord and not be worried.

Lindsey printed out an enlarged street map of the mill area in 1912 and marked the locations for the different protests and encounters with the police and militia. Then she correlated the contemporary photographs of each spot today with the locations on the map. Her hand paused on the mouse. "What's that?"

She examined the photo she had captured a couple of days before. Her heart quickened. If she wasn't mistaken, a drug transaction was taking place. The angle of the men's faces made them indistinct, but with the right software they could reveal who's who. "Lord, what am I going to do now?"

A cold sweat broke out. "Please Lord, this can't be happening." Being a good citizen by reporting the murder she'd witnessed in New Orleans had put her life in jeopardy. First, the attack by the man working for Richard Melancon. Lindsey rubbed the scar on her chest. Then she'd been taken into protective custody, cutting her off from her family. She squeezed her eyelids closed and let out a deep sigh.

The moonlight glistened on the surface of the water. Lindsey wiped her brow, the humidity made it difficult to breathe. Getting an authentic feel of what it was like in New Orleans at the end of the eighteenth century had a downside.

A couple of voices caught her attention. Two men were arguing. One man was standing in a boat; the other on a small pier. A beam of light shone on the man on the pier. The sharp lines in his jaw and cheek showed the intense anger he felt for the other man.

A flash of silver from the boat caught Lindsey's eye. The man on the pier lunged toward the other man. The boat rocked. They were entwined in battle.

Crack! A small explosion echoed in the night air.

Shaking herself back to the present, she recited the verse she'd read earlier this morning. "In God, whose word I praise . . ." She methodically dialed Marc on her cell phone. "Hi, Alice, it's Lindsey. Is Marc available?"

"Afraid not, Lindsey," Alice replied. "He's in a private meeting with a client and asked me not to disturb him."

"Okay. What about Neil? Is he free?" Lindsey paced back and forth in front of her computer screen. *I don't want to get involved with another police case.*

"Sorry, he's in there with Marc." Alice's voice lowered. "It's one of the city mayors, and he's in a bit of a trouble."

City mayors running into trouble with the law wasn't that rare of an occurrence, but to have a consultation with a criminal attorney meant a serious problem indeed.

"Can I help you with anything?" Alice asked.

Lindsey glanced back at the picture. From working with Marc on his criminal cases, her eye was educated to spot a drug transaction and how the various drugs were usually packaged. The man receiving the small bag of white powder, probably cocaine, was definitely wearing a tailored suit that form-fit his body. The guy selling the drugs seemed rather nondescript, average height and build, with no distinguishing features that she could see in the photo. With a ball cap on his head, the color of his hair was lost, and she couldn't see his eyes in the picture.

"No, thanks. Just ask Marc to call my cell phone right away."

"Sure. Are you all right?"

"I'm fine. I just need his input."

"All right. If it's an emergency, I could interrupt him. I know he'd take a call from you."

"No, it can wait." After all, she'd taken the picture days ago. For all she knew it could have been someone passing through the area.

Lindsey clicked her phone shut before she heard whether Alice had hung up. She took in a deep breath and sighed. *Why do these kinds of things always happen to me?* Would Marc appreciate her doing her civic duty again by giving evidence to the police that might at some future date bring her back to the Lawrence area? After the time she'd spent in New Orleans, she admitted she was a bit gun-shy.

Lindsey sat down, closed her eyes, and prayed. "Father, I don't know why I captured those images, and I certainly don't know what to do with them. Do I take them to the police? Do I simply ignore the fact that I have some pictures of a possible crime taking place?" She sat in silence waiting, reflecting, hoping life would not repeat itself.

Her cell phone rang; she looked at the number and saw it was Marc's cell. "Hi, babe. I hope Alice didn't drag you out of the meeting?"

"Nope, not at all. We just ended and we're heading out for some lunch. What's up?"

"I did it again." Lindsey began to pace the length of her hotel room.

Marc let out a nervous chuckle. "You'll have to be more specific, honey."

"I photographed what appears to be a cocaine purchase."

"Lins . . ." Marc's consternation was evident. "What happened?"

She stopped her pacing and looked out the hotel window. The parking lot below, the interstate off in the distance, the entire world seemed quiet and unaware of the inner battle going on within her. She filled Marc in.

"All right, print out a simple statement, take it to the authorities, and drop it off. Don't let them keep you more than a couple of minutes. If they continue to ask questions, call my cell. I'll keep it on and answer immediately."

Lindsey let out a deep sigh. "Thanks, Marc."

"You're welcome. Now, when are you coming home?"

"I'm hoping to fly home on Friday. I'd love to get my hands on some of the actual words of the strikers, other than the transcripts from the hearings."

"I'll be praying for you. Take things one step at a time, Lins. Don't let the problems from New Orleans resurface."

Lindsey heard the open door chimes of her husband's car. "Thanks. I'll let you go."

"You're never an intrusion, and next time I don't care who I'm talking with, tell Alice to interrupt. I always have time for you."

Lindsey held back from chuckling. "Well, we know that isn't exactly true. But I love you, too."

"Love ya. Bye," he said with a lilt of laughter in his voice.

Talking with Marc lessened her uneasiness. She sat down, wrote out a statement, printed off the two photos, and burned copies onto a CD.

"Why couldn't I have been content to write romance novels?"

DECEMBER 6, 1911 ~ LAWRENCE, MASS.

Sylvia stretched her aching back. "Do you like working in the office, Jenna?" She glided her hand over the brown woolen material she was stitching.

"It's too soon to tell, but I love working with numbers, and the smell of the ink and paper . . . well, they bring back my school days in England."

"You miss England?" Anna said in her accented English.

"Yes, very much. Life was hard there, though not as hard as it is here. Then again, I didn't have to work to support myself. I just had my chores."

Sylvia leaned forward and tapped her friend on the knee. "But the new job is good for you, yes?"

"Yes, I'm certain it will be. Perhaps the three of us could rent a small cottage of our own. Wouldn't that be nice?"

"Can you teach us how to read and write in English?"

"All right. We'll start with the alphabet," Jenna suggested, as the three women continued to stitch the cloth in their hands. "This is the letter *A.*" She leaned over and scratched a capital letter *A* with fabric chalk on the wooden floorboards.

In unison, Sylvia and Anna recited the Italian pronunciation for the letter *a.*

"So you can read, just not English."

They nodded their heads. "A little." Sylvia tried her hand at it. The lines were wiggly and didn't look much like Jenna's.

"Excellent," Jenna encouraged.

Sylvia narrowed her gaze at her first attempt.

"Honest, Sylvia, for your first try that isn't bad at all. Letters take practice. A hand that hasn't practiced to write straight or curved lines takes time to train, just as the hands that feed the looms. The girls just starting are slow at first and awkward. So it is with letters."

Sylvia sat straight up and tried writing the letter once again. Holding the chalk proved a bit awkward without her third finger.

"Me," Anna squealed.

Sylvia handed her the chalk they'd used earlier to draw the lines on the fabric to shape the skirt and jacket for Jenna. It suddenly struck Sylvia as odd that the company noticed that Jenna knew how to read and write. *How did they find out?* she wondered.

"Jenna, I know you said Mr. Billings called you into the office, but how did he know you could read and write?"

"Someone told him." Jenna looked down at the letter that Anna had just drawn. "Very good," she said. "Anna, your name begins with the letter *a* and ends with it as well." Jenna proceeded to write out Anna's name. "This is a capital *A,* and this is a small *a.* Both are *a*'s, but when writing a name, the first letter is a capital. The two middle letters are *n*'s," Jenna pointed out.

Sylvia traced with her finger the letters Jenna had drawn. "What does my name look like?" she inquired.

Jenna spelled out Sylvia's name. "Your last letter is an *a* also. Hear the *a*-sound. Ann*a*, Sylvi*a*..."

"Jenn*a*," Sylvia and Anna sang.

The three women giggled. "Yes, my name also ends with *a.* You ladies will learn quickly."

Sylvia's chest swelled. Maybe she could be taught, contrary to what her old school mistress in Italy had said so many years ago. If she could learn to read and write, maybe she could earn enough money to visit her family. When her family had moved farther west to the mills in Holyoke and Chicopee, Sylvia had stayed in Lawrence, believing she'd be able to make more money there. But now she wondered how her family had fared. Did they make better wages farther west? Together they'd never had much, but they did have each other. Now, she had the closeness of friends like Anna and Jenna. Although Jenna was English, Sylvia believed she could be a friend too. *If she doesn't change too much, working for the wealthy men of the company.*

Sylvia fingered the fine wool blend once again. The material was top-of-the-line, the threads woven tightly together. Jenna would look elegant in this suit. She'd look like a businesswoman ready for an important meeting. She'd look like money. She glanced at Jenna's blue eyes. *Will you be changing, my friend?*

Chapter Seven

Lindsey parked her car in front of Edgar Archer's home and handed the keys to the valet who opened the door for her. Adjusting her simple black dress, she stepped toward the front entrance.

The old colonial house stood proudly, its round column supports extending up to the second floor. The blue slate walkway hinted of an older era, a simpler time. She saw what looked like a spin mark from a child's heel and grinned. Childhood memories of spinning pirouettes on the hard heels of her new patent leather shoes brushed across her mind.

"Good evening, Ms. Marc. Welcome." The doorman, dressed in a white tailored dinner jacket, extended his arm. Lindsey slipped her hand into the crook of his elbow. He led her down the spacious hallway into a room that had large, ornately carved wooden pocket doors that slid into the walls rather than swinging open into the room. "Presenting Ms. Lindsey Marc," the doorman announced in a stately manner.

The buzz of conversation was momentarily silenced as everyone turned to acknowledge the newcomer. Lindsey felt like a flounder caught in a scallop dredge, wishing all the world for an exit. Marc was so much better at these kinds of events. She smiled.

"Welcome to my home, Mrs. Marc. May I call you Lindsey?" Her host took a step from the crowd and extended his hand.

"Please do."

Edgar Archer beamed. "And please call me Edgar." He was a middle-aged man with graying sideburns and a bit of a roguish grin. In his prime, he might have been the kind of man who would inspire romance novels, a hero with a touch of the dark side in him. But tonight he appeared to be a man of great wealth and few close friends.

Why'd you think that? Lindsey caught herself wondering. She examined the others in the room a bit more closely. Perhaps the way the man extricated himself from the crowd prompted the hasty conclusion.

"I'm so glad you could join us."

Edgar Archer led her by the elbow toward a group of three men who were deep in conversation. At the moment, she felt like Ms. Scarlet being led by Colonel Mustard to the conservatory in some twisted game of Clue. The rich wood paneling of the room only added to the illusion. "Gentlemen, may I present Mrs. Lindsey Marc."

Lindsey nodded and said, "Hello."

The room held a faint scent of cigar and leather, mingled with the aroma of festive lavender sprigs that accented the room.

"This, gentlemen,—" Edgar nodded toward a man with a thin mustache and straight, black hair combed tightly back who looked like Mr. Green on the Clue cards at home—"is Travis Beecher."

Mr. Beecher extended his hand. "Pleasure to meet you, Mrs. Marc. I enjoyed *City Streets*. What are you working on now, if I might ask?"

Lindsey smiled. "I'm researching the 1912 labor strike here in Lawrence."

"Such a tragic time," an older gentleman, perhaps in his seventies, said. "Barnaby Paige." He stepped forward and offered his hand. "My grandparents told me many a story about the strike."

"Unions had their place." The third man, a redheaded "Professor Plum" with long sideburns, smiled. "Don't get me wrong. There's no question that changes needed to be made in the mills, but the end result . . . well, I sometimes wonder." He sipped his drink and ended his musings.

"This young man is Waylan Tompkins." Edgar placed his hand on Tompkins's shoulder and paused. "My grandfather witnessed the strike from the owners' perspective. It cost the company quite a bit of money."

"Ah, but Edgar," Barnaby Paige chimed in, "the salaries were half that of other textile mills in the area at the time. The entire reason they moved the mills here from Boston was to avoid some of the higher salaries from the city."

"Yes, but the social reforms that society undertook have advanced this country," Travis Beecher added.

Lindsey turned her gaze toward Travis. Observing people had been her hobby even before she had decided to become a writer. The small gestures. How people held themselves. How a man might move his head slightly to the right while listening to someone else speak gave so many insights about his character. She was inclined to suspect that Travis was related to Barnaby. Not because they acted or responded in the same fashion, but because they shared the same forehead and shape of nose.

"Don't let me interrupt your conversation, gentlemen," she said. "I'm always interested in hearing from those directly involved, or even a generation removed, from an event."

Barnaby sidled up beside her, leaning a bit closer than she was accustomed to, but not quite invading her personal space. "Then you'll want to be talking with me. My grandparents were a part of the strike—the formation of it, actually."

"Yes, but what about the way those women organized? Who'd have thought they'd send their children away?" Waylan added, and stuffed his left hand into his pocket the way Professor Plum would. Lindsey suppressed an inward chuckle.

"I'm afraid my wife was delayed at the center she volunteers for.

She'll be arriving soon, I hope." Edgar leaned over and whispered, "May I introduce you to a few of my other guests?"

"Of course. Thank you, gentlemen. You've stirred my curiosity."

Following a healthy round of salutations, the men went back to their private discussion. Edgar escorted Lindsey around the room.

A woman who appeared to be a good ten years younger than Edgar came into the room. She smiled and greeted the guests as she approached Edgar. "Good evening, Mrs. Marc. I'm so glad you could come to our home."

Edgar wrapped his arm around his wife and introduced them. "This beautiful woman is my wife, Betty."

"Pleasure to meet you." Lindsey extended her hand.

⤖ ⤕

An hour later, Lindsey sat at a long dining table with an older woman to her right and Edgar Archer to her left. Overall, the evening had been a pleasant one, and she had tried to pay attention to those around her, rather than escape to the recesses of her mind to continue plotting the novel. It was hard to hear the tidbits of conversation and not want to write them all down immediately.

Across from her sat the local police captain, Harold Pitts, and his wife. Lindsey remembered her foolish visit to the police station earlier in the day. They hadn't wanted her pictures. Initially, there had been some interest by the desk sergeant, but after Lindsey had sat and waited for an hour or more, he came back with the thanks-but-no-thanks speech.

"Good evening again. Ruth Emery." The older woman with a regal white crown of hair smiled at Lindsey. Ruth dotted her lips with the white linen napkin. "I understand you're researching the Bread and Roses strike."

"Yes, I became interested in the strike when I ran across a story about the death of Anna Lopizzo."

"Such a shame. It's hard to believe blood was shed during the strike. My grandmother told me that they fought for what they believed was right. She was one of the few who had worked in Watertown before coming to Lawrence, so she knew how poorly they were being paid in comparison with the other mill workers."

"Your grandmother was one of the strikers?"

"Yes. Her name was Sylvia Giovanni. She came from Italy to work in the mills when she was seventeen. She traveled with a group of women, all of whom came to find their futures in America."

The gentle ping of a crystal bell sounded.

Edgar Archer took his place at the head of the table. "First, I want to thank all of you for coming this evening. Betty and I are so appreciative of your support. Second, I want to clarify for Mrs. Marc that I am indeed running for office, and though I am not asking for her support, I am honored that she would come to our home on such short notice."

Wouldn't Marc love to see my picture in the paper, endorsing a stranger for a city office. . . . Hardly! Lindsey's stomach flip-flopped.

"I promise you, Mrs. Marc, there will be no cameras upon your exiting of the building."

"Thank you." Lindsey smiled a little stiffly.

"You're welcome. Having run for city council on more than one occasion, I understand how it feels to be followed by the media."

"No comparison, Edgar," Waylan Tompkins hollered out.

The room erupted into laughter.

"So very true. Now, if I were to run for president . . ."

Waylan, the youngest member of the small group, stood up and placed a hand on his backside. "Run for your wallets boys, he's attempting another fleecing."

Again, those in the room were caught up with the gaiety of the moment.

Perhaps Lindsey had misjudged this crowd. Edgar Archer's friends, though high and influential people in the city of Lawrence, also seemed to be close enough friends that they could tease one another.

"As I was saying," Edgar continued, "we are truly honored that you've joined us tonight."

"Here, here," someone said at the far end of the table.

"A toast." Edgar held his glass to the air. "Blessings on all of you." He turned to Lindsey and added, "May your fingers be swift and your insights intriguing."

The gentle chime of crystal on crystal flitted down the table. Lindsey sipped her champagne and replaced her glass. She definitely had misjudged this man and his friends.

"Simply scrumptious, Edgar, thank you." Ruth placed her linen napkin on the table next to her plate.

After one of the finest five-course meals that Lindsey had ever experienced, she turned to the host and added her own compliment. "Yes, it was a delightful meal. Thank you for the invitation."

"I'm pleased you came. Like Ruth, my grandfather and great-grandfather worked in the mills, but they were in management." He smiled and lifted his glass to Ruth. "They were the ones the strikers were fighting against. As I've heard the accounts, the strikers had some good reasons for their disputes."

Ruth snickered. "Did you know they had to purchase their own drinking water in those hot, noisy buildings?"

Lindsey sat back and watched the two of them.

"Excuse me, nature calls." Waylan Tompkins pushed his chair back from the table. "Not that I don't enjoy this enlightening conversation." He winked. His reddish brown hair and green eyes suggested an Irish heritage, but Tompkins certainly wasn't an Irish name.

Each person at the table had a story to tell. Before the evening was over, three of the guests had offered to look through their things to see if they had anything that might apply to Lindsey's research, and Ruth Emery had extended an invitation to go through her grandmother's trunk.

It was nearly eleven-thirty when Lindsey returned to the hotel. A slight scent of citrus wafted past her nose as she opened the door to her room. The red light on the phone welcomed her back, and she punched the numbered keys to retrieve her messages.

"Hey, hon, sorry I missed your call this evening. Call me when you get back. Love ya. Bye."

The machine played the second message. A deep, gravelly voice intoned, *"Mrs. Marc, I think you should go home and plan a different book."*

DECEMBER 7, 1911 ~ LAWRENCE, MASS.

Jenna's hand trailed down her stomach as she twisted to give herself a profile view of her new brown suit in the full-length mirror. The waist-length coat with a narrow lapel felt elegant. "This is wonderful. Thank you. *Grazie,*" she added.

"*Prego,*" Anna and Sylvia replied.

Sylvia picked up the bag with her lunch from the counter. "You look wonderful. But the factory whistle will blow soon. We must get to work."

Jenna thought of Brad. He had been right not to come into the house last night. The other women would have talked if he entered the building.

Jenna paced alongside Anna and Sylvia as they headed down the cobblestone street toward the river and the mill. She held her shoulders high. A few of the others who walked by turned and eyed her new clothing. Jenna smiled.

She strutted into the factory. "I'll see you after closing, but don't wait for me. I have no idea how long I'll be working tonight."

Anna and Sylvia headed off toward their looms. The noise of the plant intruded into Jenna's thoughts. One machine after another started up. The leather straps slapped against the wheels as the giant looms came to life. Soon there would be a cloud of dust in the color of the fabrics being made for the day. In her mind's eye she could picture it so well. The noise in the office became a dull, rhythmic beat, unlike the overpowering din on the factory floor.

Jenna turned toward the offices and headed down the narrow hallway.

"Good morning," Polly Reed greeted her. "Let me see."

Jenna gave her a brief spin, showing off her new suit.

"Very nice. Here are yesterday's accounts receivable. You'll need to post them and balance the totals for the day." Polly continued with her instructions while Jenna loaded up her arms for the full day's work. "I'll be by later to see how you're doing. Any questions?"

A million, but she wouldn't ask one. "No, I think I understand it."

"Wonderful, I'll be back in"—she glanced up at the wall clock— "in an hour. That should give you time to get settled and started."

"All right." Jenna strode confidently into her office. At least she hoped she looked confident, because at the moment she didn't have an ounce of it in her. She sat down at her oak desk and placed the mound of receipts in a neat pile in front of her. Reaching for the ledger behind her, she spun around and found Brad standing in the doorway.

He held a finger to his mouth for silence. "Miss Waverly, would you come to my office at noon?"

"Yes, sir." She immediately realized she didn't know Brad's last name. Was it Wood? He said that he'd speak to his uncle about a new position. So many questions still remained about Brad. And yet, she couldn't wait to be alone with him. She needed to apologize, and noon couldn't come soon enough.

"Thank you. I'll see you there, and bring this month's expense report. I'd like to go over a few details."

"Yes, sir." Jenna's hands trembled as she reached for the next invoice.

Before Brad turned to go, she heard his hushed whisper, "You look absolutely stunning this morning."

"Thank you," she whispered back. His compliments were like a fine spring rain that refreshed and invigorated the soil after the long months of winter.

Jenna worked hard organizing and posting the invoices from the previous day. After a while, Polly Reed walked into the office and removed her jacket. "How are you coming with the invoices?"

"Slowly but surely," Jenna replied.

Polly leafed through the piles and explained the process of posting to the ledgers.

When noon came, Polly said, "You have a thirty minute break for lunch. Take care of your personal needs and eat. You did bring a lunch with you?"

"Yes, Mrs. Reed. Thank you so much for all your help."

"You're welcome, but it's my job." She put her jacket back on and adjusted it so that it sat perfectly on her shoulders. Jenna looked down at her own jacket, which was wrinkled from bending over the desk all morning. Now she understood why Mrs. Reed had taken hers off. "You'll get used to it," the older woman said.

Jenna hiked up to the third floor and hoped she would find Brad out in the open. The olive green cloth cover on the ledger darkened from the sweat of her palms. *Stop being so nervous,* she admonished herself.

"Miss Waverly," Brad's voice called from behind her. She turned and found him standing in a doorway. "Come in, please." He stepped back and allowed her to enter.

She scanned the door for his name. It wasn't there. She slipped her gaze over to his desk. It wasn't there. *Drats!*

The door closed behind her. She found herself entrapped in his arms. "My dear, sweet Jenna. I'm so sorry about last night." He captured her lips with such force that she dropped the ledger and wrapped her arms around his neck. She needed his support. She needed his love.

She wanted to kiss him, but his office wasn't the right place. Yet it was so comfortable, exciting . . . Jenna pulled back from Brad's wonderful but imposing kiss. "Stop." Her voice cracked.

"Sorry." Brad stepped back and picked up the ledger. He opened the pages and pretended to read them. "Excellent, thank you."

"Brad? What's going on here? Last night you wouldn't come into the house—not that that was a wrong decision, but still . . . you keep me at a distance and then . . ." Jenna tried to catch her breath. "Then you, you . . . I don't understand."

"I'm sorry. You're right. There's a time and a place for everything, and here in my office is not it. But I wanted a few moments with you to apologize for last night. Can we talk someplace tonight? Can I take you for a drive into the country?"

"If you're afraid of being seen with me, what's the point? I'm not from your social class, and obviously that is of more concern than your feelings for me." Jenna had never been so bold, but a man had never made her feel this way before. She wandered away from him and looked out the large window at the river below. The harsh temperatures had nearly frozen the river solid.

"Jenna, please try to understand. I do want to be with you, but there are things that my uncle would not understand. I have to be most discreet. Please say you'll meet with me. We'll discuss this later. You can't be gone from your office much longer without further suspicion."

Jenna nodded her agreement, clutched the ledger to her chest, and ran out of the room. If she'd stayed a moment longer she would have cried or done some other foolish thing. This was not the time to give in to her emotions. If Brad truly cared for her, then he'd have to deal with his family. But how could he know if he really cared for her or not? They'd only been together a couple of times.

Jenna gnawed on her fingernails. On her desk was a note from Polly Reed letting her know she wouldn't be able to help for the remainder of the day. Relief washed over Jenna. Not that she resented Polly's help, but how could she keep from showing her emotions for Brad?

The next hour dragged by. She hardly made a dent on the paperwork. Her stomach rumbled. In all the commotion, she'd forgotten to eat. Reaching for her lunch bag, Jenna pulled out her sandwich and unwrapped it. She bit off a hunk and chewed. It felt marvelous in her mouth, waking up her taste buds.

Jenna thought back on the kiss. It had been powerful—the kind that girls fantasize about, a kiss that makes a woman believe the man will sweep her off her feet and carry her away to his castle to live as the queen. Did she want to be the queen of Brad's castle?

An alarm blared, jarring Jenna from her musings. She ran to the door and joined a stream of people running toward the observation windows. "What's wrong?" she asked.

No one seemed to know. They all stood mesmerized by the swirl of activity below. The cloud of dust gradually settled as the weaving machines were shut down. Then, out of the spiraling cloud, a man in ragged and bloody clothes carried a small child. Jenna's heart caught in her chest. A thin boy lay limp in his arms. The man's grease-covered face was streaked with tears and blood. The boy was dead.

Chapter Eight

Lindsey calmed herself and prayed before she called Marc. "Hi," she said, trying not to sound nervous.

"Hi," Marc yawned. "What time is it?"

"Midnight." She sat on the bed and removed her heels.

"How was the dinner party?"

Circling the phone cord around her finger, she answered, "Fine. I managed to make some contacts with people who had relatives who were a part of the strike, both on the management and strikers' level."

"Great." She heard the bedsprings creak. "What aren't you telling me, Lins?"

"It's probably nothing." She had been trying to convince herself for the past five minutes.

"*What's* probably nothing?"

"Someone left a message and suggested I write a different story."

"Uh-oh. Tell me what happened." The sleepiness in Marc's voice was gone.

"Nothing. That's what's so strange. Even the photograph I took to the police held no interest for them."

"Lins, I'm concerned. Remember, we discussed this. I'm not letting you stay there if you're at risk in any way."

"Honey, I'm fine. It's like the pastor and counselor said, I can't go running and hiding every time someone decides to send a prank call. The newspaper article came out today saying that I was in town. It's probably some nut wanting to give me a hard time for no reason at all. He didn't threaten me. He simply suggested I go home and write another book." She tried to convince herself as much as Marc.

Marc sighed. "I still don't like it."

"I don't like it either, but I have to face minor problems like this or I'll never be free of this fear." Cradling the phone between her ear and shoulder, she stood up and pulled down the over-starched bedspread. "Pray for me. I'm a little shaky."

A calm washed over her as Marc prayed. "Promise me, if there is any further sign of trouble, you'll come home. Right away," he emphasized.

"I will. Thanks for praying." Lindsey rubbed the bottoms of her feet. "I could use you right now. My feet are killing me."

His baritone laughter relaxed her further. "Run yourself a hot bath."

"I can't. My mind is buzzing with all the information I learned at dinner." *Not to mention the phone message.* "I need to write it down before I lose it. And, let's face it, a hot bath would knock me out for the night."

"That is the general idea."

"Watch it, buster," Lindsey interrupted, "or I'll be calling you all night with the exciting things I'm writing."

He groaned. "Tell me what happened tonight to get you so excited about the story."

Good. She needed to refocus, and he knew that as well. She told him.

"Sounds like you're making progress," he said when she finished.

"I am. I love you, Marc. I miss you."

"I miss you too."

Lindsey held the phone for a moment to listen to his last breath as he hung up. There was a definite downside to research trips.

Wouldn't it be nice if Marc could retire and come with me? Maybe someday.

→ ←

Lindsey coaxed her bleary eyes open. She'd fallen asleep at the computer again. The basic bones of the novel were coming together, the central plot was forming, but it wasn't around the death of Anna Lopizzo. Instead, Lindsey found an intriguing story line developing out of the mysterious death of Jenna Waverly.

She saved the document and closed the lid to her laptop before making her way to bed. The clock read 3:48. Lindsey moaned. She had an eight o'clock appointment with Barnaby Paige. She slipped between the covers and closed her eyes.

→ ←

Fumbling for the phone, she tried to stop the continuous ring of the wake-up call. She opened one bleary eye and squinted. A little to her right . . . there. She knocked the phone off the hook.

Her body felt like lead as she tried to push herself up from the bed. She shouldn't have stayed up working last night. Marc's idea of a long, hot bath had been the right idea. Why hadn't she listened to him?

Somehow she managed to coax herself out of bed and into the bathroom. She turned on the shower and stood under the pulsing water, rinsing the smell of cigar smoke from the night before out of her hair. Leaning her head back, she let the water cascade over her. *Shoulda, coulda, woulda won't help now, girl,* she reminded herself. She lathered her hair and scrubbed.

The phone rang.

Lindsey paused with her hands full of suds. Should she answer it?

What if it's Barnaby? He can leave a message, she reasoned, and continued to whip up the rich lather. Hair washed and rinsed, she finished her shower and dried off. Wrapping herself in a towel, she went to the phone. The little red light was blinking. The message was from Barnaby. He couldn't make it. Could they reschedule?

Lindsey fell back on the bed and went back to sleep.

→ ←

She woke to the persistent ringing of the telephone. "Hello?"

"Lindsey, its Abigail. I found something on Jenna Waverly. She had a job in the mills—that's not surprising, and according to some records, she worked the looms. But I have another source that lists her as a bookkeeper for the same company."

"American Woolen Company?"

"Yup."

"I found her on a list of employees too," Lindsey said, "but only as a weaver. Interesting. Do you have any dates?" She sat up and glanced at the clock as she readjusted the towel. Noon. She'd slept the morning away. Of course, she'd also worked through the night—or most of it anyway.

"From what I can see," Abigail continued, "she only worked for a month as a bookkeeper. That was in December of 1911, just before the strike. If I have all the records right, she stopped working for the mill just before Christmas, three or four weeks before the strike."

Lindsey scratched down the information and the names of the documents, so she could recheck the information later. Then she had a better idea. "Abigail, could you e-mail me the information?"

"No problem. I hope this helps."

"Yes, it does. It makes me ask more questions, and questions are good."

Abigail giggled. "I'll have the e-mail off to you in a little bit."

"Thanks again, Abigail. You've been a blessing. Bye."

Lindsey rushed to the bathroom, looked at her flyaway hair, and winced. Turning on the tap, she cupped the water into her hand and poured it over her head, brushing through the unruly strands. With any luck she'd get her hair to stay down for an hour.

After dressing, she returned to the mirror to appraise the black denim jeans and bulky, cream-colored sweater that made up her outfit. She ran the brush through her hair one more time. *You're going to go through an attic,* she reminded herself. *You don't have to be a fashion queen.* She grabbed the briefcase that contained her laptop, the digital camera, and her tape recorder—everything she hoped she'd need for her visit with Ruth Emery.

She arrived a couple minutes past one. As she walked up the front steps toward the old colonial, she wondered, "Who is Sylvia Giovanni?"

⇥ ⇤

"Shoot," he grumbled to himself. "If she's not holed up in her room or at the library, she's visiting with someone." He tapped his fingers one at a time up and down his hand, wondering how he could get her alone in a public setting. The inn wasn't possible. They videotaped everyone coming in and out of the hotel. He needed a place secluded enough so she could disappear without notice.

DECEMBER 8, 1911 ~ LAWRENCE, MASS.

"Jenna," Brad whispered. "Over here." He hid behind the corner of the mill just past the exit.

Her heartbeat raced with excitement, then plunged instantly into sadness. Why did their relationship have to be such a big secret? They had talked about everything on their wonderful drive in the country. In so many ways they had the same point of view. Why was he hiding behind corners? She stepped off the curb and crossed the street toward him. This was foolish. She stopped.

"Jenna," he called out softly.

She stepped toward him, her mind protesting each forward step. This was wrong, this was ridiculous, and yet she continued. She longed for him. He appeared to desire her as well. But he reminded her of worsted wool still damp from the cleaning, a man who couldn't stand up for himself and for what he wanted.

"I think I solved our problem," he said. "I found a cottage just north of here in Methuen. You can live there. No one will know when I come to visit. I told the owner we were getting married this weekend. She believed me and rented the place to me for twenty dollars a month. It isn't much, but it will be a place of your own, and we could see one another and not worry." Brad's eyes pleaded for understanding.

"Are you saying we're going to get married?"

"No, not exactly. It's too soon, don't you think?" Brad ushered her to his car. "Come. I'll show you the place, then you can decide."

Jenna slipped into the car and sat rigidly in her seat. Did she want to be a kept woman? Was she ready for the implications of what he was suggesting? Was he asking for sexual favors? On the other hand, this would solve the problems with the housing situation. A woman couldn't have gentlemen callers past seven in the evening. And there were plenty of people who would squeal. Mill workers weren't the sweetest sort of women. Genteel behavior went out the door when the whistle blew. In the houses, they tried to live like civilized ladies, but who knew what civilized and genteel were anymore? Jenna certainly didn't. Learning how to serve tea with a silver tray service was not something one did while working in the mills.

"Jenna, speak to me. You haven't said a word."

"Brad are you asking me to . . . to . . ."

"To what?"

She opened and closed her fists. "You know."

Brad's face reddened. "No." His voice was gruff. "I told you, your honor is safe with me."

"But why the secret place? I don't understand. And why the façade that we're married? Why would a landlord care?"

"Jenna, there are social rules one must abide by. A lady would never entertain a man without being chaperoned. And you know that would not be possible for us. The other point to consider is that we both want to spend more time together. I can't afford to take you out to dinner every night. Our own cottage would allow us some time alone, some time to get to know each other. That's all."

Jenna closed her eyes. It all sounded so reasonable. And she rather liked the idea of her own home. She could handle the foolish desires that had crept into her mind today. Or were they so foolish? Wasn't Brad thinking the same thing, wondering if they should marry? Trying to find a way for them to be together so they could find out?

"Who's going to pay for the cottage? I don't think my salary will cover it and leave me anything to eat."

"I'll cover the cost of the cottage. Can you afford the trolley expense to work and back every day?"

"Probably. I don't know what my salary is going to be for doing the bookwork, over that of a weaver."

Brad chuckled and reached for her hand. "You'll be earning at least double, if not triple."

Then she could probably afford the rent too. But if he's offering to pay. . . . "Have you seen the place?"

"Yes. It needs some work, but at least the roof doesn't leak. The landlord took some money off for the condition of the place if I promised to do some of the repairs."

"I'll take a look . . . and if I like it, I guess I'll move in."

Brad's face beamed. The smile she loved so much reached from the front of his lips to the curl of his jawline.

Jenna didn't care what the place looked like if it would give them time together to get to know each other, to possibly marry one day. She couldn't believe her ears that he was talking marriage.

About fifteen minutes later, they arrived at a small cottage on a lot with a short front yard. The house next to it was a large two-story with a wraparound front porch. The cottage needed paint and a shutter or two repaired in the front.

The screen door is off its hinges, but who needs a screen door in winter? she reasoned, trying to convince herself. In her heart she knew this was probably another mistake, but Brad made it seem so reasonable. And wasn't reason what her parents had taught her to do?

Go ahead and try to convince yourself, Jenna. You know this is wrong. She ignored the voice in her head and reached for the crook of Brad's arm. "Show me the inside, please."

He patted the top of her hand with his own. "With pleasure."

They entered through the front door into the small living room. It had a stone fireplace and oak floorboards. They needed a bit of polish. The bedroom was small but larger than her room in the boardinghouse, with a good size closet. And to have a bathroom all to herself—Jenna couldn't think of anything more wonderful. The brief tour ended in the kitchen. "What do you think?" he asked.

"I think I love it."

He swooped her up in his arms and twirled her around in the small kitchen. "I'm so happy to hear you say that." He eased her down softly and kissed her.

Jenna melted into his kiss and returned it with equal enthusiasm.

"Uh-hum," someone cleared his throat, then coughed.

Jenna and Brad pulled away from one another.

"You'll be taking it then, Mr. White?"

"Yes," Brad agreed.

So his last name is White. Brad and Jenna White—not bad. Not bad at all.

Chapter Nine

"Lindsey, it's so nice to see you." Ruth Emery greeted her with a healthy hug, like an old friend. "I've been in the attic all morning. I've found a few things and set them aside." She ushered Lindsey into the house without taking a breath.

"Excited?" Lindsey ventured.

"Actually, I am. I haven't spent time with those memories in a long, long while. It's quite fun."

Lindsey could easily relate to those feelings. An eclectic blend of antiques and modern pieces decorated the older woman's home. Oddly enough, there was a harmony among the various items from different time periods. Lindsey eyed the snowflake patterned white silk sofa. American Rococo Revival, she assessed.

"Is that a Stanton Hall?" she asked.

"Yes. You do know your antiques. This particular piece was a gift to my grandmother from Grandfather Donovan on their twenty-fifth wedding anniversary. When they were first married, they both worked in the mills and they didn't have much. After they married they moved to Methuen. My understanding was they were able to rent a small house out there instead of an apartment. Both had lived in the boardinghouses prior to getting married. And both were involved with the strike. They were a unique couple."

Lindsey raised her eyebrows.

"Grandfather was Irish; Grandmother Italian."

"That is an interesting mix," Lindsey chuckled.

"You can say that again. When I was a small girl, I remember hearing the two of them argue. Grandpa would be silent. Grandma would be very animated. Then after she finished, grandfather would simply stand up and calmly say, "You're right, Sylvia," or, "You're wrong, Sylvia," or whatever the case might be, and he'd walk off. They loved each other with a passion. I don't see that too much these days."

Ruth led her over to a wall lined with photographs. "This is Grandma Sylvia and Grandpa James." Lindsey scanned the picture of the older couple. Sylvia had the typical dark hair, dark eyes, and olive-toned skin of the Mediterranean. James had a healthy head of dark, curly hair.

"Which one do you resemble?" Lindsey asked.

"Neither. I look more like my father's side of the family. My maiden name was Everett."

Lindsey made a mental note to check the records for James Donovan and Sylvia Giovanni to see if she could find out anything about them. Using real people in her fictional tale would add an element of authenticity to the piece. "What did they do in the mills?"

"I believe Sylvia worked on the looms, where she lost a finger, and I'm fairly certain Grandpa was a machinist, but I can't be a hundred percent sure. Grandfather left the mills in the early twenties and started a small machine shop. I can't tell you how many times I heard growing up, "Don't go to work for the mills." I did, however, work one summer in the mills and learned quickly why it was not the career choice to make. I decided to attend college and taught school for many years."

Lindsey glanced back at the photograph. Sure enough, Sylvia had only three fingers on her right hand. "What was so hard about working in the mills?"

"The noise, for one. And a dust cloud enveloped the place as soon as the machines roared to life. But that noise—it was an incredible racket. You'll have to travel down to the Lowell museum. They have a running loom, and you can hear it. Then multiply that noise by fifty to a hundred times, and that's the sound the mills made. Aside from that, it was a rough group of people to work for. You got paid by how much you produced, so if a runner didn't bring the bobbins fast enough, you heard about it in some of the most foul language imaginable." Ruth shook her head. "I imagine not much has changed. Oh, the wages are a bit better, but it's a hard way to make a living. Ah, but you didn't come to hear me wag my tongue." Ruth clapped her hands together. "Come on. The attic's up here."

Lindsey followed Ruth to a white wooden stairway leading to the second floor and eventually to the narrow attic stairs. With so much more yet to learn about these people, their lives, their way of life, she'd definitely have to go to that museum in Lowell. She wouldn't be going home by Friday. Marc wouldn't want to hear that she needed to extend her visit, but he'd understand. She tried to calculate her days. *How can I get home sooner?*

Ruth pointed to the second step from the top. "Be careful. That step is a little shaky."

The rich smells of old clothes, old books, dust, and dry heat filled Lindsey's nostrils. She scanned the attic. There were empty picture frames hanging from the rafters, old wooden sleds, a well-worn sofa, some small tables and dressers, and an overstuffed chair that had lost its stuffing in the seat. Box upon box of other items crowded the floor.

Ruth stepped over to a small table. "I put most of the items I've found so far over here."

Lindsey made her way to the table. On it were bundles of old letters postmarked during the Second World War. "Those are my parents' letters to one another. I don't know how much help they might be, if any."

"Thanks. What do you have from your grandparents?" Lindsey

held the bundle of letters in her hands. To think these were actually mailed to Europe and carried through the war. Several were well worn; others were in better condition.

"Back here is my grandmother's trunk. In it I found a poster from the strike and a flyer they handed out to release the union organizers six months later." Ruth handed the old document over to Lindsey.

It was titled, "The Spirit of Lincoln."

> *Fellow workers—Citizens—Comrades*
> *Do not let Capitalist Editors befog the present situation before you . . .*

Lindsey sat down in a wooden rocker and read the editorial opinion about the explosion in the cobbler shop and how it was linked with Mr. Wood. The threat of another strike only six months later was news to her. "Interesting."

"I thought so. Tempers were sure running high. From what I understand, other strikes around the country started organizing about then."

"Right. There were even some named Bread and Roses as a sisterhood to this one."

Ruth rummaged through the box. "This was my grandmother's wedding dress. Nothing fancy, but look at the stitching."

The hand stitching on the dress exhibited top quality workmanship. The fabric, a light linen, seemed fitting for a poor worker from the mills. "Did she make it herself?"

"I believe so." Ruth reached in and grabbed another memory. "Oh my, I forgot these were in here. This is my mother's dressing gown for the baptism and dedication ceremony."

"Baptism and dedication?"

Ruth sat down with the infant outfit on her lap. "Remember that my grandfather was Scots-Irish from Ulster."

Lindsey nodded her head.

"They're Protestants, and most Italians, like my grandmother, were Catholic. So, to compromise, they dedicated the baby in both churches. Years later, they settled on the Protestant church, but in their early years they compromised. As I mentioned, my grandmother could be quite adamant about her point of view."

Lindsey chuckled. "I can only imagine."

Ruth joined in the laughter. Her eyes sparkled with merriment. "They really were quite a pair. I loved them dearly."

She placed the tiny garment aside and reached down into the trunk once again. "Oh my goodness, look at this."

Ruth unwrapped a small leather diary from a swatch of brown woolen fabric, the type a business suit would be made from.

"Was it your grandmother's?"

"I don't know." Ruth flipped open the pages.

Lindsey held back the urge to take it from her host's hand.

"No, it belonged to someone else."

Lindsey jumped off her seat. "Who?"

DECEMBER 11, 1911 ~ METHUEN, MASS.

Jenna loved her new home. Sylvia and Anna helped her move in, and they spent the first night in the cottage with her. Neither of them knew about Brad, and it was best to keep it that way. They did think she was foolish to spend her raise on her own place, but once they saw it, they agreed that it gave a certain sense of freedom and accomplishment.

The trolley rocked on its rails. She held her bag tighter, protecting a large potato, two carrots, one onion, and a half-pound of beef shank to put together some stew. A meat-filled stew. Brad had given her a dollar to purchase food for dinner and for the house. She had rounded her shopping out with some flour, eggs, and a yeast cake to make a starter for sourdough bread.

She looked forward to spring when she could plant her own vegetables. For the rest of the winter she would need to eat a lot of beans like the other mill girls, but tonight she wanted their dinner to be special.

The trolley stopped, and she took her first step to independence. She hiked the five blocks up the hill to her cottage. The backyard edged a wooded area at the end of a dead-end street. What could be better?

She noticed Brad's car parked beside the house. Gooseflesh rose on her arms in anticipation. It had been three days since they had seen each other.

He opened the door for her. She ducked under his arm. "I can't believe it takes you that long to come home on the trolley. I've been waiting forever." He let the door slam back on its frame and reached for her waist. "I've missed you."

His lips were a sweet blend of softness and silk. She regained her equilibrium.

"I've missed you too." She placed her bag on the kitchen counter. "I went shopping for tonight's dinner."

"I ended early and did some shopping of my own." He beamed. He opened the cabinet and showed they were filled with canned goods and spices. He opened the next cabinet near the sink and a set of four glasses and place settings lined the shelves. He pulled out the drawer near the sink, which held silverware. Then he reached for the cabinet door closest to the back door and showed the various pieces of cookware he'd purchased.

"Where'd you get all this?"

"An estate sale in Boston. There are linens and towels in the bathroom, a comforter for the bed, and some fancy silk pillows for the sofa."

"Can you afford it?" *How much does he get paid? Is it any wonder the workers are talking strike, with Brad and others making so much more money?*

"Trust me, it was a steal. Most people were there for the antique furniture, paintings, and expensive pieces of pottery. I had my eye on a fancy piece of jade, but I was outbid."

"I don't know what to say."

"Say nothing. This will all be ours one day. I see it as an investment in our future."

She stepped into his arms. "Oh, Brad, do you mean that?"

He held her close. "Of course. I've thought of nothing else but you. I can't concentrate on work. My life at my uncle's house is pure boredom, which doesn't help when I'm trying to get my mind on something besides you. I don't see how I can live without you. But I know we can't be married just yet. Soon, I hope. My uncle is a powerful man, and I need to be strong enough to oppose him.

"One day I'll lather you with the finest things that money can buy. You'll have fancy linens to dress your table, the finest china to set upon it. I just need time, Jenna. I know I'm asking a lot from you, but give me some time."

She kissed his lips to silence him. "You foolish man. I've already decided to give you the time." Passion flamed in her heart and in his touch. She needed to break off the kiss. Thankfully, he did.

"Jenna, I'm concerned about the rumors of a strike with this new law, reducing the workers' hours to fifty-four a week. What are the women on the floor saying?"

"They aren't pleased. But—" Jenna hesitated. Should she tell him what the workers were discussing? "They aren't paid well."

"I know. I'd like to see them get more, but there's nothing I can do."

Jenna stepped toward the stove. She wasn't happy with Brad's lack of concern for the workers—but not two seconds ago she had confessed her belief in him. She sighed.

He coughed. "What's for dinner?"

Chapter Ten

Ruth opened the small black diary. "It says here, Jenna Waverly."

Lindsey grabbed the diary, unable to resist. "No way." Sure enough, inside the front cover, it said, "This book belongs to Jenna Waverly." "How did your grandmother know Jenna?"

"Who was she?" Ruth's salt and pepper eyebrows knit together.

"She was found under the ice on February 10, 1912."

"During the strike?"

Lindsey acknowledged the question with a simple nod of the head and thumbed through the diary for the last entry. "I wonder how your grandmother had this."

Ruth leaned back and looked inside the chest. "There's another journal, a larger one." She pulled it out and opened it. "This one belonged to my grandmother, but it's dated much later."

"May I see it?" Lindsey reached for the journal, not quite believing her good fortune. She couldn't wait to read Jenna's diary. The best thing would be to type in all the entries, but she didn't have time before she returned to Miami.

"Of course." Ruth let her fingers linger over the written words on the yellowing pages in front of her, and a tear edged her eye. "She's writing about becoming a grandma."

Lindsey pulled back her hand. "Why don't you keep reading it for a bit. I'll look over Jenna's."

"All right, but I could use a tall glass of iced tea. How about you?"

"Sounds wonderful. Is there anything else in the chest?"

"A few more items. Let's finish scavenging, then we'll bring everything down to the dining room that we want to examine more closely."

"That's a wise plan. I admit, I can get caught up in the moment. I can't believe you have Jenna's diary."

"I can't believe it's in English. My understanding was that Grandmother understood English but preferred Italian during the days of the strike. It wasn't until she married Grandpa that she really started to learn English. Her journal is written much later, and there are a few words and phrases still written in Italian."

"Wonderful. What a family treasure." Lindsey held on to Jenna's diary and leaned toward the chest. "So, what else do we have in there?"

They spent the next few minutes rummaging and found the bill of sale to the cottage that the older couple had purchased, and not rented as Ruth had assumed, shortly after they married. They came across a necklace Ruth had never seen before. *Could this also have belonged to Jenna?* Lindsey wondered.

Finally, they found the bottom of the chest and an old letter from someone with the initials Q. B. dated around the same time as the purchase of the cottage. They gathered their few clues and headed down to Ruth Emery's formal dining room. While Ruth left to fix their refreshments, Lindsey placed the items on the table. She opened the worn leather diary and began to read. It started in the summer of 1909 with Jenna's journey to America and her discovery that her aunt had died. Lindsey learned how the poor girl was forced to work in the mills, having no funds for transportation back to England. The first few days in the mills were hard on the young farm girl, but she tried to maintain a positive attitude.

As she continued to scan the pages she saw a pattern of depression forming in Jenna's entries. "Was it suicide?" Lindsey mumbled.

"What?"

"I'm sorry. I was just thinking out loud."

"Don't keep me in suspense." Ruth set the tray down with two tall glasses of iced tea and a plate of fancy cookies.

Lindsey closed the diary and set it aside, being careful not to soil it. She reached for one of the glasses. "Thank you." The fruity blend of raspberry tea whetted her appetite.

"You're welcome. Now tell me what you know about Jenna Waverly. I'm all ears. I can't believe I'm helping a mystery writer in my own home with information I didn't even know I had." Ruth grabbed her glass and offered the plate of cookies to Lindsey.

"I know precious little." Lindsey took a cookie and nibbled on a corner of it. "I know she worked for American Woolen Company."

"Mr. Wood's mill? Where my grandparents worked? Which of course makes sense if my grandmother had her diary."

"Right. And I know she was a weaver at first, but then in December of 1911 she became a bookkeeper. The fact that she could write probably had something to do with it. But how did they know? Management and the mill workers rarely talked. So how did they find out?"

"You're assuming she could work with numbers?" Ruth sat back in her chair.

"From the position she was put in, yes."

"Ah, but what if she was hired because she didn't know the numbers so well. Remember, they say Mr. Wood hired a man to blow up some of his own property to blame it on the strikers." Ruth reached for her tea.

"Hmm, interesting. Have you ever considered becoming a mystery writer?" Lindsey made a mental note to look up the accusations about Mr. Wood as she took another bite of the sweet, flaky cookie.

"Nope, just read and watch a lot of movies. I hate it when I figure out who did it in the first few minutes."

Lindsey sipped her tea and set her glass down. "Okay, we know when Jenna's body was found, and we know that the last entry in her diary is dated the second of February. We know that the authorities didn't know who she was at first and posted it in the paper. Who identified her? What happened in those eight days that caused her to die? Or was it simply an accident?"

"All good questions. What's the last entry say?"

"I don't know. You insisted we finish searching," Lindsey chuckled, "so I haven't looked yet." She placed her glass down on the coaster that Ruth had provided and wiped her hands on a paper napkin. She took in a deep breath and exhaled slowly.

Holding the small book in her hands, she closed her eyes and wondered once again what Jenna looked like. The report had said nothing more than an unidentified woman had been found. Where had she been found?

"If you don't open it soon, I'll scream," Ruth interrupted.

"Sorry."

"No you're not, but go ahead and open the thing before I take it from you," Ruth teased. "Did the police say it was murder, an accident, or suicide?"

"They didn't say." Lindsey opened to the last entry and read out loud.

Dear Lord, forgive me. I can't believe I'm with child. What will Brad say? I'm terrified, Lord. This changes all of our plans. And yet I'm amazed that there's a baby growing inside of me that was created out of our love. Oh, Father, I love him so much.

Lindsey blinked and reread the words one more time.

"She was pregnant when she died? That shoots your suicide theory, doesn't it?" Ruth held her glass with both hands.

They both continued to stare at the intimate words so elegantly penned on the page. "Who's Brad?" Lindsey mindlessly asked.

"Maybe she reveals who he is earlier in the diary," Ruth suggested. "How tragic."

"Could Brad have not been pleased with her pregnancy?" Lindsey theorized.

"Are you suggesting he rid himself of his problem, literally?" Ruth asked.

"It's a possibility." Lindsey thumbed back a few pages to December 10, 1911, and continued to read silently.

Sylvia and Anna stayed with me in my new home last night. Brad will be joining me for dinner tomorrow night. I'm so excited. I can't believe this is really happening. I know some will say this is wrong, that I shouldn't accept Brad's gift of a home. Others, in their unholy minds, will think that we are not being honorable, but we are. We're only doing what society won't let us do—spend time alone together.

Lindsey glanced over to her hostess, who was holding her grandmother's journal. "Ruth, I know this is an incredible favor, but may I keep Jenna's diary for a while? I'd like to read it all from cover to cover. I promise I'll guard it and treat it carefully. But there have to be clues in there about Jenna, about the decisions she made, and possibly about what led to her death sometime in February."

Ruth sat back in her chair and thought for a moment. She nodded her head and said, "By all means, but you'll need to keep me posted. What did you just read?"

"It's written the second night in her new home. She mentions that Sylvia and another friend, Anna, helped her move in. So that's probably how your grandmother knew her. Apparently Brad set her up in the cottage."

"Oh, dear, she was one of those." Ruth took another sip of her iced tea. "I was hoping for something not so bold, I guess."

"Actually, she claims that moving there allowed the two of them time alone."

Ruth raised her eyebrows. "Obviously."

"She didn't intend to do anything that God wouldn't approve of," Lindsey added in Jenna's defense.

"Don't know where she went to church, but back in my day, a woman and a man didn't do that unless they were married—or sinning." Ruth set her glass back on the table.

Lindsey chuckled. "I didn't say it was a wise plan. I tried to teach my boys to watch out for just that kind of a situation. People think they can handle their emotions, then get caught off guard."

"True, but if he's set her up in the house . . ."

"I know. I need to read more."

"No question." Ruth agreed. "But you're not leaving until I have some more information. Read on."

"Okay, but may I use your bathroom first?"

"It's down the hall on your left, second door." Ruth opened her grandmother's journal.

"Don't forget to tell me anything interesting you find in there." Lindsey winked.

"Unless it's a family secret," Ruth quipped.

"True, no secret is safe with a writer. It may not come out exactly like someone said, but it's bound to come out in some form or fashion."

Ruth glanced up at her and narrowed her gaze. "I'll remember that."

Lindsey chuckled inwardly on her way to the bathroom. How fortunate it had been to meet up with Ruth Emery. *Thank you Lord, I appreciate this gift. Help me be worthy of revealing this new information. Help me to be mindful of this woman, Jenna, and not judge her for her sins. Help me see the heart of the woman, and help me find out why she died.*

When she returned to the dining room she found Ruth thoroughly engrossed in her grandmother's journal. "Find any family secrets?"

Ruth jumped.

"I'm sorry. I didn't mean to startle you."

"No, no, it's just me getting older, I guess. I didn't even hear you leave the bathroom."

"Must be the interesting reading."

"Grandmother thought to write down some of her fondest memories. It's really special to read about her love for Grandpa. Not that there was any doubt, but she could be a stubborn woman. She said here . . . let me think, where was that?" Ruth slid her finger down the page. "Here it is. 'James was always an attractive man and caught a girl's fancy. But if he hadn't been more stubborn than me, we never would have been blessed with such a rich life and family.'"

"Nice. Isn't it strange how limited we are in our focus? I mean, we know we have parents and grandparents that go back many generations, but they all have their own stories, their own struggles and passions. I guess the older I am, the more I see beyond myself. But when I was young, well, there was nothing but Marc. And how the Good Lord keeps everyone's story straight is beyond me."

Ruth giggled. "It is amazing. Daniel and I were just like you and your husband. Guess we all have our romances."

"And Jenna obviously had one with Brad."

"True. I did find a reference to Sylvia's two best friends dying during the strike. She specifically mentioned Anna Lopizzo."

Lindsey sat down and took hold of Jenna's diary, turning back to the reference where Jenna had moved into the cottage. "So, the friend, Anna, who helped Jenna move in must be Anna Lopizzo. Interesting. What else did she say?" *How is it that Sylvia knew both of the women who died during the strike?* Lindsey wondered.

"Not much. I can't believe Grandmother knew Anna Lopizzo. She never mentioned it, as best I can recall, but that was many years ago, and I'm not as quick in the memory department as I once was."

Lindsey traced the crocheted lace cloth on the dining room table. It appeared old and slightly yellowed with age. "This is beautiful. Did you make it? Must have taken a long time to crochet."

"No, my Grandmother Sylvia did."

Ruth scratched down some notes.

"While you're looking through your grandmother's journal, check and see if she mentions John Rami. I can't believe she would know all three of the people who died during the time of the strike, but you never can tell." Lindsey's mind buzzed. Was Sylvia Giovanni a common denominator?

"Who's he?" Ruth asked.

Lindsey explained, then sat back in the Windsor chair. Ruth's earlier words about skeletons in the closet crossed her mind. Could Sylvia have been involved with these two women's deaths? Was her fight for the cause so great that she would sacrifice her friends?

DECEMBER 15, 1911 ~ LAWRENCE, MASS.

Jenna looked up in response to the knock on her door. Polly Reed stood in the doorway with the latest ledger sheets Jenna had just produced. "These are all wrong, Jenna."

"How so? I simply put in the information I was given."

Polly sauntered over to Jenna's desk. "Yes, but look here." She placed the sheet on her desk. "See, this column has not been adjusted by the percentage of the depreciation value, which then, in turn, makes this column of figures off by the same percentage point, minus the taxes."

Jenna's head spun as Polly explained about the value of assets going down since machinery needed to be replaced every ten years. That was easy to see. Her loom should have been replaced long ago rather than calling James Donovan to fix it every two weeks. Every time it broke down, she lost time and pay.

Polly sat back and pulled a report from a file drawer. "Here's last year's report. It shows what the value of the equipment was in 1910."

Jenna scanned the figure. It was very different from the 1911 value.

"Note this line here." Polly pointed back to the current ledger sheet.

"Add the purchase of new equipment and the cost of repairs to the current value, and it should come pretty close to last year's value."

Jenna quickly figured the numbers. They were within a few dollars. "Now I understand."

Polly smiled. "Good, so you will fix this sheet and have it to my desk before the end of the day?"

"Yes. Sorry."

"You're a quick learner, Jenna, but please ask me when you don't understand something."

"Yes, ma'am."

Polly placed the report back in the file cabinet and left Jenna to her work.

Jenna shook her head. Looking at the amount of monies set aside for equipment purchases, there shouldn't be so many problems on the factory floor. *Just do the job, Jenna. It's the floor manager's decision to fix the equipment, not yours.*

Sylvia and Anna were planning to come over for the weekend. Brad had to travel and wouldn't be back until Tuesday. The three ladies planned a time of cleaning, sewing, and cooking to set up the new house. It was too late in the year to work in the garden, but Jenna couldn't wait to plant some flowers and vegetables. Oh how she missed the fresh food from the farm.

"Miss Waverly," Mr. Billings's baritone voice echoed in the room.

"Yes, Mr. Billings, how may I help you?"

"I'm behind on my quarterlies, and I was wondering if you could give me a hand." His hands were filled with a haphazard stack of papers.

"If I can."

Mr. Billings stepped into the room. "I need you to work Sunday. I can't imagine us getting through this by the end of the day."

"I'm sorry, I have plans for the day. If you'd like, I could take some of this home and work on it there. I could bring it back on Monday morning. Would that help?"

Mr. Billings glanced at the door and back to her. "Can't hurt, I suppose. You have to make certain you don't lose a single receipt."

"I'll be careful." Jenna was surprised that Mr. Billings would ask for her help; then again, he was the one who'd had an error on his bookkeeping "test."

Billings dropped his work on her table and pointed out what he needed done. It was simple organizing and posting in the ledger. There were no percentages of depreciation or any other tricky mathematical gymnastics to go over. She could probably do it in two hours. It wouldn't make for a nice evening of girl talk with Sylvia and Anna, but it would win her points with Franklin Billings.

Although she had worked more than a week in this position, she still worried that she would be sent back to the looms. She would do anything to keep her new job. The offices were so much quieter than the noisy factory floor. There was no lint cloud to make her choke. If Jenna had learned one thing, it was that office work suited her far better than factory work.

"I'll see what I can do before I leave today," Jenna offered.

"Thank you, Miss Waverly. I appreciate your help."

"You're welcome."

He wasn't out of the office more than fifteen minutes before Polly Reed came back in. "How are those figures coming?"

"Just about done."

"Did I see Mr. Billings just leave?"

"Yes, he's asked me for some help with his quarterlies."

"Good. Maybe they'll come in without errors this time." Polly chuckled. "By the way, I have to leave early today. My daughter has an appointment with the doctor, and someone needs to watch the baby. Are you all set? Do you have any further questions?"

Jenna looked back down at the paperwork. "No. I understand what I'm supposed to do now."

"Good. I'll be here for another hour. If you have them done before

I leave, let me know. Otherwise, leave the sheets on the desk under my blotter."

Jenna nodded. "All right." She wiggled the pencil back and forth in her hand for a moment. "Mrs. Reed, I have a couple of friends who are going to my house for the weekend. Is there any way I can get word to them on the floor that I need to work a little later?"

Polly placed a hand on her hip. "You really need to be careful if you want to move up in the office work. Management doesn't like office workers mingling with the factory workers."

Jenna opened her mouth to object.

Polly held up her hand to silence her. "I understand they're your friends and you've worked with them for years. I can send a message to them this time, but in the future you might want to have a meeting place after work." Polly leaned forward and whispered, "Just to keep management from . . . you know?"

Jenna wasn't at all certain she knew, but she nodded her head in agreement. If it was anything like Brad and his problem with their social differences . . .

"What are their names and where do they work?" Polly scribbled down the information on a small piece of paper from Jenna's desk.

Jenna went back to her work with a sudden rush. If she could finish these ledger sheets, she could make a dent in Mr. Billings's quarterlies and possibly finish them before she left to go home.

⤙ ⤚

When the whistle blew for the end of the workday, Jenna saw, out of the slightly open office window, the factory workers exiting like a swarm of locusts. She glanced back at Mr. Billings's quarterlies. He was so incredibly disorganized. *How did he ever land in management?* she wondered.

Thirty minutes later, she stuffed all the receipts into a large manila envelope and grabbed a couple of extra ledger sheets and pencils. She walked over to her coat and slid her arms into the sleeves. She couldn't wait to go home. She couldn't wait to spend the weekend with her friends. She missed them. And though she loved the cottage, she was lonely there. Living in a house full of women for so many years changes a gal. Jenna was grateful for the times she had with Brad, but so far they'd been few and far between. *Why does he have to travel so much? Will he ever be ready to acknowledge our relationship publicly and—and get married?*

Calm down, she reminded herself. It had only been a couple of weeks since she and Brad had met. *Men need more time. That's all there is to it,* she decided as she exited the office.

"Jenna." James ran up to her. "Anna and Sylvia want you to know they'll be meeting you at ye place later."

"All right. Thanks." Jenna went to the trolley stop and waited. It arrived within a couple minutes. On the trolley, Jenna thought about the work she could finish before Sylvia and Anna arrived. The delay was a blessing in disguise.

A man with a long trench coat boarded the trolley at the next stop. He wore a gentleman's hat with a black ribbon around the brim. *Better dressed than the usual trolley passenger,* Jenna thought. He nodded, then took his seat in front of her. She'd grown used to the regulars, and he wasn't one of them. On the other hand, she'd never traveled at this time before. The set of his shoulders was relaxed, but his fingers tapped a nervous rhythm on his knee. He held his arms close to his body as if he wanted to avoid any physical contact with the seat or his fellow passengers.

He looks like he's never ridden a trolley before, Jenna said to herself.

The rhythmic clang of the wheels relaxed her while the gentle breeze nipped her nose. Jenna leaned down and huddled closer to herself to keep warm. At her stop, she passed the man. His highly polished black shoes gave the impression that mud would simply slide off them. She carried her bundle up the hill to the end of the street and smiled at the sight of her home.

My home. How sweet that sounded to her weary body. Inside, she placed the work envelope on the table and went to her room to change.

Back in the kitchen, she put on a kettle of water for some hot tea and set out to make vegetable soup and biscuits for dinner. A movement outside caught her eye. She leaned over the sink and looked out the window. Had she set the locks on the doors? Her hands trembled. The last house on a dead-end street, a woman alone—it wasn't the best of situations.

Is someone out there?

Chapter Eleven

He'd beaten her back to the hotel. It probably wasn't wise to have passed her—who knows, she could have turned off somewhere before the hotel, but following this woman was boring. He needed a little excitement.

"Stay focused."

From his seat in the lobby, his face shielded by the day's newspaper, he watched her enter the building through the automatic lobby door and head for the elevators. The smell of freshly brewed coffee wafted from the coffee shop. *Surely I have time for a cup of coffee and a sweet roll,* he told himself. He folded the newspaper and walked over to the Coffee Café. Finding a table that afforded him a view of the lobby, he ordered a cappuccino mocha and opened the sports section to check last night's scores. Inhaling the sweet aroma of his coffee, he settled in to await the results of his latest handiwork. "Yeah, this should do just fine."

⇢ ⇠

Lindsey's heart skipped a beat. The door to her hotel room banged the wall as she stopped mid-stride. Her research papers littered the floor, and the cushions from the sofa lay tossed aside. Everything was out of place. Frozen, she reached for her cell phone and auto-dialed Marc's cell.

"Hey, honey, what's up?" Marc's cheery voice allowed her to take a breath.

"You won't believe this, but someone's ransacked my room." She surveyed the mess once again.

"What? Are you all right? Have you reported it?"

Lindsey stepped back into the carpeted hallway. "I'm fine. I haven't even entered the room. I called you first."

"All right, go to the next floor, down the hall, anywhere. Just get to safety as soon as possible," Marc ordered.

Lindsey obeyed. Who would possibly want to tear apart a writer's room? She reached instinctively into her purse and clutched Jenna's journal. Thankfully that hadn't been in the room at the time. She heard Marc's voice calling her. She placed the phone back to her ear.

"Lins, are you there?"

"Hi. Sorry."

"Go to the lobby. I've called the hotel. They're informing the authorities. Have you witnessed any other criminal activity?"

"None, I swear." Fear drenched her body in a cold sweat. "It has to be some strange coincidence. I found something today, but no one knows except Ruth Emery."

"What on earth did you find?"

"A journal written by the woman who drowned in the river. Jenna Waverly."

"Oh, honey, not again."

"Marc, there's no reason to think it's personal." She mentally worked through the logical steps her counselor told her to do when unexpected stressful situations occurred. "Do you think it could have been some thieves looking for money?"

"Except for the message yesterday."

A wave of nausea tossed in the pit of her stomach.

Marc sighed. "On the other hand, you're probably right. We can both tend to overreact. Let's see what the cops say, okay? Where are you now?"

"I'm in the lobby. The manager is here along with a couple of front desk workers. I'll call you when I know something."

"Okay, keep me posted. I'll be praying."

Without asking, he knew the fears she was battling. Marc was probably fighting a few of his own. New Orleans had been a difficult time for Marc and the boys as well.

A man in a long-sleeved, white shirt and dark tie quickened his pace toward her. "Mrs. Taylor?" She glanced at the name on his brass badge: John Randall. Manager. "I'm so sorry," he said. "I've called the police. They should be here shortly. Is there anything missing?" He was a young man, perhaps in his late twenties or early thirties.

"I don't know. I—I didn't go into the room."

The manager paced back and forth. "I don't know what to say. Nothing like this has ever happened before."

So it wasn't a common occurrence that just happened to hit my room. "Have any of the other occupants found their rooms broken into?"

"Not that I'm aware of. We could go up and check."

We? Wouldn't Marc love to hear that. "I think we should wait for the police to arrive, then let them check."

"Ah, right. Good idea." He glanced out the front windows.

Lindsey mentally calculated what she had in her room. Her laptop, digital camera, and recorder were with her in her briefcase. Most of the information in the room was in the form of photocopies and books relating to the strike, all recoverable material.

"We'll switch you to another room at no charge."

"Thank you. I would like a similar one, if you don't mind."

"I'll put you up in a suite. I'm really sorry about this. I don't believe we've ever had a break-in before. Of course, I've only been working for this hotel for less than a year," he rambled on. He played with the keys in his front pocket.

His nervous behavior would fit a guilty man as easily as a frightened one. Lindsey studied him. He'd make an interesting character for a novel. He has all the classic behavioral quirks, she mused.

The police arrived in short order. They examined the room, and Lindsey found nothing missing. No other room on the same floor had been touched. All indications were that it was a random act. Nevertheless, Lindsey was relieved to be moving to a different room—especially when the hotel manager opened the door to the VIP suite. Not only was it twice the size of the room she'd been in, with a living area apart from the bedroom, it also had a conference table.

"What a blessing," she murmured. "Thank you, Lord." With all her paperwork and the timeline she was creating, the extra space would be extremely helpful.

She closed the door behind the manager and his assistant and pressed the send button to call Marc.

"How are you?" he asked.

"Okay. It's nerve-racking, but they moved me to a nice suite." Stepping farther into the room, she sat down on the sofa. In front of her, a large screen television filled most of the sectioned wall. Three stuffed chairs and a square shaped coffee table rounded out the sitting area in the suite.

"I'm not crazy about you staying at that same hotel, Lins, VIP suite or not," Marc said. "I know I shouldn't be worried, but with the death threats we received during the New Orleans trial, I don't want you taking any chances."

"I'm not thrilled about it either, but according to the police, it's a random break-in. There were no written threats. Probably some kids looking for money or something they could hawk." She slipped her shoes off. Propping her feet on the coffee table, she leaned back on the brown leather sofa. They discussed the possibility of the break-in being a random act, the threatening phone call the other night, and the wisdom of moving to a more secure location.

Lindsey held the back of her neck and stretched it. Her muscles were tight and stiff. "Okay, I'll move tomorrow. I'll register under my maiden name. That should keep me safe."

Fifteen minutes later, they ended their conversation, and Lindsey took advantage of the whirlpool bath, allowing the weariness and excitement of the long day to ease from her body. She knew better than to give in to the urge to start reading Jenna's journal tonight. She wouldn't sleep a wink until she finished it.

❧ ❧

The wake-up call startled Lindsey. She lifted the receiver and dropped it without listening to the automated response. The message light flashed on her phone.

She called the front desk.

"Are there some messages for me?"

"Yes, Mrs. Taylor. The management has blocked all incoming calls to your room, and they want to express their profound apologies for what happened yesterday. They hope you've found the new room satisfactory and hope you will continue your stay free of charge while you're in the area."

The rest of my stay? That seems a bit over the top.

"Also, Edgar Archer left a small package at the front desk for you."

Perhaps she should change her name and stay at this hotel. No one but a few on the staff would know. She could even check out of her hotel room to convince whoever might be watching her that she'd left. If someone really was watching. A new rental car could be brought to the hotel to further the disguise. She'd have to call Marc and ask what he thought of the prospect.

"Thank you," she answered the operator. "Please let the staff know I'll be checking out."

"But . . ."

"I'll speak with the manager."

"Yes, Mrs. Taylor. I'll switch you over to him right now."

"Thank you."

While her call was transferred, she dialed Marc on her cell phone. "Honey, I have something I want to run by you."

"Hello?" the manager's voice came on the phone.

"Please hang on for a moment," Lindsey said. She cupped her hand over the phone and quickly relayed her plan to Marc.

"All right. But if there's the slightest indication of any further trouble, you're leaving there immediately. Agreed?"

"Agreed, bye."

"Bye." Marc hung up.

"Mr. Randall, I'm sorry I had to put you on hold."

"Mrs. Taylor, I'm sorry you feel you must leave our hotel. I can assure you tha—"

Lindsey interrupted and shared her plan. The manager was more than happy to accommodate her, even arranging a new rental car in her mother's name. Within two hours, she had checked out of the hotel, purchased a red wig, exchanged her car, and called in a registration under her maiden name for the same hotel's suite—all without leaving her room.

With everything in place, Lindsey dressed, donned her wig, and exited the hotel. She decided that a drive north to Maine for an overnight visit with her parents would be in order, if for no other reason than to give some distance from her stay at the hotel. At a rest stop about an hour away from her parents' exit, Lindsey stretched her legs and sat down at a picnic table under a tree. She scanned the Maine coastline, taking in the scenic view.

Totally different from South Florida, she mused. The water's darker, the shore lined with large boulders of granite—and there isn't a pelican in sight.

The fresh scent of pine filled the air. She extended her legs and feet and leaned against the top of the picnic table. It felt good to breathe and not be recognized. She retrieved Jenna's journal from her purse and began to read.

Jenna had come to this country at the age of fifteen only to discover that her aunt had passed away. No provision had been made for the young woman who was now a stranger in a strange land. The first entries were a swirl of confusion.

Well, at least she spoke English. Can you imagine those Italian girls? She read on.

DECEMBER 16, 1911 ~ METHUEN, MASS.

"Jenna," Sylvia beamed. "The house is looking nice." Jenna had never felt so proud as at this moment.

"Thank you. I love it."

Anna peeked around the corner. "With your own fireplace and wood stove . . . no cold now."

Jenna laughed. "I may have them, but I've nothing to burn in them."

"Ah," Sylvia sighed. "How much is wood these days?"

"More than I can afford. But come next winter, I'll be prepared." With Brad here every evening she hadn't felt the cold. They'd huddle together on the sofa and talk for hours. With each passing day, she fell more and more in love with him. His three-day business trip only deepened the ache and longing within her.

Jenna roamed toward the rear of the house. "Come see how I've started to fix my bedroom. The closet has few clothes to put in it."

The girls followed her with excitement.

"How can you afford all this, and where did you get the furniture?" Sylvia asked.

Jenna found herself telling half-truths to her friends again, as she had the first night when they'd helped her move in. "They came with the place." *Sort of.*

"It's a darling house." Anna sat down on the bed. "How can you pay for it?"

"It'll cost just about all my earnings, but I can manage. Next year, I hope to plant a garden and have enough food to keep me through the winter. Do you think I can keep a couple of chickens in the backyard?"

"Chickens?" Sylvia scrunched up her nose. "Why?"

"For their eggs. There's nothing like fresh farm eggs in the morning."

"You are a farm girl, yes." Sylvia laughed. "Next you'll want a pig as well."

"I wouldn't mind. I just don't know if I could feed it."

Sylvia continued to laugh. "You're hopeless."

The springs creaked as Anna stood up from the bed. "Where's the material? Let's start those curtains. A woman should not live alone without curtains on the windows." She left the room and ambled toward the kitchen.

"I can't believe your good fortune. How'd you ever hear about it?" Sylvia asked.

Jenna braced herself to lie once again but realized she didn't need to. "Someone at the office mentioned it. I know it's a struggle, but I think it's worth it, don't you?"

Anna scanned the knotty pine cupboards and white porcelain sink. "Yes, I think it is. This is why we talk strike. To have our *pan é rose,* our bread and comfort too."

Sylvia sat down at the table. *"Si."*

"Jenna, you see the books. Can the owners afford to pay us more?"

"Don't ask me. I'm not allowed to speak about financial matters regarding the company." *But, I want to. I'm so sorry, my friends.*

"No numbers, just a yes or no if Mr. Wood can afford to pay us better."

Anna placed her hand on Sylvia's forearm. "We should not ask. We no want to ruin Jenna's job."

Sylvia sighed. "*Si,* I'm sorry."

The three women worked late into the night cutting and sewing the new curtains. Finally, Anna and Sylvia went to sleep on Jenna's bed. Jenna stayed up a little longer and went to work on the paperwork she'd brought home.

She worked until the figures started to blur before heading for the sofa.

Chapter Twelve

Lindsey reread Jenna's impression of the mills compared to life on a farm. *Confining* probably described her feelings best. She wrote little after she realized she had no choice but to work there. Jenna had given up hope.

Closing the journal, Lindsey leaned back and looked out to sea. She inhaled the salty air and tried to imagine all the hope and dreams that energized immigrants to make a new life for themselves in the land of promise and opportunity. Jenna seemed like so many others who came before her, and yet so different in other ways. Most came knowing how much hard work would be involved. Most knew that accommodations would not be spacious, although in some cases it was more than they had in their own countries. Jenna, on the other hand, had had her own room on a farm in wide-open spaces. To be left alone and so young in a strange city with no other choice than to work in the mills . . . well, Lindsey certainly understood the young girl's frustration. Some of the early entries referred to her faith, but those became fewer and fewer as time went on. If only she had clung to God, perhaps Jenna would not have ended up alone in an icy river.

Lindsey's cell phone rang, bringing her back to the present day. "Hello," she answered without looking at the caller ID.

"Lindsey, where are you?" The panic in her mother's voice was palpable.

"Hi, Mom. I'm at a rest stop—been reading for a while." Lindsey glanced at her wristwatch. She should have arrived an hour ago at her folks' home. "Sorry."

"Well, just as long as you're okay. You could give a person heart failure. I just received a phone call from a total stranger."

"What?" Lindsey jumped up.

"Someone was looking for you. I told him you weren't here. He wouldn't leave his name. I don't like this, Lindsey. What have you gotten yourself into?"

"Nothing. I promise. I don't understand why you'd be called."

"Well, your father is cleaning the shotgun, just in case."

Oh brother. "Mom, tell Dad to put away his shotgun. Nothing is the matter, it's just some strange coincidence." *On the other hand, who would be calling Mom and Dad, looking for me? Something doesn't add up.* Nothing she'd come across or even witnessed should bring this kind of suspicious behavior. *Perhaps we're all just a little bit paranoid after New Orleans.*

"Mom, answer me this, do you occasionally receive calls for me or asking for information about me?"

"Occasionally, but not that often. Just local reporters."

"See, that's my point. It can't have anything to do with the hotel room being ransacked." *Thankfully, I didn't tell them about the phone call telling me to leave town.*

"You're probably right." Lindsey heard her mother's hand go over the phone and her mumble, "Michael, put the gun away. Lindsey says there's nothing to be concerned about." Silence followed for a moment, then her mother added, "Marc works for them. If he believed Lindsey was in trouble, he would have sent her home."

Lindsey rolled her eyes heavenward. *Lord, help me calm my parents . . . and myself.* "Mom, I'm fine. I'll be there shortly."

"All right, dear. Drive safely."

"Not a problem. Love you."

"Love you, too."

She couldn't deny the obvious any longer. Someone wanted her out of the way. But who, and why? She hadn't unearthed any deep, dark secrets. She glanced down at Jenna's journal. Or had she? Were the clues to Jenna's death in this small book? Had she known what was happening before she died? But there were no entries for eight days prior to her death, unless she drowned on February second and the body hadn't been recovered until the tenth. *A body would probably remain in good shape in nearly frozen water. Though I guess it might swell some,* she thought. She decided to double-check with a coroner.

Lindsey flipped the old journal open to the second-to-last entry and scanned it. *Nothing unusual.* She closed the small book and headed back to her car. *No need keeping the folks waiting any longer.*

> ← ←

He'd been fortunate to be listening in the hotel lobby when the replacement rental was ordered. He had enough time to remove the tracking device and successfully mount it on the new car before she left.

Glancing at the fuel gauge, he noticed that his car was almost empty. He inhaled the last of his cigarette and tossed it out the window. A small pile of butts had collected on the edge of the off-ramp. He'd been sitting for nearly two hours with the engine running. The indicator light still hadn't gone on. He tapped it once again. Nope, she still hadn't moved.

It's possible she turned around and went back to Lawrence, he reasoned.

He'd been having this argument with himself for the past hour. How long could a person sit at a rest area without facilities? He'd been inclined to pull over behind her, but he would have been too noticeable in this secluded stop. He didn't need to be spotted.

He'd been warned not to kill the woman. But if he found the right opportunity where an "accident" could happen—he drummed his fingers on the steering wheel—it might be beneficial.

DECEMBER 16, 1911 ~ METHUEN, MASS.

Jenna slipped out from under the sheets on the sofa. She'd heard a noise outside. Reaching for the broom that stood in the corner, she moved into the next room. Anna and Sylvia were sound asleep in her bedroom.

Crack. A dry twig snapped outside the kitchen door. This time she knew she wasn't just imagining it.

Jenna grasped the broom handle a bit more tightly and positioned her arms for a swing. The back door squeaked open. Jenna froze. Her heart raced. She could hear the blood pounding in her ears.

A man's hand reached around the door.

Jenna aimed the broomstick.

A dark wool overcoat came into view.

"Brad?" She lowered the broomstick.

He poked his head in and smiled. "Hi. I just returned from my business trip."

"It's three o'clock in the morning."

"Sorry, but I had to see you to let you know I was in town and that I could spend the day with you tomorrow. I was going to sleep on the sofa . . ."

"Brad, I have guests."

"What?" his voice rose.

"Shh. Anna and Sylvia are spending the weekend. They're help-ing me make curtains and such."

"Oh." His shoulders relaxed. "I'll leave." He placed his hand on the doorknob. "Can I see you tomorrow?"

"Yes. *No* . . . I don't know. The girls were planning on spending the entire weekend. I could ask them to go home, but wouldn't that raise suspicions? Sylvia's already asking questions about how I can afford this place, the furniture. I don't like keeping our relationship a secret from my friends."

He came to her and held her in an embrace. "I know, my precious flower. I'm sorry." He lightly brushed a few stray hairs from her forehead. "Just a little longer and we'll be able to be together. I promise."

Jenna's heart raced. "Oh, Brad. I love you. I want to be with you."

"I love you too, but we have to do this right. My uncle is a powerful man, and with all the talk of the workers wanting to strike, he's been quite irritable around the house. You have to allow me time to prepare him."

"I know."

He leaned down and kissed her. Jenna felt alive and vibrant in his arms. How could a woman love a man so much in such a short time? She didn't know, but she couldn't argue with it. In his arms, it felt like they had always been together and time didn't matter.

"I love you," he whispered as he pulled away. "I'll come by on Sunday evening. Enjoy the time with your friends."

"I'm sorry."

"Nonsense. I think it's wonderful that you want to turn this place into a home. I'll see you Sunday night."

"Good night." The door closed silently between them. Jenna stood and stared at it for a moment. Why couldn't she just be honest and tell her friends? He did have a point about the gossip wheel in the factory, but Anna and Sylvia would never tell anyone. She sighed, crept quietly back into the shadowed living room, and slipped back under the covers. The bedroom door remained shut. No one had awakened to hear Brad come in. They were safe for a little longer. But how long could she fend off Sylvia's questions? Anna didn't seem to notice, or at least didn't speak her questions aloud if she did. Sylvia, on the other hand, was a straightforward, deal-with-it-now kind of person. Jenna smiled. *Perhaps that's why I like her so much.*

⇻ ⇺

They worked most of Sunday finishing up the curtains they had started. With the scrap material and some old dresses, they began braiding a rug. Jenna would add to it as time and scraps permitted.

In the afternoon, they repaired to the kitchen to do some cooking. It was a luxury they didn't have in the boardinghouse. They baked homemade breads and a pot of stew for dinner. Anna and Sylvia taught Jenna to make pasta, and soon it was strung all over the house to dry.

As much as Jenna enjoyed what they were doing, her mind kept coming back to Brad and his hopes of spending the day with her. Somehow, the time with her two friends didn't quite compare. Perhaps it wasn't a good thing to love a man so much that you couldn't think of anything but him.

"Jenna," Sylvia's voice cut through the fog in her mind. "What's the matter with you? Are you sick?"

"Sorry. I'm fine. I was just thinking how wonderful it is to have friends like you." Lying was becoming a habit.

"It's been fun, but I need rest to return to those looms. They rattle your bones." Sylvia yawned.

Anna hung the last of the pasta. "I should nap too."

Jenna stretched out a long yawn. "That's not a bad idea."

"I sleep on the sofa tonight, Jenna. You have your bed," Anna offered.

"Thanks, but I'm fine." *What if Brad comes back?* She didn't think he would, but he had his own key. Locking the door wouldn't make a difference.

Having seen that man outside her window the other day had made her nervous. She didn't want to be left alone, and she was grateful that Anna and Sylvia were there for the night.

"May I have a cup of hot tea, to warm the bones before bed? If you please, Jenna." Anna asked.

"I think that might be nice."

Sylvia opened the cupboard.

Jenna froze. She'd pulled all the ingredients out for the baking earlier this morning, hoping to keep Sylvia and Anna from noticing her full cupboard. They had brought the sack of flour they'd used for the pasta making.

"Look at all this food." Sylvia turned and put her hands on her hips. "Jenna, I know you can't afford this—even if you are working in the office now. Who pays for all this? And don't tell me it was here when you rented the house."

Chapter Thirteen

If reporters were hunting her down, there was no point in putting her folks through a media frenzy, Lindsey decided. After a quick call to her parents and some assurance that she'd be careful, she pulled back onto the highway, heading south. Besides, taking a day away from her research would delay her return to Miami.

Her cell phone rang again.

"Hello," she answered on her hands-free set.

"Hey, Mom. What's with the break-in to your hotel room?"

"How did you hear about that?"

"It was on the news."

Lindsey tightened her grasp on the steering wheel. "What?"

"Yup." Jeff chuckled. "You're a hot news item. People are real curious about you since the trial in New Orleans."

A beep sounded in Lindsey's ear. She pulled to the side of the road. "Hang on, I have another call coming in."

She switched to the second call. "Hello." The car rocked as a semi sped past her, followed by a red sports car.

"We've got a problem," Marc said.

"I heard. I'm on the phone with Jeff now."

"Your publicist should be shot," Marc sighed.

"How'd he find out about it?" Lindsey noticed a dark sedan slow down before it passed her. *A courteous driver, how nice,* she mused.

"I have no idea, but I'm tracking that down now. Call me when you're off the phone with Jeff."

"No problem." She switched back to Jeff. "Hey, son, that was Dad."

"He heard it too, huh?"

"Apparently. Did I make the national news?"

"Yup." Jeff chuckled.

Ending her conversation with Jeff, Lindsey put on the news radio station and within two minutes she heard the sound bite related to the break-in. "So much for a low profile in Lawrence," she quipped. She blew a wisp of hair from her face. She placed another call to her parents and told them that a reporter must have called looking for her.

Pulling back onto the highway, she continued south toward Lawrence. There was only one way to fight the media, and that was to deal with them head-on.

Of all the silly things to have happened. Lindsey glanced in the rearview mirror. *Lord, help me deal with this and deflate it as soon as possible.*

She called her publicist. "Hi, Stan. Lindsey. Did you have a hand in all this?"

"No," he laughed, "but I'm going to have a ball launching your new book. What's it called?"

"*Bread and Roses,* and I hope we don't have to go through another New Orleans *City Streets* experience."

"Hey, come on, that was wonderful timing, if I do say so myself."

"Yes, you would say so," Lindsey chuckled. "Okay, how can I spin this and take the heat off of me? I need a couple more days to dig up some information. Unfortunately, I don't know if all my contacts will allow me to make copies of their materials or take the originals back to Miami."

"Hmm, let me think." Lindsey could hear the tapping of a pencil on a stack of paper, a familiar trait of Stan's. "Okay, here's what I know. The police found nothing missing from your hotel room. More than likely, it was kids or someone looking for something valuable to steal, right?"

"Right. How on earth did something so minor make national news?"

"Because someone had a slow day and saw big bucks. The photo of you carrying your paperwork out of the room was priceless."

"They have photographs?"

"Only one that I'm aware of, but it's the backdrop on all the reports I've seen."

Lindsey did not remember a photographer's flashes going off as she exited her room. *Whoever it was must have come with the police, and I just didn't notice them.* "Oh boy," she said out loud. "I did go to the police station this week. Obviously, someone noticed me."

"Okay, the way I see it . . ." Stan had more marketing savvy in his pinkie than Lindsey had in her entire body. He continued to discuss how to handle the media.

Lindsey thought out loud. "This research trip has been difficult enough, without all this distraction. So many of the mill workers didn't read or write. Many started working when they were kids."

"Bring that up. Swing the media hounds to the real reason you're there and away from the nonsense of someone breaking into your hotel room. Then get your work done as fast as you can and go home. The sooner you're working on the book, the better it will be for putting this story to rest. But most of all, be safe, Lindsey. I remember those threats that came during the trial. They weren't pretty."

"There've been no. . . ." Her words trailed off.

"What's happened? What are you not telling me?" Stan insisted.

"Oh, it's nothing. Someone left a message for me to write a different book and leave town."

"What on earth for? You didn't witness anything this time, did you?"

"Well-l-l-l-l . . ."

"No way. What did you see?" Stan let out a nervous chuckle.

"It had nothing to do with anything. It was a simple drug deal, and the police weren't even interested in the pictures I took."

Stan whistled. "I don't like this, Lindsey. I don't like it at all."

"Marc knows, and he isn't concerned." Lindsey gripped the steering wheel tighter. "Well, not overly concerned." She put on the blinkers and signaled her exit. A dark green sedan behind her did the same. Hadn't that car passed her earlier? Fear prickled her spine.

"Stan, I'm almost at the hotel. I'll call you later."

Instead of driving directly to the Lawrence Inn, she turned toward the center of town and placed a call to the police station. She continued on over the Merrimack River toward the old American Woolen factory. After some fancy turning and returning through the old streets, she glanced in the rearview mirror. She seemed to have lost her tail. Maybe they weren't even following her. The highway exit to the bridge was a fairly common route.

Lindsey headed back to the hotel. She needed to get a handle on her emotions and portray calmness for the reporters, if they were still there. A small group of people stood outside the lobby entrance as she pulled up. She had taken two steps from the car before they spotted her. She took a couple more steps, then paused, as Stan had suggested.

"Ms. Marc, aren't you afraid to come back to the same hotel? Didn't you check out this morning?"

"The police assured me that it was a simple attempt at theft. Nothing was stolen and, more than likely, it was someone looking for a quick buck. Yes, I did check out this morning. I had planned on visiting my parents, but I turned around once I learned I'd made media headlines. Who'd have thought that researching a book on the Bread and Roses strike would garner so much attention before I actually wrote the book?"

"What specifically are you writing about in reference to the strike?" asked a thin reporter in a tweed jacket. He looked like a throwback to the sixties. He jabbed a microphone toward her face.

Lindsey smiled and began to explain. This was exactly what Stan wanted.

"One of the unique things about this strike," she concluded, "was that it banded together women from many different countries who didn't understand each other's language, yet who somehow managed to create a unified front. That isn't to say that the men didn't strike also."

The small crowd wrote or recorded her statements. Another reporter brought it back to their purpose.

"Do you think the break-in was related in some way to the Melancon trial?"

"That hardly seems likely. Richard Melancon is serving time in the Louisiana state prison. What interest could he possibly have in the Bread and Roses strike of 1912?" Of course, she knew that revenge was not out of the question with someone like Richard Melancon, but she hadn't been the only one to testify against him.

"When will this book be coming out?" Derrick Hutchinson came to her rescue and gave her the perfect question to end the interview.

"Next March. However, if I don't get to writing it, my publisher will do more than ransack my hotel room. Good night all."

As she slipped away from the eager reporters, she made a mental note to send the PR on *Bread and Roses* to Derrick.

Letting out a deep breath, she went to the front desk. "Evening, Mrs. Taylor. Welcome back." The young woman taking registrations simply handed her the room key.

"Thank you. The list of acceptable calls to my room is the same. Please don't let anyone else get through to me."

"We understand. Management wants to thank you for returning and trusting us after the unfortunate break-in."

"You're welcome." Lindsey palmed the key and headed toward the elevator. Inside, she did something she normally wouldn't do. She pushed the button for two floors below hers, exited and walked up. She couldn't be sure that she wasn't being watched from the lobby, and she would have been easy to spot during the press interview.

Inside her room, she called Marc. Together they discussed the possibility of Richard Melancon being behind the threatening phone call and the room being rummaged through. Both agreed that it made little sense. He had been found guilty and would have spent time behind bars even without her testimony. He wouldn't jeopardize his possible release on parole by threatening her after the warning the judge and his own legal team gave him at the time of his sentencing. And although she had witnessed the killing, she had also admitted that Melancon was not without some justification, in a twisted sort of way.

Lindsey turned the water on to fill the whirlpool bath, then went to her paperwork, still neatly laid out on the table as she had left it earlier this morning. She popped a strawberry in her mouth from the fruit basket the management had sent up the night before.

Grabbing her purse, she placed Jenna's journal on top of one of the piles, then reached for it again on a sudden impulse. Quickly, she thumbed through to the page where she had left off. Jenna had written sporadically over several years, but she had started writing regularly again from November 3, 1911, until eight days before she was found dead.

Why did she suddenly start back up?

DECEMBER 17, 1911 - METHUEN, MASS.

"Jenna, who paid for all this food?" Sylvia repeated.

"I did." Jenna looked down at the floor.

"There's a man, isn't there? Who is he? Why do you sell yourself for this life?"

Anna came up beside Sylvia and placed a calming hand on her shoulder.

Jenna forced back her tears. "It's not like that. I love him. Nothing sinful is going on. We just can't spend any time together because . . ."

"Because he's management," Sylvia supplied.

Jenna shook her head and collapsed in the seat.

"He's the one I saw you staring at a few weeks ago, isn't he? Mr. Wood's nephew?"

Jenna acknowledged with a single nod of the head.

Sylvia let out a deep sigh. "Mr. Wood would not like his nephew with a weaver."

"That's the problem. Brad and I want to be together, but he needs time to arrange things so his uncle won't be furious. I know what you're thinking, but he's never made a forward move toward me. He treats me like a lady. He's the one who helped me get my new position. But he asked me not to tell anyone. He's so afraid that the mill grapevine would hum right to his uncle's ears."

"The lips would flap." Sylvia sat down.

"Does he love you?" Anna asked. She sat down opposite Sylvia and put her arm around Jenna.

"Yes. We plan on getting married as soon as possible. I just have to give him time to work things out."

Sylvia shook her head. "I don't know. It doesn't seem right."

"I pay for the trolley; he pays the rent. He bought all the furnishings."

"He can afford it," Sylvia grumbled.

"Sylvia," Anna chastised.

"Sorry. It ain't proper," Sylvia defended.

"I was raised proper enough in England and I know this doesn't fit the acceptable behavior, but what else can we do? I can't invite him into the boardinghouse. Everyone would talk and report it to his uncle. There are only so many restaurants we can go to without someone noticing us, and he can't afford to go out to eat every night, no matter what you might think."

Sylvia patted her on the hand. "I know. Not a good situation. Perhaps one of us should move in and chaperone."

"You can't. The landlord thinks we're married."

"What?"

"Brad rented the cottage. He said we were getting married the weekend after I moved in. He also told her he wanted a safe place for his bride because he traveled a lot."

"Does he stay all night?"

"No!" Jenna couldn't believe Sylvia was being so forward. But then again, Sylvia was always this forward, unlike Jenna's English friends, who were always so careful with what they said and to whom they said it. Unless, of course, they were gossiping; then all etiquette went out the window. She lowered her voice and said, "No, he doesn't stay all night, but he has left his automobile here a time or two. I only hope we can be married soon. Then we won't have to play these foolish games."

"I hope so too," Anna smiled. "With strike talk, Mr. Wood is not in so agreeable mood."

"Brad rarely talks about his uncle, but he's said something very similar."

"Management knows we talk about striking?" Sylvia sat back in her chair.

"Of course. You know how the grapevine is."

"Did you tell him?" Sylvia asked.

Anger burned deep in the pit of Jenna's stomach. It was one thing to be straightforward, it was another thing to be rude. "No," she spat.

"Sylvia!" Anna scolded.

Sylvia apologized, but Jenna turned and walked into the bathroom without another word.

After Sylvia and Anna went to bed, Jenna padded out to the sofa and settled in for the night. But sleep was elusive. She tossed and turned, uncomfortable with the tension that had developed between them. Not to mention how Brad would feel once he discovered she'd revealed their secret.

＞ ＜

The next morning, when Sylvia and Anna left for Mass at the Catholic Church, Jenna felt a pang of guilt. At home in England, her family would have attended services at the chapel in the village. She had tried to go to church when she first came to America, but without her aunt to encourage her, she had soon lapsed into the habit of sleeping in late on Sunday mornings. After six long days in the factory, she reasoned, she could use a day of true rest. She couldn't remember exactly when she had stopped going, but it had been a long time.

Her thoughts shifted to Brad. She was sure he would try to come by today, although she had no way to tell him that her friends had left. She ran through the house and set up a dinner for two, just in case.

He'll think that the girls would want to get back before dark, won't he? she hoped.

A shiver of apprehension flickered over her skin and traveled up her arm. *Was it right to want Brad so much?* They weren't married, and they were still getting acquainted. And yet, they seemed to know so much about each other. They talked about everything. She couldn't stop thinking about him all weekend.

Her only fear was letting him know that Sylvia and Anna knew about their relationship. Would he understand? Would he be upset? Would he break things off before his uncle could find out?

Jenna began to pace.

As the day whiled away, with still no sign of Brad, Jenna went into her bedroom to lie down. She would not cry. Brad had no way of knowing when the girls would leave. *What if he had to go out on business again?* she wondered.

She leaned over and reached for the journal she kept in the small drawer of her nightstand. She found comfort in writing all her thoughts and the many events that happened in her life since meeting Brad. It was hard to believe that one man could change her life so much.

Jenna began to write.

A loud crash thumped against the back wall of the cottage. Jenna shrieked.

Chapter Fourteen

Early the next morning, Lindsey set out for her appointment with Barnaby Paige. When she was settled in his parlor with a cup of hot tea, he began recounting stories he'd heard from his grandparents about the soup kitchens and meals that were sacrificed to keep the strike going.

No wonder observers and reporters at the time sensed such solidarity among the workers, Lindsey thought. Lack of food seemed to be a motivating factor behind why the strikers sent their children to New York. An adult might be able to deal with a hungry belly, but watching and hearing their children's pleas for food would have been difficult. Help had come from the union organizers, but mostly after the strike began.

Two hours later, she left to meet with Edgar Archer. He had mentioned that he'd found some material in the family archives that referred to Mr. Wood, the owner of the American Woolen Company.

As she drove up the Archers' driveway in the daylight, she could see that their property had once been a grand estate with stables, guest quarters, and gardens. But comparatively little land remained, and other homes now occupied the area.

Lindsey shook herself back to the present. *Stay focused,* she reminded herself. *You need to finish these interviews and get home before anything else happens.* Coincidence or not, the events of the past twenty-four hours had her rattled.

The key verse from her morning devotions—2 Timothy 1:7—flowed through her mind: "For God did not give us a spirit of timidity, but a spirit of power, of love and of self-discipline." She closed her eyes, took in a deep breath, and let it out slowly, reminding herself not to be overly concerned.

Gathering her briefcase, she got out of the car and walked up the blue slate sidewalk to the front door. Unlike the other night, a butler didn't greet her. Instead, Edgar and his wife, Betty, extended a warm welcome.

The scent of a floral arrangement on a side table under an antique mirror filled the entryway. Betty looped her arm through Lindsey's and led her to the front sitting parlor. "We caught that horrid news of the break-in at the hotel. Are you all right?"

"I'm fine, thank you."

"May I get you something to drink?" Edgar offered.

"No, thank you. I'm fine."

"We took the liberty of putting together a light lunch. We hope you'll join us," Betty offered.

Lindsey smiled. "Thank you."

Edgar sat down in the chair to the left of the divan where Betty and Lindsey had settled. "I'm well aware of the history of the mills and the strike, Mrs. Taylor. And I know the role my great-grandfather, others in upper management, and the mill owners at the time played in it. However, they weren't all bad men."

"I appreciate your willingness to share with me, Edgar, and I understand your perspective. But from everything I've read about the conditions in the mills, the owners didn't seem to have much regard for the rights of the workers."

"*Rights,* as we now understand them, weren't a part of the vocabulary back then," Edgar admitted without batting an eye. "The goal was to produce goods at the lowest possible cost to earn the greatest profit. Bringing in the immigrant workers allowed men like my great-grandfather to run and operate the mills profitably. The boardinghouses were a good plan, but not enough were built, and far more workers came than were originally expected. They established very strict guidelines for the girls, to protect their virtue, but many things were overlooked.

"Phineas Archer, my great-grandfather, respected William Wood. Wood was a stern man, and when he felt he was right he would never waver from his decisions. This made him a strong businessman, but this attitude obviously has its weaknesses, like not listening to the wise counsel of his officers."

"Were the police on the take from the mill owners?"

"I don't know. Of course, there are no records of such transactions. But the police had a vested interest in keeping the peace, and a few extra dollars here and there no doubt would have kept them motivated."

Lindsey pulled out her recorder. "May I record our conversation to refer to later?"

"Of course, we have nothing to hide. All of this happened way before our time," Betty purred.

"Just don't use it against me in my political campaign," Edgar chuckled.

Lindsey made a mental note. As a politician, Edgar might be inclined to spin anything he said to give Lindsey what she wanted to hear—or what he thought she might want to hear. "Are you familiar with the death of Anna Lopizzo?" she asked.

"It was such a tragedy. Tempers were running high all over the city. People were being beaten, and the police and militia were acting out of fear because of the sheer volume of strikers."

"Who do you think killed her, the police or the strikers?"

"Don't know. It could have happened either way." Edgar stood up. "Excuse me, I'd like a cup of coffee." He handed her a small bundle of old manila envelopes. "Take a look through these while I get myself a cup. Are you sure I can't get you anything—coffee, tea, soda, water?"

"Nothing, thanks."

Betty leaned over and pointed at the small bundle her husband had given to Lindsey. "These are some clippings from Edgar's grandfather's collection that relate to the strike. There were no personal journals that we've ever seen. However, I did find these." Betty opened the second manila envelope from the top and pulled out some smaller envelopes with postmarks on them. She handed them over to Lindsey.

Lindsey steadied her hands and took the small bundle. "Who are they to, and who are they from?"

"I'm not sure, but we think they are from a distant cousin who lived on Martha's Vineyard at the time of the strike. They're addressed to a Quincy Ludlum. He's possibly their son. They're personal letters about the family, except for this last one. The parents are concerned about a correspondence they had from Mr. Wood.

"My guess is that Quincy lived for a short time in this house, but did something to fall out of favor with Mr. Wood, his employer. He probably sympathized with the strikers. If so, I can't imagine that Edgar's great-grandfather would have allowed Quincy to stay here."

Lindsey made a mental note to go over the list of employees at the American Woolen mill once again and look for Phineas Archer and Quincy Ludlum. Lindsey opened the old letters and skimmed them. They told of the family's decision to stay on the Vineyard but were happy that Quincy was enjoying his apprenticeship with Mr. Wood.

Edgar reentered the room with a silver tray, a couple of cups of coffee, creamer, sugar bowl, and a bottle of water. "I know you said you were fine, but I brought some bottled water just in case."

Lindsey glanced up from the letters in her hand. "Isn't it sad that the workers were charged for their drinking water?"

"Yes," Edgar answered, and placed the tray on the coffee table. "The river was so polluted that the water had to be shipped in."

"But—" Lindsey protested, but Edgar held up a single finger.

"I didn't say I approved. But it's easier to look back now and see what should have been done to prevent the strike. And yet, there's a certain satisfaction in being an American and seeing how much our country has grown by recognizing these kinds of wrongs and making laws to prevent them from happening again. It's unfortunate this kind of treatment, and worse, continues all around the world today."

"True. I found it interesting that the water was a huge issue for the congressional hearings. Each of the transcripts I've read had the same question about the water asked more than once to the same person giving testimony."

"It's probably why so many public and private buildings have water coolers on nearly every floor today," Edgar suggested.

"Hadn't thought about that." Lindsey pointed to the water. "May I?"

Edgar chuckled and handed the clear plastic bottle to her. "You'd think Congress would have been more concerned with the age of the children working in the mills. Obviously, the child labor laws were written years later. Still, you would think the hazards of children working would be far more important to them than water," Edgar suggested.

"On the other hand"—Lindsey held up the bottle—"this is a basic necessity for life, and from what I understand, those mills were very hot, not to mention the clouds of lint flying in the air."

"Even after the laws were changed and the unions organized, you had dust, and those machines were extremely loud." Edgar took his cup of coffee and leaned back in his chair. "The mills aren't as crowded with workers today, and with better ventilation systems, those huge lint clouds are a thing of the past."

"What else do you have in these envelopes?" Lindsey asked.

"Not much; some bits and pieces. I made a copy of an old report to the shareholders to give you an idea of the operating budget they were working with back then."

"Thank you. That will be a big help."

Betty leaned over and pulled a book from the bottom of the pile. "This is *Mills, Mansions, and Mergers,* written by Edward G. Roddy. In there you might learn a little more about William Wood and his vision. It tells about the Shawsheen Village and his master plan to expand the American Woolen Company from Lawrence into Andover where he would build an entire community for his employees."

This was news. Lindsey hadn't learned much about William M. Wood yet.

Edgar put his coffee cup down on the tray. "You might also be surprised to learn that Wood was the son of poor Portuguese immigrants born on Martha's Vineyard. His father was a crewman on a whaling ship. He died when William was only twelve. The child left school and went to work to help support his family. As you're probably well aware, that is just how things were done back then."

"My grandfather had to go to work when he was eight to help support his family. I do understand the process," Lindsey acknowledged.

"Also, and we don't like to talk about it much, Mr. Wood ended his own life in 1926. He had suffered a stroke in 1924, which forced him to retire. He had built the company from nothing to an enterprise that owned sixty mills and employed forty thousand people."

"Impressive," Lindsey admitted.

Edgar looked over the rim of his glasses.

"Not the suicide, the company," she amended.

"I realize most people feel that Mr. Wood was the cause of the strikes. And they are probably right, but he was a good man, a hard-working man, and he had a real talent for building a strong business. World War I helped the company grow with lots of war contracts. Roddy's book will probably give you some helpful insight into the kind of businessman he was."

"Thank you. I really appreciate all this information."

"You're welcome."

They ended their discussion on upper management and the strike and retired to the patio that overlooked the river. Lindsey stayed through lunch but left as soon as socially polite.

With her hand on the knob of the thick oak wood doorknob, Lindsey asked, "Oh, Edgar, if you don't mind my asking, how did you learn that I was in town?"

"Travis Beecher called and said you were in Lawrence. After that, I made some inquiries and found where you were staying."

Travis Beecher? So how did he know? Lindsey wondered. "Ah, thanks. And thanks again for all your help and the material you've given me."

Edgar draped his arm over his wife's shoulder. "You're welcome. It was our pleasure."

She ran down to Lowell and visited the museum, taking her digital video camera along with her. She quickly scanned all the plaques. By manipulating the image on her computer, she could read the information later. Inside the room where the antique loom operated, she was amazed at the deafening sound the machine made. That noise, multiplied by ten, forget a hundred, would take some getting used to, she imagined.

Lindsey drove into the hotel parking lot at 8 P.M. An even larger group of reporters was waiting outside the front entrance. A hotel security officer greeted her at her car.

"Mrs. Taylor, there's been another break-in."

DECEMBER 18, 1911 ~ LAWRENCE, MASS.

Sylvia leaned over and whispered to Anna, "I don't like it. I'm worried about her."

"Pardon?" Anna shouted back.

"Later." Sylvia glanced up at the clock. The whistle would be blowing in fifteen minutes. All day she couldn't stop thinking about Jenna and her new home. She didn't like the idea of her being a kept woman. She understood on some level the couple's need to have a place where they could spend time together, but this just didn't seem proper. She'd seen too many women over the years try to work their way up by giving favors to men in management. Some would get a promotion in the factory, but she'd never seen a weaver switch from the floor to upstairs management.

And yet, why would Jenna lie about her relationship with Brad White? Maybe he was an honorable man. Maybe he really did love Jenna and want to marry her, just as Jenna said. But men weren't to be trusted. At least, not men you've barely met.

James smiled as he rambled by her loom. She returned the smile. She liked him, but he was Irish and she was Italian. After two years of smiling and making light conversation with one another, Sylvia was just beginning to trust James. How could Jenna trust Brad so completely, so quickly?

Sylvia changed the bobbin of white wool thread and readied the next one, getting her loom prepared for tomorrow. Over the years, she'd learned that she could produce a bit more each day if she prepared the night before. The extra production had helped to raise her pay by a few cents per week. In the end, it would be worth those few extra pennies, nickels, and dimes, which now filled three mason jars under the floor-boards beneath her bed. She hoped to use the money for something special, but she might need it for food if the strike became a reality. Given Mr. Wood's disposition toward the workers and their need for a pay increase, she couldn't help but believe they would be striking.

Why can't he pay what workers get at other mills? she wondered.

She remembered someone telling her that Mr. Wood had started out working in the mills when he was a boy, but Sylvia didn't believe he had. *How could a person who's worked the mills not know the needs and conditions of the workers?* It was just the boss's way of getting a person to think twice before striking. She had also started saving a handful of beans each week in preparation for the strike. James had said, "A person ought to be careful these days, not foolish like Jenna, spending all her new money at once."

A week without much food would be hard, but two weeks would be worse. She couldn't imagine the strike going on much longer than that. The girls in her boardinghouse all talked about the strike, but no one really expected it to happen.

Sylvia looked over at her friend, Anna. Thirty-four years old and what does she have to show for her life? Nothing. Absolutely nothing. *And I'm only ten years behind her. What will I have to show for my life? There's no man, no children . . .*

The closing whistle blew. The looms came to a grinding halt. Slowly, Sylvia's ears began to throb. Abrupt silence seemed to hurt just as much as the constant slapping of the leather straps turning the massive looms. The dust cloud gradually settled. Sylvia looped her arm around Anna's. "Come on, we have to figure out a way to stop Jenna before it's too late."

"What?" Anna set her legs like lead and didn't budge a step farther.

"I have been thinking about it all day. It is not right. Someone has to warn her."

Anna brushed the dust off her sleeves. "It is not my affair, neither is it yours." Anna continued in Italian as a team of the Polish girls strolled past. "She is a grown woman. She can decide for herself."

"She is only eighteen. She can not possibly know what life is about. I am really concerned, Anna."

Her eyebrows arched as she saw the redheaded stranger, whom Jenna had admitted was Brad, march out onto the floor and head straight toward them.

Chapter Fifteen

Lindsey followed the security officer into the lobby of the hotel while dialing Marc on her cell phone. As soon as Marc heard what had happened, he said, "You're flying home tonight."

"Honey, I haven't spoken with anyone yet, but trust me, I'm safe. There's a hotel security person with me right now, and I'm going to leave the hotel and stay with a friend."

"Who?"

"I don't know. I haven't thought it out yet." *Perhaps, I could ask Ruth Emery or Abigail Adams.*

"I still don't like it."

"Neither do I. But they didn't break into my room, just the same room I was in before."

"Lins, I want you where you're safe."

"I am." She prayed silently and hoped it was true. "I haven't had any other phone calls or messages. This is probably some sick kid's idea of having fun with me. Honestly, I haven't witnessed any murder, and the one I've uncovered from 1912 still doesn't have a suspect. Even if it did, he's six feet under by now. There's nothing to be afraid of." She tried to convince herself as much as Marc. "I did two interviews and visited the Lowell museum today. I have precious little I need to do tomorrow. I'm hoping to finish up enough to leave tomorrow night."

"All right, then, I'm coming up there. You're in danger. I don't like it, and I'm not going to stand by and—"

"Marc, let me talk with the hotel and the police and find out what's happened, then I'll call you back."

"Lins," Marc groaned.

"Mrs. Taylor?" the security officer gestured her toward the front doors.

"Honey, I have to go. I'll call you in a few minutes."

"Promise me you'll be careful," Marc pleaded.

"I will. I told you I have a security officer here with me right now."

"Is he carrying?"

Lindsey gave the officer a cursory visual exam for the bulge of a weapon beneath his jacket. "I don't know."

"Be careful."

"I will." She snapped the phone shut. "Sorry, about that."

"Can't say I blame him. If you were my wife, I'd probably be saying the same thing." He tipped his hat.

Lindsey chuckled. "Okay. So tell me, where are my belongings?"

"Still in your room. I'm to escort you to your room and stand guard while you pack. Mr. Randall, the manager, is terribly sorry for the inconvenience and has credited your credit card for all your expenses while you've been staying with us."

That's one way to get a free stay in a hotel—not! Lindsey quipped to herself.

Inside her room, everything was in place. She carefully packed up her papers. After having organized them the night before, she didn't want to go through that process again.

Her phone rang.

"Hello." Lindsey balanced the phone on her shoulder with her head.

"Mrs. Taylor, I'm so sorry. I don't know what to say."

Lindsey recognized the manager's voice. "It isn't your fault."

He let out a nervous cough. "Actually, it may be. We spotted one of our employees rummaging through your old room today."

"An employee?" Lindsey sat down on the edge of the bed.

"He claims he was offered five hundred dollars from a magazine for any piece of evidence that proved you were working on something other than the Bread and Roses strike."

"That's crazy. I was honest with the media. Would he have access to a key?"

"He worked in the kitchen, so the key to a patron's room is out of the question. Obviously, his employment has been terminated and the police have been notified."

Lindsey rubbed the back of her neck and sighed. "Thank you."

"As I said, I am terribly sorry. He confessed to today's break-in but refuses to admit he broke in the first time. I honestly don't know whether to believe him or not."

"Apology accepted. These things happen."

After Lindsey hung up, she put on her hands-free headset and called Marc on her cell phone.

"Is your room okay?" Marc asked, starting right into conversation.

"It's fine. The manager caught the guy. It was a hotel employee who was offered five hundred dollars from some rag mag for any evidence that showed I was working on another story besides Bread and Roses."

"You're kidding."

"Afraid not. So you see, I'm perfectly safe. And as much as I'd love to have you here, it isn't necessary." *And if I keep telling myself the same thing, maybe my heart rate will go back to normal.*

"Maybe, but I still don't like it. I want you home as soon as possible. You've been there for nearly two weeks."

"Ten days, and I was wonderfully interrupted for three of them," she giggled.

Marc chuckled. "It was a nice weekend. I miss you, Lins."

"I miss you too. If I put in some solid hours tomorrow at the historical society, I might be able to take the last flight out of Logan. Would you believe I still haven't talked to anyone about the river and dam freezing up in winter?"

"I can believe it. You've been busy tracking down a lot of elements."

She could never thank the Lord enough for such an understanding husband. "I love you."

"I love you too. Let me know where you go, and call me before you go to bed tonight."

Lindsey chuckled. "Yes, Master," she teased.

"Lins, that's not fair."

"I was just teasing."

She could hear Marc shuffling some papers. He was fine. Now if she could get her own body to relax. They said their good-byes, she put the last of her papers in her briefcase, and packed her clothes and toiletries.

Whom shall I ask to stay with? she wondered. She thought of a cousin who lived down the highway in Westford, Massachusetts. It would be a drive back and forth to Lawrence each day, but not too long. She looked up her cousin's number and dialed.

⇢ ⇠

"Morning, Lindsey. Sleep well?" Judy asked the next day, pouring herself a cup of coffee.

"Yes, thanks. I should have called you in the beginning."

"What's family for?" Judy lifted the pot. "Wanna cup?"

"Thanks." Lindsey and Judy had spent several hours the night before catching up on family, kids, and life. Judy was her second cousin, and it would take a reporter a lot of digging to find Lindsey here.

"You're welcome to spend another night. I won't change the bed just in case."

"If all goes well, I hope to catch the last flight home tonight. Hard to say. I did some searching on the Internet regarding William M. Wood and found out some interesting tidbits."

"Like?" Judy placed a full mug in front of Lindsey, then sat down across from her. "Have a bagel. Cream cheese or butter?"

"Cream cheese, if you have any."

"In the fridge." Judy started to jump up.

Lindsey held out a hand to her. "That's okay, I can get it." She opened the refrigerator and rummaged through. "Mr. Wood was a very smart businessman, for one. Second, he was born on Martha's Vineyard to Portuguese immigrants, as Edgar Archer told me. His father died when he was twelve, and he went to work to support his family."

"Interesting. You'd think he'd be more aware of how unrealistic the salaries were."

"I think that's where the problem lay. He probably figured he did it, so why couldn't someone else—with the proper motivation."

Judy chuckled. "True Yankee attitude."

"And then some." Lindsey slathered her bagel with the cream cheese.

"I'd love to tag along with you, but I need to work. You know where the key is and the security code, right?"

"Yup, I'll lock up on my way out. If you don't mind, I think I'd like to spend a couple hours here just putting some thoughts on paper and my notes in order."

"Not a problem. Anything else, just give me a ring." Judy finished off her bagel. She was dressed in a trim business suit with pastel flowers on the jacket and skirt. Her hair and makeup were in place, with the exception of the lipstick, which Lindsey felt certain she would be applying in her car before she entered the bank.

They embraced. "It was great seeing you again, and please do visit when you're in the area. With the kids all grown now, I enjoy the company."

"I'll remember that. And please come on down and thaw out for a couple weeks this winter. Most folks are able to swim and enjoy the beach in January."

"That sounds wonderful. I'll probably take you up on it sometime."

They said good-bye.

Two hours later, Lindsey had her suitcases packed and the computer in her rental car. As she drove out of her cousin's housing complex she glanced in her rearview mirror.

＞ ＜

He watched the red indicator light as he pulled his car to the side of the road and shut off the engine. After following the woman down to Westford and figuring she was tucked in safely for the night, he had gone home for a good night's sleep. If nothing else, he needed a shower and shave.

He had thought about giving up the surveillance. There seemed to be little to warrant his attention. Her stop at the police station had been fruitless. No one had taken her seriously, his sources told him. No one on the force seemed to know who she was and what she'd been involved with last year. If they had, perhaps they would have taken more interest in her photographs. *There's no question this woman has a nose for trouble.*

He saw her rental car turn onto the block ahead of him, and he fired up the ignition on the Corvette. He shouldn't have driven his own car today, but the rentals just didn't have the same feel.

After he had followed her for several miles, she began to slow down. He matched her speed. When she slowed even further, he decided to take a calculated risk and pass her.

After he passed her, he watched her in his rearview mirror. *She's on the phone again.*

He shook his head. *Women.*

DECEMBER 17, 1911 ~ METHUEN, MASS.

Jenna's whole body shook as she crept out to her backyard to check on the loud noise.

Who's out here?

Gingerly, she trekked forward, gliding her hand against the rough exterior of the shingled cottage. Before she poked her head around the corner, she listened. Not hearing a sound, she took in a deep breath and stepped forward. Seeing no one and nothing out of place, she stepped closer to the rear bedroom window.

A five-foot board that had leaned against the back of the house was now on the ground. She held the lantern over the board's landing spot. She stood on the board and drew the light in closer to the cottage. On one shingle she saw a fresh scratch. Something had been out here.

She leaned the lantern closer to the ground, casting the beam around in a search for footprints.

Who would be outside my bedroom window? Is there a thief in the area? She couldn't recall having heard of anything amiss in the neighborhood. Of course, she hadn't talked with any of the neighbors yet.

No footprints showed in the frozen earth, not even her own. *Maybe a raccoon knocked over the board?*

Jenna retreated into the house. Brad should have been here by now. With the lateness of the hour, there was little hope he'd make it tonight. She wrote in her journal about confiding in Sylvia and Anna with a nagging doubt. Maybe she wasn't doing the right thing, living by herself.

> ⤳ ⤶

The next morning, Jenna made herself busy at work. Between the routine office work and balancing the ledgers, the morning passed quickly. When the lunch bell whistled, it took her by surprise.

Around two in the afternoon, Brad popped in with an assortment of ledger sheets. They pretended to pore over the sheets, scanning the papers and casting glances at each other.

"Where were you last night?" she whispered.

"I'm sorry, I couldn't make it. I had a horrible weekend with my uncle. He insisted I entertain his friends up from Boston."

Jenna glanced up. "Brad, I told Sylvia and Anna about us."

"What?" his voice strained not to yell.

"They figured it out. They knew I couldn't afford everything in the cottage, and when they opened the cupboards and saw all the food, well, I just couldn't come up with a good enough lie. They promise not to say a word."

"I don't like it, Jenna. If they say one thing to the wrong person . . ." He closed his eyes and sighed. Picking up the papers, he whispered, "We'll speak on the matter tonight."

"I'm sorry. I love you."

He reached over and placed his hand on hers. "I love you too."

"I'll have a nice dinner for us."

"Don't. I'll be late. I have a few matters I'll need to take care of first. But I will be there."

Jenna nodded. Catching a glimpse of Polly Reed walking down the hallway, Jenna raised her voice. "I hope that helps."

"Thank you, Miss Waverly. I appreciate the time." Brad picked up on her cue immediately.

"Good afternoon," Brad greeted Polly as he stepped back to allow her to enter before he exited. *A perfect gentlemen.* Jenna suppressed a smile and looked to her desk to remind herself what she had been doing before Brad came in.

"Afternoon," Polly nodded. Every hair on her head stayed in place. "Jenna, how are those figures from yesterday's shipping coming?"

"All done and on your desk."

A broad smile spread across Mrs. Reed's face. "Is that young man still having trouble understanding the books?"

"Not really, he just wanted to be sure he understood it correctly. He seems to be a fast learner."

"I thought so, but isn't this the third time he's been to your office?"

"Yes, but each time it's been a different matter."

"Perhaps it's another matter all together," Polly winked.

Jenna flushed. She refused to answer. If she did, she'd be lying, and she'd lied so many times now she was beginning to lose count.

"Just be careful, dear. He's upper management. I don't want to see you get hurt."

"I'll be careful." Jenna already knew she'd be hurt if anything were to come between her and Brad.

Polly gave Jenna some work to do for the remainder of the day, but Jenna's mind kept drifting back to Brad. Was he angry? Had she ever seen him truly angry? There was that one time outside the boardinghouse, but he hadn't ranted and raved. *Even if he's still angry, I think I'll be able to handle it. Brad's gentle nature won't allow him to be anything less than a perfect gentleman.*

By closing, Jenna had finished off what normally would have taken her only an hour to accomplish. She filed the ledgers back in their places and readied herself for the cold winter air. Of all the items she had purchased, a new wool coat was not one of them. From this point forward, she should start saving for a coat. Thankfully, the woolen suit jacket helped her weather the elements, but with temperatures this cold this early in the season, no doubt the rest of the winter would be freezing.

Jenna boarded the streetcar and huddled behind the seat. She caught sight of Brad entering his car outside of Hartig's barbershop. *Is that Sylvia and Anna with him?*

Jenna started to shake. *Oh God, please don't let them get fired.*

Chapter Sixteen

Lindsey tightened her grasp on the steering wheel. She glanced again at her rearview mirror.

Turn for turn a blue car had been following since she'd left her cousin Judy's street. *Did they follow me from the hotel? Who? Why? What information do they think I have? Think, Lindsey, think!*

Images from the past surfaced, memories of another street, another city. A shiver of fear tightened her spine. *Please God, keep me safe,* she prayed.

She drove onto I-495. The blue car followed, now eight or ten car lengths behind.

She called Marc. After a brief explanation of what was happening, he encouraged her to go to the police station.

"Try and get a tag number, Lins. It's probably a rental and won't matter, but you never know."

"All right, I'll try." But how? With license plates on the rear of the automobile, how could she? *If I jam on the brakes, they'd probably stop right behind me.*

"Why are they following me?"

"I don't know, but I don't like it." She heard a muffling sound as Marc covered the mouthpiece of the phone, but she could still hear him say, "Alice, cancel the rest of my appointments." Then he was back on the line. "Lins, I'm taking the next flight up there."

"Marc, you won't believe this. They just turned off."

"What? Are you certain?"

"I don't know. Maybe I'm just paranoid from all the other things that have happened in the past."

"Possibly, but I still want you to report it to the police."

"Do you really think I should report this? I'll be caught up with paperwork for hours, and they'll just laugh at me." Lindsey continued to check her rearview mirror, looking for any sign of the blue sedan.

"Marc, stay. I'm fine. I'm just jittery; it wasn't even the same car. I had a lovely visit with Judy. If at all possible, I'll be out on the last flight tonight."

A long sigh tickled her ears. She loved that he loved and cared for her so much that he was willing to drop everything to come to her rescue. Her very own knight in shining armor. "I love you," she added.

"I love you too." Marc let out an exasperated breath. "You're certain you're safe?"

"I think so. The car isn't behind me. I better go so I can finish up my work and get home to Miami tonight. I think the last flight leaves around nine."

"All right. I'll see you *tonight,*" he emphasized.

→ ←

Two hours later, Lindsey stopped for lunch at a restaurant next door to the Lawrence Historical State Park. As she was eating, and clicking through her notes on the laptop, the fine hairs on the back of her neck rose. Slowly she panned the small restaurant. A teen on in-line skates passed the large plate glass window, his pink hair a throwback to punk rock days. Across the street, she noticed a man in a bright yellow jacket with a red ski cap on his head.

Odd, for a warm spring day up north.

She took a deep breath to settle her nerves, but her senses were on overdrive. *What am I reacting to?*

She glanced back at the computer and stabbed a grape tomato from her salad. The small hairs rose once again. Lindsey scanned the area for a second time.

Something isn't right. But what? The oddly dressed man was no longer visible. She glanced over to her parked car. A man of medium height and build was hooding his face with his hands and peering into the driver's door window.

What is he looking for? Lindsey ran down a list of items still in the car. *The briefcase with all my research!* Her heart sank in her chest. Should she go out? Should she confront the man? Was he just a thief looking for a quick buck? Or was it more sinister? Was there really someone after her?

Frozen from fear, she clung to her chair and watched.

The man moved on to the rear window on the driver's side. His hands never left his face and he made no attempt to place his hand on the door handle.

Lindsey watched him as he meandered around the car. He dropped from sight for a moment, then popped up on the passenger side, reprising his Peeping Tom efforts. Lindsey reached into her briefcase and pulled out her digital camera. She aimed and waited for the right shot when he lifted his head.

Click. She switched to view the image. *Missed!* She aimed and waited for another shot. The man disappeared between the cars once again.

Her anger started to rise. Lindsey left her food and research on the table and stepped outside of the restaurant. "Hey," she hollered. "Anything I can help you with?"

The man scurried off. She ran across the street and quickly scanned the underside of her car to see if he had placed anything there during his disappearing acts. After a cursory search, she decided that nothing seemed out of place. She counted down her anger as she hustled across the street toward the restaurant, took a deep cleansing breath, and opened the front door. "Calm me, Lord and give me peace," she prayed.

Sitting back down at her table, she glanced at the picture currently on the computer screen. It was a timeline from the museum, noting the significant events of the strike.

"January 31, former mayor's son arrested for planting dynamite in dye shop to discredit strikers."

Lindsey paused. *Is this information important to my story?* She drummed her fingers. *Two days after Anna's death. Did management deliberately set up the strikers?*

Another thought captured her attention. She quickly scanned her notes on William M. Wood. "Yes," she caught herself speaking out loud. "Explosives were found on or near the mills three times during the strike. Two Wood employees, Ernest Pittman and John Breen, confessed, but Wood was also indicted because they worked for him. There was a long trial, and a grand jury eventually found Wood not guilty."

Lindsey tapped the table with her fingers.

"Mrs. Marc?" an unfamiliar voice jarred her from the past.

"Hello?" An elderly woman with brilliant blue eyes shuffled up beside her. Age spots unevenly decorated her face and forearms.

"I'm sorry to bother you. I saw in the paper that you were writing a book about the Bread and Roses strike."

"Yes, I am. Would you like to join me?" Lindsey offered.

The old woman looked over to her right and then sat down beside Lindsey. "I don't mean to tell you your business and all, but what exactly are you trying to prove? If you don't mind my asking?"

Lindsey closed her laptop. "I don't know if I can prove anything. I'd love to come up with a reasonable explanation as to who killed Anna Lopizzo. However, I write fiction based on truth, so whatever conclusions or implications I include in my story, however reasonable they may be, are not proof one way or the other."

"There's no one alive who can tell you who killed her. Folks have been pretty well divided since it happened. Depends on which part of the street your family stood on at the time." She leaned forward and squinted. "Why all the hubbub if you're just turning up that old story?"

"I haven't figured that out myself." Lindsey smiled.

The woman leaned back. "My mother worked in the mills at the time of the strike. I was born not too long after it was over."

The older woman appeared in excellent health for someone in her nineties, Lindsey assessed.

"On mother's deathbed she confessed a terrible secret she couldn't take to the grave. Now, I'm not so sure I should tell you this or not. So, I want to know exactly who you are and what you're going to be writing about."

"I'll try, but I don't know exactly what I'm going to write."

Lindsey gave a truncated version of the story thus far, leaving out the details of Jenna Waverly. "I love communicating biblical truth in a way that entertains and challenges the reader."

The older woman used the table to help herself up. "If you want to learn my mother's secret you can come by my place at nine tonight. Not a minute before, or I'll pretend I don't know you." As she lifted her hand, it revealed a small white napkin folded in half lying on the table. "Never met a writer before. Thank you for your time," she said in full voice.

"You're welcome. The pleasure is all mine," Lindsey replied. *Is this woman crazy, or does she really have a secret to tell?*

Slowly, the woman ambled over to a table where a gentleman perhaps in his late sixties or early seventies sat with a middle-aged woman. Lindsey guessed them to be the woman's son and possibly her granddaughter. Once the older woman was settled, Lindsey reached for the folded napkin. Inside it had an address and a message: "Secrets went to the graves."

She stuffed the napkin into her rear jeans pocket and looked up the address on the map software she had installed on her computer.

The decision as to whether or not she'd be going to the stranger's house wasn't even a question. Turning down a solid lead would be like cutting a major artery. Suicide.

But who is this woman? What secret might her mother have taken to her deathbed? And what bearing will it have on my story? Lindsey glanced over to the woman's table once again. In the car she had two copies of *City Streets*. She called for the waiter, explained she'd be right back, and asked him to watch over her belongings. She ran across the street to the red sedan, opened the trunk, and pulled a copy of the book out of her suitcase.

With the book in hand, she headed back to the restaurant. As her foot landed on the sidewalk, a tremendous blow from the left sent a blaze of pain through her side as she fell to the ground. A fresh surge of pain raced along her right side with the sudden impact. Her forehead hit the pavement with a crack. She looked up. The kid on in-line skates stumbled to his feet.

Everything went black.

DECEMBER 18, 1911 ~ METHUEN, MASS.

Jenna paced back and forth waiting for Brad. Her mind swirled with worry about Anna and Sylvia. She prayed that Brad wouldn't fire them. Then she tried to remind herself of how kind and generous a person Brad was. Exhausted from the inward battle, she still longed to see him. *How much longer?* she wondered.

A car pulled into the driveway. She looked up at the clock. Seven. She closed her eyes and gathered her thoughts. A blast of cold air entered the kitchen as Brad opened the door. He smiled at her. "Hey there, beautiful. I'm home."

How could she be mad at that face, that sweet, adorable face?

"I've been worried."

"About what?"

"I saw you with Anna and Sylvia today."

He removed his overcoat and draped it over a chair. "I see. And what do you think was going on?"

"Oh, Brad, I don't know. That's what has been spinning in my mind like the spools of wool on a loom all evening. I was worried that you'd fire them for knowing about us."

Brad chuckled. "The thought had crossed my mind, but then I came to my senses. If I fired them, they would have all the reason in the world to talk about us. However, if I tried to befriend them, they might help us keep our secret. My father taught me that a little sugar goes a long way." He winked. "Now, where's my sugar?" He opened his arms.

She ran into his embrace and held him tight. The fresh cool winter air hung on his clothes, but it wasn't strong enough to overcome his unique musky scent.

"Now, don't be asking me too many details. Christmas is coming, you know."

Christmas? She had completely forgotten. What could she make that would be special for Brad? He had virtually anything he needed. She could knit him a sweater, but would it be difficult for him to explain where he'd gotten it? "I haven't thought about Christmas."

Brad lifted her chin and kissed her. "I figured out a way for us to get married. I still couldn't live with you for a while but . . ."

"Really?" she interrupted. "When? Where? How?"

The rumble of his laughter calmed her. "Later, I'm starved. What's for dinner? It smells great."

Jenna left his arms and went over to the oven. She removed the cast iron pot. The bubbling brew smelled heavenly. "I knew when I saw you with Sylvia and Anna that you might not eat, so I fixed up enough for both of us."

"I knew there was a reason I loved you." He winked.

"It's a scalloped potato recipe with bits of ham. I'm afraid I spent a bit more than I should have on the ham."

"Nonsense. A man loves his meat. Especially this man. I'll leave you a few dollars in the cookie jar for more meat. I saw some great chickens in the Lacillade's window."

"I know the place. I'll pick one up tomorrow. I can make a chicken pot pie and soup from one chicken." She ladled a healthy helping of their dinner onto his plate, then a much smaller amount onto her own.

They settled down for a quiet meal before retiring to the front room. Brad lit a fire in the fireplace and joined Jenna on the sofa. Jenna snuggled up beside him. He wrapped his arm around her and kissed the top of her head. It felt so right being in his arms. "I love you," she whispered.

"I love you too."

They shared a kiss that stirred the flames of passion hotter than the fire before them. Brad pulled away first. "Jenna, I must tell you my plans."

The cool air on her swollen lips reminded her they were not truly one yet. *When, oh, when?* she pleaded. She tried to focus on Brad's words, not him.

"I think I've figured out a way for us to get married without my uncle being aware. First, we'd have to plan this very carefully. I'm scheduled to visit my family on the Vineyard for the Christmas holiday. I can return a few days early, and we can drive over to Middleton and find a justice of the peace. I'm fairly certain my uncle has no connections in Middleton. There are no company mills there. What do you think?"

Jenna didn't know what to think. *A secret marriage, what is that?* "It sounds like you're still unable to stand up to your family."

"No, Jenna, honey, it's not like that at all. Okay, maybe it is, but it's not the reason I'm asking you to do this. Honey, I can't keep coming over here night after night only to return to my uncle's home. I want you too much. I don't want to go to my uncle's. I want to love you as a husband should and not feel guilty about it."

Jenna blushed. Hadn't she wanted the same? "But why the secret?"

"Because I can't afford a house and the appropriate caretakers that would fit my social standing. My salary, while a lot higher than yours, is still not high enough for a man in my position. If we were to make our marriage known, I would dishonor you by having you living in this small cottage, however quaint it may be. And I certainly would not want to subject you to my uncle's home, however grand it may be."

"But I love this little cottage. It fits me." Jenna smiled and placed a loving hand on his chest.

"And I love it too. But I would do an injustice to you. And then there is the matter of your social standing. I will need to come up with an acceptable heritage for you and your family. Yes, it's snobbish, but you don't know my uncle."

Jenna honestly didn't know William Wood, but she had heard that he was a child of an immigrant family himself. Why wouldn't he understand?

Brad took her hands into his, caressing them gently with his thumbs. "Honey, I love you, I want to be your husband. I want to be the father of your children. But I have to do this very carefully. One day we can tell the truth. But for now, and until you've been accepted, it will have to be a secret. We simply cannot marry until all the other things are in place."

"Living a lie?"

"Not exactly, but I can see how you would think that."

"I don't understand. How is it that when we acknowledge our marriage people won't know who I really am. I work for the same company."

"That's the first thing to stop once we are married. You cannot work."

"I don't like it, Brad. Not one bit. If I'm to be your wife, I want to be your wife. Why would I have to stop working?"

"Jenna, I have nothing. I have no inheritance coming. My father has spent it all on a few bad investments. I want better for my children. I don't want to see them working in the mills. I want to provide a good home, a good education, give them everything that will help them better themselves in this world. You've worked the inside of those mills. Do you want that for our children?"

"No."

"Honey, I love you. I don't care who you are or where you came from. It's you I fell in love with. It's you I will marry. If I have to fool my uncle for a short time to be with the woman I love, so be it. But I will provide for you and our children so they will never have to work the mills, so they will have a life of comfort. I have to. As a good provider, I must."

Jenna pushed herself away from Brad and shuffled over to the fire. "My father was a good man. We didn't have much, but we were a happy family."

Brad closed the distance of the room between them. Placing his hands on her shoulders, he turned her around to face him. "My sweet rose, I did not mean to offend you or your parents. I simply wanted to get married sooner than later. However, if we can't do it now, I'll wait the two years and then we'll be able to marry."

"Two years?" she cried. Tears flowed down her cheek.

He brushed them away with his thumbs. "Oh my precious, I'm so terribly sorry. I did not mean to hurt you. I just want us to be as husband and wife, to be one with you. Forgive me for my thoughtlessness."

Jenna sniffed.

He held her close. She wrapped him tighter in her embrace. She kissed the base of his neck. He groaned and captured her mouth with his own. The passions that flamed earlier came back in an intensity Jenna had never known. She wanted nothing more than to be one with this man.

She closed her eyes, ignored her upbringing and everything she knew was right.

Chapter Seventeen

Lindsey woke to the sound of an ambulance. Her body ached from head to toe. A crowd of strangers huddled around her.

"Ms. Marc, Ms. Marc, are you all right?" someone called out. She couldn't quite focus on who or where they were. She lifted her hand to her head. Small pieces of dirt and grit scratched her forehead.

She glanced up, but the sunlight blinded her. A sea of blurred images hovered over her.

The ambulance siren roared, then abruptly cut off.

"Ms. Marc, I'll watch your things," a male voice called out.

EMTs in their blue uniforms checked Lindsey's pulse, listened to her breathing, and checked the dilation of her eyes. Her head throbbed. Slowly her vision began to clear. She heard the EMTs' orders and responded briefly to their questions.

"You might have a concussion, Ms. Marc. We're going to take you to the hospital and have you checked out."

Lindsey nodded. *Big mistake.*

"Please, retrieve my computer and purse from the restaurant," she pleaded.

"No problem," the female attendant responded and left.

They lifted her onto a stretcher with wheels. *I never realized how narrow these things really are,* she thought as one of the EMTs connected an IV to her left arm.

The female attendant came up with the waiter and cleared her throat. "There seems to be a problem."

The waiter looked down at the ground and then back up to her. "I'm so sorry, ma'am. Someone stole your laptop."

"What?" Lindsey pushed herself up from the bed. Dizziness took over. She grasped the sides. The elderly woman she'd spoken to moments before looked worried. Her male companion came up beside her and offered his arm for her support.

"I'm so sorry. I ran out with everyone else when you were hit. When I went back in, it was gone. Your briefcase was still there and your purse," he offered.

"Great." Lindsey closed her eyes to ease the dizziness.

"What kind of computer is it?" the waiter asked. "I'll report it to the police."

Lindsey gave him the details on the late model Macintosh. "Oh, one more thing. It has an identifying sticker on the bottom with the logo from my Web page."

The waiter nodded. "Don't worry, Ms. Marc. I'll tell the police."

Lindsey lay back on the gurney. On top of the pain throbbing through her body, she had now lost all of her notes. Well, maybe not all her notes. There still were the hard copies. Then she thought back on the man who had hung around her car. "Oh no, let me up. I have to check my car."

"I'm sure it can wait, Ms. Marc."

"You don't understand. All of my notes—I can't afford to have them stolen. There's a . . . a one-of-a-kind item that can't possibly be replaced. Please, I must check it out."

"Give me your keys and tell me where it is." The female attendant held out her hand.

"The red Toyota across the street, in the trunk, in the smallest suitcase. There's a small black journal in the inside top pocket." Lindsey handed the woman the keys and grasped the gurney to stabilize herself. Her ears rang a pulsing whine.

The kid on in-line skates stood over her. "I'm sorry." He rubbed his chest trying to ease his own pain from the impact. "I wasn't looking." He looked down at his feet still encased in a pair of in-line skates. "There was a major babe walking on the other side of the street . . ." He cleared his throat. "I wasn't looking. Sorry."

Lindsey smiled weakly. If she hadn't been the mother of two sons, she probably wouldn't recognize the irony of the situation. "I understand, but I'll need your name and how to get in touch with you. My insurance company will want to speak with you. Unless you carry insurance, then I can file a claim with your company."

"Insurance? I ain't got a car."

Obviously. Perhaps it was a good thing, thinking of the damage he'd done on just a pair of in-line skates.

"I've taken his statement, ma'am." A police officer came into her field of vision.

"Would you also take that man's statement as well," she asked, indicating the waiter, "and anyone else who might have seen the person who stole my laptop?" Lindsey moaned. Her head throbbed. She had never experienced a headache like this before. She blinked, trying to keep her focus.

"He'll do his job." The medical technician patted her on the shoulder. "Relax, just in case you have a concussion."

Just then the female EMT came up waving Jenna's journal. Lindsey accepted it with relief. Everything else was replaceable—time-consuming, but replaceable. "Marc. Where's my phone? I need to call my husband."

"Later," the male EMT ordered. "We need to get you to the hospital, stat."

Lindsey rolled her eyes and groaned. Even that simple act hurt. She closed her eyes and smiled.

Maybe I'll only lose a day or two at the most.

Still, it was a day or two too many.

Marc won't be pleased.

✣ ✣

Judy came to the hospital and picked her up after five hours in the emergency room. They retrieved the rental car and returned to Judy's house for the night.

Lindsey spent the next morning calling insurance companies, filing claims, asking the police to make copies of the accident and theft reports, and purchasing a new laptop computer. She managed to download the drivers for the camera and video camera from the products' Web sites. For lunch she had a salad and a handful of pills. She ached in spots she didn't know could ache.

Following lunch, she sorted through her briefcase and came across the address written on the napkin by the elderly lady in the restaurant the day before. Her mind immediately erupted with questions: *Have I lost the possibility of learning this woman's secret? Do I need to wait until nine tonight to find it out? Will it be safe to go out at that hour? Should I take a chance?*

With printed-out directions from her cousin's house to the address on the napkin, she slid behind the wheel of the Toyota and drove to Lawrence.

When she reached the final line in the street-by-street directions, she found an old, stately home standing majestically atop a hill overlooking the Merrimack River. It was a mid-to-late Victorian, painted in eggshell white with blue trim edged with a fine line of an accenting off-white, almost yellow. The old shutters were painted to perfection. A modern addition on the left matched the original building. The finely manicured appearance of the lawn spoke to the owner's pride in the upkeep of the property.

A contrasting monument to the modern world—a plastic play gym for children—stood to the right of the house. It had two swings, a slide, and hand-over-hand bar rails across the top. Lindsey smiled. The earthy scent of rich soil filled the air, mixed with lilac and cedar.

Ambling up the red brick walkway between precisely edged flowerbeds to the front door, she knocked and took a step back. Potted plants lined the entryway, giving the house a warm, family feel.

The door opened a fraction. "May I help you?" a small voice answered. Lindsey couldn't see the child but had no doubt one was there.

"Yes, I hope so. My name is Lindsey Marc and . . ."

"Mom," the child yelled. "Lizzy Marc is here."

Before she could finish, a woman in her twenties with long brown hair and a fair complexion appeared at the door. "May I help you?"

"I'm sorry to bother you. My name is Lindsey Marc. I was at a restaurant yesterday and . . ."

"Oh my goodness. Come on in. Mother, Grandpa and Gram were telling me all about your accident."

Lindsey smiled. She'd found the right house. The question was, would the elderly woman be able to share with her at this hour. "I'm sorry to impose. Someone stole my laptop . . ."

"Mother said that too. I'm so sorry to hear it. Let me get my great-grandmother; she's the only one home who was at the restaurant yesterday. Perhaps she saw something. She's getting on in years but is still as sharp as a tack. Can't pull a thing over on that woman." The young mother left the room laughing.

Lindsey stood in the grand hall, gazing up at a sweeping staircase that curled gracefully to the second floor. The crystal chandelier— *I'd hate to have to clean it*—harkened to earlier days.

"Why, hello, Mrs. Marc." The elderly woman appeared as Lindsey pulled her gaze down from the chandelier. "I'm so glad to see you're up on your feet. That young man should have his hide tanned for such nonsense."

"I'd be the first in line with the paddle." Lindsey chuckled. "If I could lift it. I'm pretty sore."

"I bet you are. Casey, would you please bring Mrs. Marc and me some iced tea with lemon?"

"Sure, Gram. Anything else?" The elderly woman glanced over. Lindsey shook her head ever so carefully.

"Come, sit down in the front parlor." The strength of the woman's grip on her elbow surprised Lindsey. Her hostess escorted her to the left front section of the room. A brick fireplace with a maple mantel stood proudly in the middle. The rear section had a grand piano.

"What did the doctor say?" the woman asked, sitting down on the divan.

"A mild concussion. No other real injuries, just that I'd be sore. May I ask you your name?"

"I'm so sorry. My name is Anna Ludlum Scott."

"Are you related to a Quincy Ludlum?"

Anna's eyes watered. "He was my father."

"Gram," Casey announced, as she sauntered in with a tray and two tall glasses of iced tea, "I'm afraid I have to watch your namesake before she terrorizes the new puppy."

"That's perfectly all right, dear. I believe I can answer any questions Mrs. Marc might have."

"Okay." Casey headed out of the front room. "Holler if you need anything."

"Casey is my great-granddaughter. The little terror to puppies is my great-great-granddaughter, Anna, who happens to be named after me, and I'm afraid she may just have more of me in her than Casey deserves."

A subtle chuckle of understanding escaped from Lindsey's throat. "Do all five generations live in this house?"

"No. My granddaughter, Casey's mother, lives across town with her husband. Donald, my son, lives here with his wife, but they travel a lot; and when Casey's young marriage failed, they asked her to come and live here so she could keep an eye out for me. The house is large enough that we don't get under each other's feet too often."

"It's a beautiful home."

"My father purchased it when I was a year old. I've lived here nearly all my life. I spent my college years in England. When I returned home, I fell in love with an artist, and father built an addition. So we always had a roof over our heads. Eventually, my husband, God rest his soul, began to make money with his art. But if it hadn't been for father's generous heart, I don't know how we would have survived. My three brothers and two sisters moved out when they married."

"It's nice to have a house stay in the family like that." The paintings on the walls seemed the perfect accent for the room and its furnishings. Lindsey wondered if Anna's husband might have painted them.

"Yes, it is. I wouldn't be surprised if it becomes young Anna's one day." The elderly Anna leaned over. "But you didn't come here to discuss my children, did you?"

"No. Your message stirred my curiosity. Have you decided if I'm worthy to know your mother's secret?"

"I have a journal that my mother wrote. She had hidden it under the floorboards of the back bedroom's closet. She began writing it when she was expecting me."

"Was that during the strike?"

"Yes. She was friends with Anna Lopizzo, the woman who was shot. My namesake."

"Did she write about Anna's death? Did she suspect someone in particular? The police, the strikers?" Lindsey leaned forward in her chair.

"No, nothing like that. The journal is very personal. Her innermost thoughts."

"I'd love to see it."

"Well, dear, that is the problem. You see, after yesterday, when someone took your laptop, I grew afraid mother's journal could be stolen from you. I'm not saying it was your fault, but with the break-ins at the hotel, the laptop . . ."

Lindsey could think of a few other reasons. "May I read it here?"

"No, that simply won't do either."

Then why am I here? she wanted to scream. But with a throbbing headache, who needed the extra noise? Lindsey stood up and gathered her purse. "I'm sorry to have bothered you."

"Please sit. The journal would keep you here too long. My son does not know the secret. No one in my family does, except me, which is why I had wanted you to come last evening. I didn't expect you to visit, after witnessing your accident.

"I'm old enough that if I simply tell you what my mother wrote, some could write it off as the ramblings of an old woman. If, however, you see the journal and make copies of its pages, then it's no longer my ramblings but my mother's recorded statements of the events that happened."

Lindsey rubbed her forehead just above the bridge of her nose. Either the headache from the concussion was increasing or else Anna Ludlum Scott's very roundabout way of speaking was taking its toll. Probably it was a combination of the two.

"I'm sorry. Let me do this. I'll bring out the journal and you can look at it."

Beggars can't be choosers. Lindsey waited patiently while the older woman left the room to retrieve the mysterious journal. Had her parents done something illegal to buy this house?

When Anna returned, she sat down beside Lindsey on the divan and handed her a small black leather journal similar to Jenna's.

Lindsey opened the thin cover. The first entry was March 14, 1912. It began, "Beverly Ludlum. My new life begins today."

"Was that your mother's name? Beverly? Was she married on March fourteenth?"

"No, she was married March thirtieth. I was born in September."

"Oh." Lindsey knew that couldn't be the secret. Anna would have figured that out many years ago. She rolled the name *Beverly Ludlum* around. She couldn't recall coming across the name before. "I'm sorry. I don't understand what's so secretive about her new life beginning as your mother."

"That's not it. The secret is that Beverly wasn't her real name."

"It wasn't? What was it then?" Lindsey asked.

"I don't know. She died trying to tell me. She waited too long. I've read the journal, and there was only one person with whom she remained friends after she changed her name. From what I gathered in the journal, no one else knew her real name."

"I'm still not sure what the importance or the great secret is. People change their names all the time." Lindsey lightly thumbed through the pages.

"Mother confessed that someone died for her sake."

Lindsey cocked her head toward Anna. "How?"

DECEMBER 19, 1911 - LAWRENCE, MASS.

Jenna nervously worked over the figures. After last night, and Brad's sudden departure, she felt guilty. Morally, she knew she'd been wrong. Brad had kissed her and told her he loved her before he left. But she still felt alone, empty, and . . . cheap. She knew that God didn't approve of what she had done. There was a sick feeling in the bottom of her stomach of having lost something she could never get back.

But would it be right to secretly get married and not tell anyone? Wouldn't that also be wrong?

Rubbing her temples, she closed her eyelids to shield the light. The mammoth headache she had from all the worry was going to drive her insane. If only she could run upstairs to Brad's office and know for certain that he didn't hate her or think any less of her for what they had done. But she couldn't. She would have to wait.

"Miss Waverly, please come to my office." Mr. Billings stood in the doorway with a rather somber face. Polly Reed stood behind him with a grave expression.

Jenna put down her pencil and followed Mrs. Reed and Mr. Billings to his office. "There's been a complaint filed against you, Miss Waverly, and I'm afraid Mr. Wood can't allow such behavior from his employees. I've been ordered to give you your salary for the rest of this week and next week."

"What did I do? If I may ask." Jenna held onto the chair to keep from fainting.

"Mr. Ludlum said you were less than honest with your bookwork, and when he confronted you, you tried to cover it up with inappropriate favors."

"What?" *Who's Mr. Ludlum?* Jenna wanted to scream. She wanted to run to Brad's office, but what could he do? Besides, anything he did would expose their relationship. No, she couldn't do a thing except take her pay and go home.

"I'm sorry, Miss Waverly. My hands are tied." Mr. Billings sat down at his desk. He pulled out a moneybox, counted out her salary for two weeks, and added a ten dollar bill from his own wallet. "I truly am sorry, especially with Christmas a few days off. You were good with the numbers, Jenna. Perhaps too good."

Stunned, Jenna accepted the cash and headed to her office. Polly Reed followed her. Inside Jenna's office, Polly said, "I warned you not to get too friendly with upper management."

"Honestly, I don't know what anyone is talking about. I didn't do a thing."

"Perhaps that is why," Polly snapped back.

Jenna narrowed her gaze. *Is she suggesting that I was asked to give sexual favors and didn't?* No one had made any such suggestions, unless she'd been ignorant to it. This was nonsense.

"I'm to escort you out of the building."

"You can't be serious."

Polly crossed her arms across her chest. Apparently he was.

Jenna took in a deep breath, exhaled it slowly, and stood up straight, holding her shoulders square. She marched out of the Wood mill with all the dignity she could muster. She would not give anyone the pleasure of seeing her cry.

Outside, she sat down on the bench and waited for the streetcar. *What am I going to do? Where am I going to get another job?* Having tasted the world of office work over that of laboring in the mills, there was no question what kind of job she'd like to have. But who would hire her to do bookwork? No doubt her record was permanently scarred for having been fired because of dishonest bookkeeping. It wasn't fair. Life wasn't fair.

Last night all seemed right with the world, she and Brad were. . . . Maybe things weren't right with the world. *Oh God, I don't understand. How can loving a man be so wrong?* The blast of a car horn aroused her from her pleading.

"Brad!" she jumped up, wiping the tears from her eyes.

He pulled his car to the curb. "Quick, get in."

Jenna hustled into the car, "You heard? Who's Mr. Ludlum?"

"What do you mean, who's Mr. Ludlum?" Brad turned his head to the left as he hit the gas pedal.

"I don't know who he is, and he's claiming all sorts of horrible things about me."

"Jenna, you can't be serious. I'm Mr. Ludlum."

"What?"

"What do you mean, 'what'? Who do you think I am?"

"I thought you were Brad White, Mr. Wood's nephew."

"No, I'm not Mr. Wood's nephew, and White was the name I gave the landlord to keep the place a secret from my uncle."

Jenna wiped the tears from her eyes. Clenching her fists, she looked straight ahead. "Why? Why would you say such horrible things to have me fired?"

"Honey, I'm sorry. I didn't know what else to do."

Jenna could think of a million things but held her tongue. She felt so betrayed, so used. *How could he do this to me?* "I don't understand."

"Trust me, Jenna. You and I both know I can't have you working for the company and have you be my wife."

"We're not married," she huffed.

"We will be." He reached over to place his hand on her knee. "I love you, Jenna."

She wanted to scream. She loved him too, but at this present moment she couldn't think of a nice word to say to him. "Where are you taking me?"

"Middleton. Before I leave for the Vineyard, you're going to be mine, all mine."

Jenna glanced over. He drove the car with singular focus. The little muscle at the corner of his jaw twitched. "Why?"

"Because we're going to the justice of the peace, and we're going to be married."

Chapter Eighteen

"Mother wrote that she had nightmares about taking advantage of a woman's death, and that only she, Father, and one other person knew what truly had happened." Anna's eyelids slipped shut.

"What kind of nightmares?"

"In her journal she said she had them over and over again that first year. Mother's other journals only speak of these nightmares on occasion. However, she never wrote down what they were." Anna leaned forward. "Here's the strange thing. When I was very little, I remember seeing Mother in tears, rocking back and forth.

"At the time, I thought she was sick. But looking back, I wonder if she possibly was having the nightmare."

Lindsey glanced over at her hostess. "Did your father come from Martha's Vineyard?"

Anna sat up straight and folded her hands in her lap. "Yes. How'd you know that?"

"I came across some letters addressed to him," Lindsey said as she continued to thumb through the pages of Beverly Ludlum's journal. Not wanting to reveal how curious she was about Quincy Ludlum, Lindsey tried to soak up all she could from the little book. The first thing she noticed was the penmanship. It lacked Jenna's graceful lines.

"Where?" Anna asked. "Who were they from? Who has them? Would they mind parting with them?"

Lindsey gave her a reassuring smile. "They were from your grandparents. I can ask the owners if they wouldn't mind giving you the letters. They seemed not to know who your father was. The letters were just something they found in the house that were dated around the time period I was looking into."

Anna's eyes sparkled. "Would you inquire on my behalf? That would be wonderful. I don't recall having anything of my grandparents', although we summered on the Vineyard for many years."

Lindsey glanced down at the pages. Reading further, she could find little relating to the strike. Instead, Beverly wrote a lot about the growing child inside her and her prayers that God would not curse the child for the sins of the parents. She glanced eye to eye with her host once again. "I don't know if I can really help you. I think you're holding something back. I think you suspect you know who your mother really was."

Anna scanned the open hallway. "You're absolutely correct. I do have my suspicions, but I can't prove it. I'd love to, but I'm getting on in years, and getting out and about tracking old files is a bit difficult."

Lindsey closed the journal and held it tightly between her hands. "Anna, I can't promise that the journal won't be stolen. But if you let me borrow it, I'll do what I can to uncover your mother's true identity."

"When I spoke with you, that was my original goal. I was also hoping you'd come across something unusual during the strike that might point to who my mother was."

"Why do you think she changed her name during the strike?"

"The journal, for one." Anna's voice dropped to a whisper. "My parents' late marriage, for another. Today, that sort of thing happens all the time. Back then, you rarely heard about it."

"Do you know where your mother was from?" Lindsey prayed she would remember every word of their conversation.

"Not really. The first entry mentions being on Martha's Vineyard. She didn't like the mills, that much is clear from her writings, especially the problem she had with Father working in the upper management and the struggle the laborers had for a decent wage and better working conditions. In her later journals, she made peace with Father's job because he fought for the workers. That made her terribly proud of him."

"What about your maternal grandparents, did you ever meet them?"

"No. When I was in college . . ."

"Mother?" Donald entered the front sitting room. "I didn't know we had guests." He apologized, extending his hand. "Donald Scott. A pleasure to have you in our home, Ms. Marc."

The gentleman from the restaurant seemed quite at home here. His hair was more white than gray. Lindsey clasped his hand. "Call me Lindsey."

"Lindsey," he amended. "You look in pretty reasonable condition considering the beating you took yesterday. Mother and I decided I should bring up a bill at the city council meeting to restrict in-line skaters from sidewalks. What brings you to our home?" he asked.

Anna answered, "The accident, son. She was hoping we saw something."

"I regret we were not paying attention." Donald coughed and cleared his throat. "I called 9-1-1 as soon as I saw the young man hit you."

Lindsey smiled. "Thank you. I wondered how they arrived so quickly."

"My pleasure. Mother tells me you're writing on the Bread and Roses strike. Grandfather worked in the mills, but I'm confident Mother has shared with you his recollections."

"Did you work in the mills?" Lindsey asked.

Donald leaned back on his heels. "I don't believe you could have grown up in Lawrence and not worked in the mills. My grandfather had me start on the bottom floor washing the wool. Let me tell you, that is backbreaking work. And the smell—have you ever smelled wet wool? Magnify that a hundred percent. I'd shower in the mill before I left, and I'd shower again once I arrived home. I applied myself to my studies after that. Accounting better suited me."

Lindsey chuckled. "I heard a similar story from another local gal who worked one summer and had her fill of the mills."

Donald continued in the gaiety. "Most my age and younger had a similar experience. I know some continued in the mills. But a high percentage of us chose college."

Anna looked adoringly toward her son.

"I won't pester you. I have some work to go over. Tax season, you know. Very busy time."

"Ugh, don't remind me."

Donald exited the room with a smirk.

Lindsey's cell phone rang. "Excuse me, Anna. Hello? . . . Abigail, what's up?"

"You know that Jenna Waverly you asked me to look up?"

"Yes." Lindsey glanced over to her hostess.

"She was married in Middleton on December 21 to Quincy Ludlum."

"Interesting." *Jenna only wrote in her journal about her love for Brad. How did she know Quincy?* Lindsey would have to read Jenna's journal, specifically December 21, to see why she married Quincy Ludlum. If it weren't for the journals, Lindsey might have thought that Jenna was Beverly, but the handwriting didn't match. And of course, Jenna was dead months before Anna was born.

Does Anna know that her father married another woman before he married her mother? Lindsey glanced over to her host and back to the book in her hand. *I need to read this journal.* She fondled the old leather volume.

Lindsey gave Anna a shrug of her shoulders and a brief smile. "Abigail, I can't talk right now. Can I call you back?"

"Of course, or I can e-mail you the information. I have a copy of the marriage record and can e-mail it as a jpeg file."

"That would be wonderful, thank you." Lindsey said good-bye and snapped her phone shut. "Sorry about that. I have a gal doing some research for me."

Anna fidgeted with a white lace handkerchief in her hands. "I understand, and I won't keep you. I just thought you might be able to help me figure out what happened, and why my mother changed her name. And why it bothered her so that she had."

"Were your parents previously married before they married each other?"

"No." Anna said.

Interesting. Anna doesn't know. So, did Beverly take advantage of Jenna's death to marry Quincy? And what happened to Brad?

"Do you know who the friend was who knew your mother before she changed her name?" Lindsey asked.

"Only the initials *S. J. D.* They're in the journal," Anna replied.

S. J. D. Sylvia? No. Her name was Giovanni in 1912.

"Then you'll let me take it?"

JANUARY 5, 1912 ~ METHUEN, MASS.

Brad slammed the door as he entered the cottage.

"What's the matter?" Jenna asked. He had left for Martha's Vineyard the same day she'd been fired and the same day they married. He'd returned late last night, but only long enough to tell her he was back and would be home for dinner tonight.

"Mr. Wood decided that because the workers worked fewer hours, they were to be paid less."

Jenna held back on the embrace she wanted to give her husband.

They had been married for sixteen days and hadn't lived together yet. "Less? They're not going to like that."

Brad gripped the back of the chair with both hands and squeezed. "I could do nothing. My uncle would have put my head on the chopping block if I voiced my opinions to Mr. Wood and the rest of the board. Wood has also increased the speed of the machines to increase production, which means there will be more injuries. Remember that boy who died a few weeks back?"

Jenna remembered all too well the limp body being carried through the descending cloud of lint dust. She simply nodded.

"That was after the machine speed was picked up last time. I see more accidents and deaths if it's increased again. I don't like it, Jenna. I'm concerned about the workers. I think they're going to do another work slowdown."

Jenna held her tongue. She chose not to tell him everything she knew. Sylvia and Anna had been over during the holidays, and the talk of a strike was increasing. The workers had heard about the new law, and some had feared Mr. Wood would do just what he had done—pay them less.

"Honey"—he pulled her into his arms—"I'm sorry, I shouldn't be bringing the office home. It's our first night together since we married, and here I am talking business when I should be telling my bride how beautiful she is." He lowered his head and his lips met hers.

Jenna savored the kiss.

"I've missed you," he said against her ear. "I've missed you so much." He held her tight.

She didn't fight it and nuzzled her nose into the base of his neck. "I've missed you too. It was horrible to be here all alone for so many days. If you hadn't fired me, I would have at least had work to go to."

"You needed to leave the office. I want your face to be gone from people's minds as soon as possible. Did you purchase the hair dye?"

"Yes, but I don't understand why, Brad. Why all the secrecy?"

"You're going to have to trust me on this, Jenna. I know it seems odd, but until people have forgotten you, I can't introduce you as my wife. We'll travel to the Vineyard in the spring. My folks are anxious to meet you . . ."

"You told your parents?" Jenna pulled away to arm's length so she could look at Brad's face.

"Yes, they know we're married. They didn't understand my not bringing you with me to the Vineyard for Christmas, though."

"I like 'em already," Jenna said.

Brad pulled her close again. "Honey, like I said, you have to trust me on this. I need for you to keep a low profile for a while, at least until I can get Polly Reed and Billings transferred to another mill. And even then you'll have to stay away from the laborers. I can't transfer everyone who ever knew you."

"I still don't like this."

"I know." Brad held her hands and let out a long sigh. "Jenna, my uncle arranged a date for me last night. I didn't want to tell you so you wouldn't be upset. But if Sylvia or Anna saw me out with another woman . . . well, I wanted you to hear it from me. It was not my desire."

Jenna pulled her hands out of his.

"Jenna, I promise. I did nothing. I swear. I attended dinner with the woman with my aunt and uncle."

Jenna shook.

Brad stepped toward her and held her close. "Oh, my sweet, sweet rose. I would never do anything to hurt you. Trust me, she means nothing to me, and I'll never see her again."

"Can you spend the night?" Jenna asked in a small voice.

"Not tonight, but my uncle and aunt are planning a trip to Maine for the weekend. They're leaving in the morning. I'll come over as soon as they leave. Do you believe me?"

Jenna sighed. "Yes." She squeezed her eyes shut. Tomorrow he would be all hers.

"Dinner smells great, but I'd like to wait." He pulled her back into his arms and lifted her off her feet, carrying her to their bedroom. In his arms she trusted him.

She wrapped her arms around his neck and whispered in his ear, "I've missed you."

Chapter Nineteen

Lindsey left Anna Ludlum Scott's home and drove to Campagnone Common, a local park, to stretch her legs. As she strolled along the pathway, she called Abigail Adams. "Abigail, I'd like you to do another search for me."

"I'd be happy to."

Lindsey smiled at the eagerness in the librarian's voice. "See what you can find out about this Quincy Ludlum's second wife, Beverly." She explained where and when they'd been married. "Could you read me the marriage record from Middleton?"

"Just a minute." Lindsey heard the shuffling of papers and then Abigail's voice again. "December 21, 1918, Quincy Bradley Ludlum and Jenna Waverly."

"What?" Lindsey shrieked. "Did you say 'Quincy Bradley Ludlum'?"

"Yes." Abigail's voice wavered.

"So Quincy and Brad are the same person," Lindsey mused. "That explains a lot." But it didn't explain why Brad would remarry so soon after Jenna's death.

The little beep in Lindsey's phone indicated she was receiving another call. She was expecting Marc. "Thanks, Abigail. I'll get back to you."

Lindsey clicked the button to transfer the call.

"Don't you think it's time you left town before something more serious happens to you?" a voice said.

Her foot faltered and she tumbled down to the sidewalk.

A sinister laugh could be heard on the phone as she clicked it shut. Whoever it was saw her fall. She quickly pulled her digital camera from her pocket and began to click in a circle around her. Maybe she could capture the man or his vehicle.

Her hands froze as she saw the same dark sedan pull away from the curb across the street and off to her left. She snapped a picture in the hopes of photographing his license plate. But the red blur of a passing car blocked the shot.

"Are you all right?" An elderly gentleman reached down to offer her a hand up. Ironically, he was balancing himself with a cane.

"Thank you, I'm fine. I just tripped."

"These old sidewalks are tough to get around on sometimes," he offered with a smile, then narrowed his gaze on her. "Hey, are you that writer who's come to write about the Bread and Roses strike?"

"Yes," she admitted with some hesitation, unsure if she should be happy or not to be recognized. She brushed the grit and debris off her pant legs.

"Miserable strike, my parents said. Ain't seen nothing like it again in these parts. Why do you like writing about such ugly times?" The gentleman had a slender build and was hunched over from age. Lindsey guessed he had probably stood close to six feet tall in his younger days.

She straightened her jacket and stood up. "I like trying to solve old mysteries. I try not to magnify the ugliness."

"Seems to me it's best to leave old wounds closed. You never know what you'll run across."

"Like murder?" She realized too late she had let her inner thoughts slip out.

"Murder? Who was murdered?"

"You mean besides Anna Lopizzo and John Rami?" Good cover, she hoped.

A wayward grin creased the old man's face. "Did you figure out who did it? Seems to me, when I was in grade school, we had many classes trying to answer the same questions and never came up with an answer. Good ol' social studies."

"I can just imagine a teacher or two talking about your local history."

"Obviously, Lawrence became a unionized city. And teachers have their own union too. Naturally, we learned about the strike, but also its many ramifications for socialism and what it managed to help change in America, and how we treat employees and children."

Do I really want to get into a political discussion here? Lindsey decided to turn the tables. "So, who do you think killed Anna?"

"Can't say. It's plausible either way. There certainly was a lot of nonsense going on at the time. Tell ya the truth, though, I think the police were more scared of the strikers than the strikers were of them. Which is always a dangerous thing when authority isn't recognized. Good or bad, we need order in society."

"I couldn't agree more. What's your name? If you don't mind me asking."

"Vincent Scheilfer. My grandfather owned the apothecary on the corners of Essex Street and Franklin in the late eighteen hundreds."

"Did you work in the mills?"

"Never did. Never had a desire to."

Lindsey smiled. "You're rare in these parts."

"Not any more. Lots of the young folks never worked the mills. Take a look at them." He spanned his hand along the river. "Most of the plants are empty, and several only use a few floors. Many have been converted into office space and smaller businesses. I believe I read where someone purchased the old American Woolen plant and plans on subdividing it into condos. Can't be certain. My memory ain't what it used to be."

Lindsey liked Vincent. "It's been a pleasure meeting you."

"Likewise. Be careful on these old sidewalks," he added with a wink.

Lindsey watched the old man wobble away. She jumped when her cell phone rang again. This time she looked at the caller ID. It was the Lawrence Police Department. "Hello," she answered.

"Mrs. Taylor, the captain has been going over those pictures you brought in last week and, well, he'd like to talk with you about them, if you don't mind."

With her eyes closed, Lindsey pinched the bridge of her nose. Would she ever be free to leave this town? She thought back on the workers and what they were striking for. Had they felt as locked into this place as she presently did?

Lindsey glanced at her watch. The crystal cover was cracked. *What else could go wrong? Wait, scratch that thought.* "Tell the captain I'll be there in an hour."

She quickened her pace to the rental car. Should she get a third one? Would it matter? Somehow they knew where she was. How else could they keep . . . *A bug. Did they put a bug on my car? And who are* they?

Taking a deep breath, she blew the hair from her face and dialed Marc.

"Hi, honey," he answered.

"Hi. I've run into some problems."

"Are you okay?"

"Yes, but they're watching me." She leaned against the car.

"Who? Forget who. Drive to Logan and get on the next flight home."

"I can't. The police captain just asked to see me about the photographs I took last week."

Marc whistled, then paused. "Lins, I'm really concerned now. I don't want this turning into another mess like New Orleans."

"Believe me, I'm not interested in that either, but something is going on. I must have someone scared. The mystery is developing around Jenna Waverly. . . ." She filled Marc in on her discoveries of the day. "By the way, Quincy and Brad are one and the same."

"So you're leaning toward Brad as the killer?"

"Appears that way. Jenna loved Brad with a blind passion from what I can tell from her journal. He could have convinced her of anything."

"But why would he marry her and then kill her?"

Lindsey continued to keep a vigil of the area while talking with Marc. "Because she wasn't the right social class. Of course, Jenna mentions that in her journal too. He said it was his uncle who would have a problem with her."

"Well, who's his uncle?"

"I'm leaning toward Edgar Archer's great-grandfather, Phineas Archer. I know Quincy stayed in the Archer's home. There are letters to that effect. According to Jenna's journal, Brad stayed in his uncle's home. That would seem to make Phineas Archer Brad's uncle. But if that's the case, how did Brad buy the house that his daughter still lives in today so soon after Jenna's death?"

She could hear Marc clicking his pen. "You might want to check whether or not Quincy Ludlum took out a life insurance policy on Jenna."

"You don't think—?" Lindsey grabbed the door handle of the rental car and scanned the area once again.

"Anything is possible."

"Okay, if that's so, then why would someone care if I revealed it now? The statute of limitations is long past. She's dead, he's dead, his second wife is dead. Why would they care?"

Marc gave a hearty laugh, "That, my dear, is why I hired you to do my research so many years ago. You're thorough, and that's paid off well for your novels."

Lindsey settled in the seat of the car. "Thanks, I think."

"Lins, I don't like it that things are getting worse up there. Exactly what happened?"

Lindsey went on to explain the call on her cell phone. Fighting off the fear of being tracked like an animal, she kept her voice steady.

"Go to Logan after you visit with the police. We can go back up there together to finish your research later," he urged.

She agreed, and they chatted until her nerves had settled. Lindsey ended the conversation with a chuckle and a final plea from Marc to be extra careful. She popped the car into gear and headed for the police station. The desk sergeant directed her to Captain Pitts's office.

"Mrs. Taylor, it's good to see you again," said Captain Pitts as he half stood up from behind his desk and extended his hand. "Thank you for coming in." He seemed so different in uniform from how he had appeared at Edgar Archer's home a few nights ago.

Lindsey shook the captain's hand and took a seat across from him. "What can I do for you?" she asked. Only then did she notice a thin man with dark, tied-back hair slouching with a practiced air of indifference over by the window. The little hairs on the back of her neck rose.

⇢ ⇠

"Drats," he mumbled. He had no choice but to sit and wait. Was it possible she was working on something other than Bread and Roses? Had her time in New Orleans pointed to a drug ring in Lawrence? Could she possibly be a threat?

He rubbed his hands together. He was in the perfect place if an order came down.

"Yes, sir, she's my future. I can feel it in my bones."

JANUARY 5, 1912 ～ METHUEN, MASS.

"Sylvia, it's not like that," Jenna argued. "We're married."

"You're what? When?"

Brad fastened his robe. "Ladies, come on in. We'll be with you in a moment." Brad escorted Jenna back to the bedroom where they could change into clothing suitable for guests.

"Did you know they were coming over?" Brad asked as he reached for his trousers.

"No, it's a surprise visit. I didn't tell them we were married over the Christmas holiday, just like you asked. I suppose that's why they felt comfortable just coming over." Jenna reached for her dress.

"I'm sure they're angry their paychecks were shortened."

"No doubt." Jenna slipped her housedress over her head. "Can you help me with the back buttons?"

"Sure." His hands were warm and strong. "These are tiny buttons," he complained.

Jenna laughed. "You have no idea how small they can get."

"Promise me you won't put tiny buttons on my clothes in the future."

"I promise."

He kissed the nape of her neck. "I love you," he whispered.

Jenna turned in his arms and kissed him. "I love you too. But we'd better go put out the fires with Sylvia and Anna."

An hour later, Sylvia still wasn't satisfied with the story. She didn't like the secrecy, and Jenna couldn't blame her, because she felt the same way. Anna, on the other hand, seemed content with it. The two friends had come over after church to spend a quiet day in the cottage with Jenna, not thinking they might be walking in on something or that Jenna might have other plans. Instead, Brad invited the two women to come along for a drive.

Jenna was relieved when Sylvia and Anna declined. She didn't have much interest in seeing the countryside, anyway. Being wrapped in Brad's arms far exceeded any other pleasure in life. After her friends had left, she and Brad sat quietly beside the fire.

"Brad, I've been thinking." Jenna pushed herself up from his chest.

"What's that, dear?"

"What if I go to Martha's Vineyard for the year and simply return as your wife. Who would remember me after a year?"

"Plenty, I'm afraid. Look, this job is important for our future, for our children's futures. We need to stay with the plan."

"But I don't like the plan. Why can't we simply tell your uncle I am who I am? We're in love and married."

"You really haven't met my uncle have you?" Brad let out a nervous chuckle.

"No, who is he? I didn't even know your real name until you told me."

"My uncle is . . ."

Brad was interrupted by an insistent banging at the back door. "Police. Open up."

Chapter Twenty

"Mrs. Taylor, this is Detective Harris. He's been working undercover for the past year in the narcotics division. He'd like to ask you
a few questions." Captain Pitts motioned to the man standing by
the window. His posture, his build, and the silhouette of his angular
nose reminded her of one of the men in the photographs she'd taken
down at the river.

"Detective," she nodded. "What would you like to know?"

He blew a puff of cigarette smoke from the corner of his mouth
and stepped forward. "How far are you in your research on the drug
trafficking in this area?"

"I haven't done any."

His gaze pierced her, challenging her to tell the truth, looking for
the least bit of hesitation in her response. Lindsey stared back with
equal fervor. "I'm here researching the 1912 strike."

He placed his hands on the corner of the captain's desk and leaned
toward her. "Yeah, yeah, I read the newspapers. What were you doing taking photographs of a drug purchase?"

Lindsey stood. "Sir, am I being accused of something?"

"Harris, cut Mrs. Taylor some slack." Captain Pitts said then directed his attention to Lindsey. "Please forgive his—uh, forthright-
ness. Working undercover sometimes diminishes their social skills."
He cast a sideways glance toward Detective Harris.

Letting out a deep sigh, Harris leaned back on his heels and raised his hands in surrender. "All right, sorry."

"So, is this the reason I've been followed?" She asked.

"Followed?" they said in unison.

"Yes. I believe a tracking device was placed on my car yesterday just before I was blindsided by the young man on his in-line skates."

The two men looked at each other and the captain stood. "Please sit down, Mrs. Taylor." He pushed the intercom button. "Send in Rick Atherton."

"Did you tell the officer at the scene of the accident about this tracking device?" Captain Pitts asked Lindsey as he grabbed a yellow legal pad from the corner of his desk and sat back down. It was the first time anyone at the police station had seemed interested in what she had to say.

"No, I didn't realize it was there until today when whoever wants me out of town called my cell phone."

"You've been threatened?" The captain began taking notes.

"Twice. 'Encouraged' to write another book is more like it. But the call earlier today, on my cell phone, resembled more of a threat, suggesting I should go home."

"Did you report this?" Detective Harris said incredulously.

A tall, dark-haired officer knocked on the door and stepped into the office. Captain Pitts acknowledged the man and said to Lindsey, "Mrs. Taylor, this is Officer Atherton. Please, give him the make and model of your car and where it's parked." Armed with this information, the officer left to inspect the car for a possible tracking device.

Lindsey answered the question as if the interruption had not occurred. "I'm not sure if I mentioned it at the hotel at the time of the break-in or not."

"Mrs. Taylor, are you telling us you've received threatening phone calls, your hotel room was broken into, and now you believe you're being followed?" Detective Harris asked.

"Yes, but—"

"But what? Are you in the habit of having these kinds of experiences?" he pushed further.

Lindsey swallowed hard. Wouldn't Marc love the reprimand she was getting from the police? "I wouldn't say it's a habit, but I've experienced it a time or two, yes."

Detective Harris lifted his hands in the air and grunted.

Captain Pitts rubbed the back of his neck. "Mrs. Taylor,"—the captain's voice spun out like fine silk. *He definitely has learned the political side of his job,* Lindsey mused—"What you photographed could put a year of Detective Harris's work down the drain. If these guys have the slightest indication that you saw them, never mind photographed them—"

"My computer," Lindsey gasped.

"Your computer?" The two officers looked at each other, at Lindsey, and back at one another again.

"It was stolen yesterday when I was injured. I have no idea who stole it. And I'm certain that recovering it was given a low profile."

Detective Harris looked like he'd prefer to have his hands around her throat. "So, let me get this straight, you've got these pictures in your computer. Are they labeled?"

"Not really, I just send them to a file folder in which all the research goes for each particular book."

"And is your file labeled the same as the name of the book you've been telling every reporter within a hundred-mile radius you're working on?"

Lindsey let out a nervous cough. "Yes."

"Great. Just great." Detective Harris turned his back to Lindsey. "Captain, we need to pull Steve out before they kill him."

"Agreed."

The angry detective hustled out of the room faster than a squirrel with its tail on fire.

Whom had she captured on film?

JANUARY 11, 1912 ~ LAWRENCE, MASS.

Sylvia and Anna clung to one another in the meeting hall. The room was packed, like an overflowing bucket of wool that had just come up from the cleaning room. Sylvia looped her arm around Anna's. The crowd pushed them in every direction. A huge man stepped on Sylvia's foot. "Er-r-r-r." She held back screaming at the lug.

"Are you all right?" Anna asked in Italian.

"I will be. Let us make room for others."

"There is no more room. They are hanging off the rafters now." Anna pointed.

"I will not sit while they take my pay!" A woman with a leathery face yelled in Italian. Cheers went up around the room. Sylvia offered her own agreement.

"We need to do another slowdown," a lanky man sitting on the edge of the platform suggested.

"We must strike!" A man shouted from the center of the crowd.

"Strike! Strike! Strike!" The chant rippled through the room.

A thin, older man stood on the left side of the building toward the platform. "The machines are too fast. My daughter almost lost her hand."

"Strike, strike, strike!" The room swelled with another round of excitement. Sylvia spotted Donna and Lucia from her boardinghouse.

"Strike!" Sylvia called out, raising her fist to the air.

A woman standing at the front on the platform lifted her hands to hush the crowd. "If we strike, we need to prepare. We need solidarity. We need the Irish, the Syrians, every ethnic group working here. But the Italians, we need to be first."

"Strike! Strike!" The crowd roared.

The woman held her hands up once again. "We will send for some union organizers to come help us."

The room hushed as others joined the woman on the platform, and the plan was laid out. By the end of the evening, it was decided. The Italians would strike.

Sylvia and Anna walked back to the boardinghouse together, taking in the fresh air. Anna looked over to Sylvia. "Why does it have to be this way?" she asked in her native tongue.

"Because Mr. Wood is cheap and heartless," Sylvia fumed. "If he had just paid attention to the slowdowns last year. . . . But no, instead he sped up the machines, and now more people are getting injured and killed."

"I know, I know." Anna looked toward the sky. "Do you think it is peaceful in heaven?"

"With all those trumpets blasting? I doubt it. But I do not think people will be going hungry up there, either."

Anna smiled and looped her arm around Sylvia's waist. "You are a good friend. But you have been very hard on Jenna. Why is that?"

"She is so young. I hate to see her ruin her life on a man who is just going to drop her."

"Why do you say that? He married her, did he not? He would not have done that if he did not love her."

Sylvia sighed. "Maybe you are right. I do not trust men."

"I noticed. James Donovan has been trying to get your attention for months, possibly longer."

"I know, and he is a fairly handsome guy for an Irishman." Sylvia winked.

Anna swatted her arm. "You have a bit of the devil in you, Sylvia Giovanni."

"You might just be right."

"How do you like working at the other mill?" Anna asked. "At least now you know it was Brad who had you transferred, and it was not something you did wrong."

"I do not know. Something does not ring true, but I cannot put my finger on it. On the other hand, Jenna seems very much in love and very happy."

Anna sighed. "That is quite apparent. I cannot believe we marched in and found them in their nightclothes. It was nearly noon." She giggled. "But I guess they are newlyweds."

Sylvia felt the heat rush to her face. "I am not ignorant." They turned the corner and continued on toward the boardinghouse.

"You sure are acting it."

"You know, life was simpler when I did not have such close friends," Sylvia teased.

"But you did not know how abrasive you could be before you had friends," Anna challenged.

"I would say I am still pretty prickly. Why do you and Jenna put up with me?"

"Because we like your honest and straightforward approach."

"Changing the subject, how are you set for food for the strike?" Sylvia clutched her coat tighter. Her nose tingled from the cold.

"I will be all right for a while. How about you?"

"I do not have much, but I will get by." She didn't want to reveal her secret stash to anyone, but she knew she'd share with Anna, if necessary. "It is too bad we cannot wait for summer to strike. Jenna's plans for a garden might have fed us well."

"I do not think we can survive until summer," Anna said. "Too many lives will be lost if we keep up this pace at the mill."

"Yes. That is why we must stay united and strike now. I just hope Joseph Ettor can help us organize," Sylvia said. "He has done so much for the unions in New York." As she took hold of the handrail on the front steps of the boardinghouse, she dropped her voice to just above a whisper. "We better not talk about the strike inside the house. We do not know who will be with us or against us."

Anna turned to Sylvia and cocked her head. "We need others to join us."

Chapter Twenty-one

"Captain?" Officer Atherton knocked and entered with two small items in his hand. "Found these on the lady's car."

The captain took the offered items.

"This is really very strange," the officer said. "This one here"—he pointed to a miniature circuit board, approximately an inch square in size, with a couple of computerized chips on it—"is high-end stuff, costs anywhere from a grand up to three. This other one," he pointed to the bulkier one with a huge magnet on it, "is very low tech, goes for around thirty bucks."

"Are you suggesting there are two people tracking this woman?"

"It looks that way."

The captain locked eyes with his subordinate. "If you hadn't removed them," he said gravely, "we might have been able to triangulate where the signal is going." Captain Pitts sat down in his chair and pushed the long strands of hair covering his bald spot back into place.

A chagrined expression crossed Atherton's face. "I s'pose I could put 'em back. But if they're watching the car, they would've already seen me nosing around and know their device is cooked."

"Well, let's at least have someone watch the vehicle for further signs of tampering."

"Yes, sir."

Lindsey sat back in the chair. *Who would want to follow me?* In her mind she reviewed what she could remember about the photographs she had taken down by the river. She concentrated on the people and the passing of the money and drugs. She now knew that one of the men was Detective Harris, having met him face-to-face, but who was the other man?

Taking a deep breath, she fought off the increasing fear. Perhaps she should go home to Miami and come back in a month or so with Marc.

"May I use your laptop?" she asked Captain Pitts.

He folded his hands, placing them on the desk. "I'm afraid my laptop is not for public use. I have sensitive files in there. And the mayor would have my hide if I were to let a writer into those files."

Lindsey sat back. "I understand. May I run to my car and get mine?"

"I thought you said yours was stolen?"

"It was. I replaced it. A writer can't be without a computer when doing research. I like to have everything at my fingertips."

"What do you want your computer for? Weren't all your files stolen with the old one?"

Lindsey smiled. "After having my system crash and losing my work one time too many, I got in the habit of backing everything up to a USB flash drive several times a day. A writer can't be too careful." She tapped the side of her purse. "I've got all my Bread and Roses files right here."

"Okay, that's fine," the captain said, "but what are you trying to look up?"

"I'd like to get a second look at those photos I took. Maybe I'll recognize the other man in the picture."

"Detective Harris knows who it is."

"Yeah, but I thought maybe if I could see him, perhaps I could place him. Why would he be after me, following me? What threat could I possibly be? Was there something else in that photograph we weren't aware of?" Lindsey rubbed the back of her neck. "But here's the odd thing. The computer was stolen *after* the bug was put on my car. Why?"

She took a swig from her water bottle and replaced it firmly on the table. "And since there are possibly two people tracking me, I'd like to see if I captured anyone else in those photographs. Maybe these threats have nothing to do with my research of the strike. Maybe this is all because I was in the wrong place at the wrong time." *Like New Orleans,* she added to herself.

"You raise some interesting questions." Captain Pitts sat back in his old wooden swivel desk chair. "Go ahead, get your computer, and let's see if we can put an end to this nonsense once and for all."

Lindsey shouldered her purse and left the captain's office. As she walked she rummaged through her bag and pulled out her cell phone—then tossed it back in. *No sense calling Marc until I leave for the airport.*

She glanced at her wristwatch. It was almost five o'clock. There was no way she'd be getting home tonight. *Why is it I always run into these kinds of situations, Lord?* she silently prayed. *Wouldn't it be nice to write a novel where my life isn't threatened? And now even the police are upset with me.* She reached in her purse once again; she'd have to call Marc.

"Where are you going?" Detective Harris's gruff voice startled her.

"Captain Pitts said I could get my laptop from the car."

The detective came up beside her and grabbed her elbow, gently but firmly. "I'll escort you."

She pulled her arm free and pressed the send button on her cell phone. Marc's line was busy. She hung up the phone and headed to the rental, with Detective Harris at her side.

The sun hung slightly over the tops of the budding trees. A swirl of wind spun around her, and Lindsey shivered. She clicked the remote for the trunk, pulled out her briefcase, and retrieved a sweater from her suitcase. The cool air was playing havoc with her system. Each night she fought the onset of a cold. Each night she'd take some medication and coat her neck and chest with a vapor rub. Marc hated the smell. She grinned at the thought. Taking a moment to put on her sweater, she set the briefcase momentarily back in the trunk. Something fell out of the sweater's pocket, and she bent down to pick it up. At the same moment, a strange noise, a metallic ping, registered just above her head.

"Get down!" someone yelled.

Detective Harris grabbed her and held her to the ground. Police officers took positions behind their vehicles with their weapons at the ready.

Lindsey curled up on the pavement and cried out for the Lord's protection.

> ⤞ ⤝

An hour later, her hands were still shaking. Whoever fired the shot had only fired once. Reporters stormed the police station in record time when they heard that Lindsey had been shot at. There was definitely a story here, and they were bound and determined to find it.

What had she uncovered? Determined to get to the bottom of things, Captain Pitts had sent a police officer in combat gear to retrieve all of Lindsey's luggage. Even Detective Harris had taken a sudden concern with Lindsey's welfare.

In the conference room, she laid out her files. Detective Harris sifted through the materials to determine what she did and did not know about his drug case.

"Did you ever think about becoming a detective?" he asked.

"Nope. I like the research, but I've had enough of criminal investigations from working for my husband. He's an attorney. Researching historical mysteries is enough for me."

"But isn't that essentially a criminal investigation?"

"Yes, but . . ." How could she answer him? He did have a point. "Fictionalizing a historical mystery allows me to always get my man, whereas in real life, that doesn't always happen."

"True. Life is messy."

"Very." Lindsey looked at an enlarged photograph of the drug purchase, courtesy of the technicians in the police lab. "I've met this man." She pointed to the other man in the picture with Detective Harris.

"How?"

"I had dinner the other night at Edgar Archer's house. He was one of the dinner guests. Let me see if I can remember his name." She paused for a moment, "Waylan Tompkins."

"Good memory. Okay, tell me what he knows about your research into the Bread and Roses strike."

"Just about everything that I knew after a few days. We had a good conversation. However, he doesn't know about Jenna Waverly's death or that Ruth supplied me with her journal."

"Tompkins isn't the man I'm after. The buy you photographed was merely a preliminary step to establish myself as a quality dealer. Tompkins represents a chance to get into some of the richer clientele in the city."

Her cell phone rang. "Hi, honey," she answered.

"Where are you? Are you safe? It's on the news, Lins. Don't tell me nothing happened."

Lindsey let out a nervous cough and cleared her throat. "I'm fine. I'm in the middle of the police station in a conference room being baby-sat by a detective."

"Good. I want you to get a police escort to the airport and come on home. This is crazy, Lindsey. I don't want to—"

"I want to come home, too, honey, but—"

Detective Harris motioned to let him talk with Marc. She handed the phone over.

"Mr. Taylor, this is Detective Harris with the Lawrence Police Department . . ."

Lindsey closed her eyes and prayed. She would not be free to leave town tonight. Perhaps tomorrow. Captain Pitts made it quite clear she wasn't going anywhere without his protection. No one was able to determine if the shot had been a warning shot or simply a bad one. Either way, it was something Lindsey wanted to avoid in the future.

"We'll put her up for the night in a secure location. We'll have her exit the building in a wig to try to limit her exposure," Detective Harris went on to explain.

"We're not exactly sure," Harris said.

"Someone's using some pretty high-tech stuff, " he added.

"Yes, sir. We'll take good care of her." Detective Harris smiled. "Just a moment." He handed the phone back to Lindsey.

"Hi," she said as casually as she could muster. She knew exactly what was going through Marc's mind.

"Lins, I'm worried, but I'm trying to trust the Lord for your safety. It's so hard when you're so far away."

"It's difficult this close to it too. If the guy was aiming for me, God made certain the bullet missed. If, however, it was a warning shot, the message is clear. I want to be home with you, but I also need to let these officers know what I know about this situation." Lindsey got up and walked to the other end of the room to give herself a little privacy.

"Okay, I understand," Marc said. "I'm not happy, but there's little we can do. Call me when you're getting ready for bed. You can fill me in later. In the meantime, do exactly as the police tell you."

"Not a problem." Lindsey chuckled. "I have some new reading material for the night." She told him about Beverly Ludlum's journal.

"I'll call the boys and your folks so they'll know what's going on. Love you tons, Lins. Stay safe."

"You too. Love ya. Good night." She clicked the phone shut and savored his last words. *Dear God in heaven, get us through this.*

Detective Harris cleared his throat. "You okay?"

"Fine." She turned around and faced him. How could anyone be okay when someone was shooting at them for no apparent reason? Obviously someone had a reason, but it completely eluded Lindsey. Whoever was stalking her probably had their fears heightened by her visit to the police station.

"Liar," he smiled.

"I'm trying to think positive thoughts."

"Nothing positive about this. You're in it up to your pretty little neck, if you ask me." He looked down at her papers. "Who do you think killed Anna Lopizzo?"

➤ ❖

"I can't believe I missed." He jammed the rifle back into its case and slipped back into the apartment building. His sources in the police station said she'd been in Pitts' office for thirty minutes.

He'd been fortunate to find an unoccupied apartment overlooking the police station. Ruffling through the refrigerator he pulled out a bottle of tonic water and sat down in the living room in front of the television. "Just when I was about to give up . . . this happens."

He twisted off the top of the bottle of beer; fizz escaped. *What to do, what to do?*

JANUARY 12, 1912 ~ METHUEN, MASS.

"Jenna, I'm home," Brad hollered.

"I'm in the bedroom."

It had been a week since the police had come to their home looking for an intruder who had been spotted in the neighborhood. The police had checked each day and found nothing. Jenna was beginning to relax. Sleeping had been sporadic at best. It hadn't surprised her when she woke up feeling poorly this morning. "I'm sick. I think I've come down with the flu."

Brad stood in the entryway. "Anything I can get you?"

"A cup of tea would be nice," she replied, and pulled the covers up to her nose. "And could you add some wood to the stove?"

"Sure. Anything else, my love?" He winked.

His presence alone made her feel a hundred times better. "Nothing that I can think of. How was your day?"

"Did you hear from Sylvia or Anna?"

"No, why?"

"The Italians went on strike today. There was some violence in the streets. A few other ethnic groups joined them. Their demands are out of the question, but these things usually start out bad."

"How's Mr. Wood taking it?"

"He isn't pleased, but he thinks they'll be back to work by the end of the week, two at the most. He's certain they can't survive too long without a paycheck."

Jenna sat up in the bed. "He really doesn't understand the needs of the workers, does he?"

Brad leaned against the bedpost. "That's the odd thing. He was a common laborer in a factory. He knows what it's like. I think he believes that if he could make something of his life, others should too."

"How can they when they can't save for the future?"

"That seems to be the question of the day. I honestly don't think he believed the workers would actually strike in the first place. He probably thought it would work itself out, like last summer's slowdowns."

Jenna wagged her head. "I've seen the books, Brad. He can afford to pay the workers better than he does."

"I know, dear. But I also see what he's trying to accomplish, the business venture he's attempting to create. It's a hard call, but you're right, he could probably pay better and still develop his plan."

Jenna smiled. At least Brad understood the plight of the workers. *Perhaps there's still time for him to talk reason to Mr. Wood.*

She reached out to him and he sat down on the bed beside her. She ran her fingers through his red curls. "You need a haircut."

"I was hoping my wife could give me a trim."

"Hmm, never cut a man's hair before."

"There's always a first time." He smiled and kissed her on the tip of her nose. "Let me make that tea." He pushed himself up from the bed. "The color is returning to your cheeks."

"You're medicine to the soul, dear."

Brad laughed. "I hope you always feel that way."

Jenna snuggled under the covers. It was good to have him home. Life was so boring without him. Tonight she would speak to him about getting a job, any job, something to keep her busy during the day while he was at work. The cottage was just so big, and a gal could clean only so many times.

✧ ✧

An hour later a very excited Sylvia and Anna showed up at the cottage. "You should have been there, Jenna. It was amazing."

"I not like the fisticuffs," Anna admitted.

"What was it like on the inside?" Sylvia asked Brad.

Brad looked over to Jenna before answering. "I'm afraid that wouldn't be fair to say, Sylvia."

"I suppose, and it wouldn't be right for me to share what we voted on either," Sylvia replied.

"Precisely why I haven't asked you," Brad said with a smile.

Jenna didn't know how Sylvia would take that. Anna spoke up first. "We can't share one another's plans. Perhaps we shouldn't visit during the strike," she suggested.

"Ladies, I'm not striking. You can come during the day when Brad's not home if that would be more comfortable." Jenna couldn't accept that she might lose what little contact she had with her friends.

Brad wrapped his arm around his wife's shoulders. "I think we can all agree not to talk about the strike when we're together. Friendship is far more important, and Jenna needs her friends."

How could he know her so well in such a short time? But that had always been a part of their relationship, a mutual understanding without having spoken a word to each other.

"You're right, Mr. Ludlum. I'm sorry I asked." Sylvia smiled.

"Honesty will get us through this, ladies. Now, if you will excuse me, I have some work to do before I leave for my uncle's."

Sylvia tossed her head from side to side. "You haven't told him yet?"

Brad looked down at his feet, then back at Sylvia, "We have a plan but it will take some time to implement."

Sylvia turned her focus back to Jenna. "How do you stand it?"

"I'm learning, but it's difficult."

"If I ever marry, I want my husband in my bed every night," Anna said, letting the words slip from her mouth.

Jenna couldn't believe her ears. Sylvia and Jenna looked at each other, and all three broke out in laughter.

Chapter Twenty-two

Lindsey reached for a second cold slice of pizza and bit off a piece. What she wouldn't give for a nice chicken Caesar salad.

Detective Harris stretched. "Can we call it a night?" he asked.

"Huh? What time is it?"

"Ten, but who's counting?" he quipped. "Do you get lost in your research like this very often?"

"All too often, I'm afraid. Just ask my husband." She took another bite of the pizza and closed the laptop. All night she had wanted to get to the two journals but hadn't been able to.

"I know I said this about an hour ago, but I think whoever this guy is, he thinks you have some information that would expose him and his activities, which makes him very dangerous. But what he doesn't know is that you're clueless. If there's something in these photographs, I can't see it. And just because you met Waylan Tompkins, well, it isn't enough to cause anyone much trouble. When it comes to his cocaine use, it's strictly for entertainment. Guys like him are a dime a dozen. The ones I'm after are the suppliers and their bosses."

She hadn't seen any signs of drug addiction in Waylan that evening, but she hadn't been looking for it either. Lindsey stood up and placed her hands on her hips. "And there's nothing in the historical research that would bring this kind of threat. After all, I'm dealing with events that are nearly a hundred years old. No one would be left alive from that time. Even their children are mostly gone. It still doesn't make sense."

"Definitely, but my brain is gonzo. I need some sleep. Officer Cheryl Dailey will take you to the safe house for the night, then return you in the morning."

Lindsey nodded. "I'm going to bring my work, if you don't mind. I do have a deadline I need to keep in mind."

He groaned. "Avoid the word *dead.*"

A sliver of ice-cold fear slid straight into her heart. Lindsey piled up her papers in order, set them in their folders, and placed them in her briefcase. She stuck the two journals in her purse and put the computer memory stick around her neck for safekeeping. "All set." She yawned.

"Don't get me started." Detective Harris yawned in return. "I have a thirty-minute drive before I get home."

"Lawrence isn't that big of a city." Lindsey zipped up the briefcase.

"I live in Middleton."

"Middleton? Interesting."

"Why?" Detective Harris held the door open for her.

"One of the couples I'm looking into was married in Middleton in 1911. December 21, to be precise."

Lindsey walked through the opened door and entered the hallway. The fluorescent lights hummed in the otherwise quiet corridor.

"Tell Officer Dailey that Mrs. Taylor is ready to leave," Detective Harris ordered a younger officer.

"Yes, sir." The young man with highly polished shoes stood to attention and scurried out of the room.

Rookie, she thought.

"I'll see you in the morning, Mrs. Taylor. Good night." Detective Harris sauntered out the front doors, zipping up his jacket.

"Mrs. Taylor, follow me." An African-American female officer who appeared to be in her early thirties motioned for her to head toward the rear of the building.

"Oh no, wait." Lindsey pulled her cell phone from her purse. "They said to leave this at the station."

Officer Dailey smiled and took the cell phone from Lindsey. She stepped into the conference room and left it on the table. Lindsey noted the muscular build of the female officer.

"Detective Harris was going to give me his phone for the night so I could call my husband."

"You can use mine. I have free roaming and nighttime minutes," she offered.

"Thank you."

They went into a smaller room where Lindsey was given some clothes to change into and a wig to put on, along with oversized work boots and thick, white cotton socks. "Am I supposed to look like a homeless person?"

"Sort of. That way I can help usher you out, holding on to you and your belongings without anyone being the wiser. At least that's the plan. The captain was quite emphatic about keeping you safe."

"I see." Lindsey understood, but it still went against her grain to look deliberately frumpy. She did as instructed, and the officer put Lindsey's briefcase in an old brown paper bag and covered it with her clothing.

Catching a glimpse of herself in the mirror made Lindsey realize she wouldn't even recognize herself. She sniffed the sleeve of the sweater. A faint odor of mustiness and stale beer finished off the disguise. She couldn't wait to shower.

"Okay, I'm going to need you to shuffle your feet, swagger a bit, give the impression you're unsteady."

"All right." In reality, that wasn't much of a strain. She hadn't been outside the police station since she'd been shot at. Not only did she still feel shaky, but her joints were also stiff from sitting in a too-hard chair. *Lord, make it impossible for them to follow me, whoever they may be,* she prayed.

Isolation and the evening chill in the room left Lindsey feeling very alone after she arrived at the safe house. Officer Dailey had given her privacy to make her calls and take a shower. The room had the same drab paint as the one in New Orleans.

Lindsey retrieved her purse, pulled out one of the journals, and opened it. It was Jenna's. She thumbed through to December 21.

What a day, Jenna wrote. *Today I was fired. Today I learned that Brad's real name is Quincy Ludlum. How I ever believed him to be Mr. Wood's nephew, I don't know. I'm happy we are married now, but I don't understand why Brad felt the need to have me fired.*

"He fired her?" Lindsey said out loud.

"What?" Officer Dailey appeared at the doorway to Lindsey's room.

"Sorry." She held up the small black journal. "Research."

"Oh." She leaned against the door jam. "You write about historical crimes, right?"

"Primarily. I started writing romances, but my heart was always into mysteries. I also love history, so I just blended the two."

"Interesting. Most mystery novels aren't like real police work. But then again, there's a lot of mundane activity in the investigation of crimes."

"What do you like to read?" Lindsey closed the book in her hand, keeping her thumb at the place she'd been reading.

"Mysteries. Once in a while I'll read a romance. They're light, but fun every now and again. Unfortunately, there isn't much romance in a cop's life."

"Are you married?" Lindsey asked.

"Divorced."

"Sorry to hear that."

"It happens." She shrugged her shoulders. "The clock is ticking, so I best let you do whatever you want to do before you retire for the evening."

"Thank you."

"Not a problem. Good night."

Lindsey listened to the officer's footsteps as she trekked confidently down the hall to the front room of the apartment. *I guess her marriage is not an issue to be discussed.* She opened the journal and continued to read.

Ten minutes later, Lindsey realized she was nodding off to sleep. Jenna was talking about the strike, about the secret marriage, and wondering when Brad would tell his uncle they had married. Jenna mentioned that Brad had a plan to bring her into the family, but she never elaborated on it.

Lindsey made a mental note to contact Ruth Emery to see if she had found anything in her grandmother's journal referring to the time of the strike. She slipped under the covers and sniffed the clean sheets. Finally, she relaxed for the evening.

An explosion rocked the windows and walls.

Lindsey bolted upright from her slumber.

Outside the window across from the bed, a huge fireball rose in the black night sky.

JANUARY 18, 1912 ~ LAWRENCE, MASS.

Sylvia clung to Anna. Fifteen thousand people had marched on Monday, another ten thousand on Wednesday. Tempers were hot despite the frigid temperatures that penetrated their thin overcoats, reminding them of why they were out on strike. Sylvia wasn't sure how many were marching today. Tomorrow would mark an entire week out on strike. They'd been told it would take time, and there would be no paychecks today.

"Are you eating?" Sylvia asked in Italian, keeping her voice low.

"I had some beans and molasses today. Thanks for the beans."

"You are welcome." After the first day of the strike, Sylvia had realized that her little stash of food wouldn't go far, but it was more than others had. Choosing when and with whom to share the food and money continued to nag at her conscience. "I have volunteered to work in the soup kitchen this weekend."

"That will be warmer than out here." Anna shivered.

Sylvia held her tighter. "Why do you not volunteer with me?"

"I might just do that."

The police cordoned off the crowd. They stopped the leaders in the front band of strikers. People murmured, asking what was going on. Soon a wave of sound washed over them as word came through that their permit to parade had been revoked.

"They cannot do that," a young woman, perhaps in her twenties, cried out.

"Do what?" Sylvia asked.

"They stopped the march, revoking our right to protest. Said our permit was no longer valid."

"They can't do that!" people shouted.

"I thought this was a free country," Sylvia groused.

Slowly, the crowd started to dissolve and work their way back to their homes along the sidewalk in front of the mills. She and Anna decided to go back to the house and warm up before they went back on the street.

"There are a lot more strikers than policemen," Anna said as they entered the house and shut the cold out behind them. She pulled her gloves off and warmed them over the small stove in the kitchen. "Do you suppose Brad let Jenna get a job?"

"I don't know. I doubt it. He controls her too much."

"She seems so lonely," Anna added.

"I think you are right, but why the secrecy? The man I marry had better be proud to have me as his wife, whether his family approves or not."

"Any man who stands up to you can stand up to his parents." Anna winked and placed a teapot on the warm stove.

"I will take that as a compliment," Sylvia chuckled.

"I like you the way you are, Sylvia. But Brad does not know you. Even though he told us his reasons and asked us to keep their secret for Jenna's sake, you have been hard on him. He did not have to marry Jenna. He chose to."

Sylvia sighed. "Perhaps you are right. I do not know. It just happened so fast."

"Yes, but they are happy. Think back to the old country. There the woman meets her husband on their wedding day or the day before. Marriages are all arranged. You understood the different classes in our homeland, but you do not understand or accept it here. Why?"

A boardinghouse sister came in, dressed in her bedclothes and holding a handkerchief to her nose.

Sylvia paused, reaching for the teacups. "Donna, would you like some tea? Are you feeling any better?"

"*Si*, tea would be nice." She coughed. "I feel a little better." Sylvia poured Donna a cup.

"*Grazie.*" Donna carried her tea to her room.

Sylvia thought about what Anna had said about the old country and Brad. *Why* does *it bother me?* "Regarding Brad, I do not know. I guess I never trusted him from the first moment I saw him eyeing Jenna. He looked like he was looking for trouble."

"But that is not true. He has married Jenna."

"Who married Jenna?" Another housemate asked as she walked into the kitchen.

Chapter Twenty-three

"Stay down," Officer Dailey came running in with her gun poised.

"What was that?" Lindsey asked.

"Don't know. Keep a low profile. I don't know if it's simply a coincidence or if someone is trying to smoke us out. Either case, you're staying down until I get an all clear from the station."

Lindsey nodded. *That explosion couldn't have been meant for me. No one knows I'm here. It had to be some freak coincidence.* Even she and Marc didn't know the address. Going home to Miami looked sweeter every minute. They sat in the darkness, still and silent. A faint smell of smoke mingled with the cool, damp spring air.

A car engine whined.

Lindsey's ear rang. She glanced at the nightstand and watched the numbers flip on the old digital clock.

A dog barked.

The faucet in the bathroom dripped.

The window vibrated in its frame. Lindsey curled her fingers around the comforter, clutching and unclutching the fabric, counting every second.

Her heart thumped in her chest.

Another droplet of water fell from the faucet.

Two minutes crept past before Officer Dailey placed a call to the station. The two-way on her cellular crackled. A stream of numbers was spouted and she disconnected the transmission.

"Everything appears to be fine, but we're to sit tight for a bit longer," Officer Dailey informed her.

"I wasn't planning on going anywhere." Lindsey began to perspire. Her mind flitted back to New Orleans. She'd been put in protective custody there too. Healing from the knife wound had been the easy part. Healing from the psychological damage had never completely taken hold. Her body started to shake. The room she stayed in had been similar—drab paint, nothing on the walls, a bed, a dresser, and a couple of nightstands. The musty smells of the humid New Orleans nights came alive. She was no longer in Lawrence but back in that room, that horrible and yet safe room. Her throat thickened. She wanted her freedom; she wanted to scream.

Lindsey took in a deep pull of air. It was cooler, cleaner than New Orleans. She squeezed her eyes shut and felt the soft ribbon of the blanket between her fingers. Slowly she let out a deep breath. She was back in Lawrence, away from the nightmare.

Father, reveal to the authorities who is behind this threat, she prayed. *If someone is out to kill me, would they risk such a high level of attack? Wouldn't they come in silently?*

"Officer Dailey," Lindsey whispered. "I can't believe anyone would blow up something just to get to me. It doesn't make sense."

"From what I know of this case, nothing makes sense. But I agree, we should have a definite word soon, and then we can let down our guard."

"Thanks."

The officer's phone rang. "Hello," she answered. "Understood, thank you."

Lindsey watched the woman holster her weapon and stand up. "There was an explosion at a restaurant down the street. Appears to be related to the heater, but there'll be an investigation. I'm going to take a look around the perimeter; then I'll resume my post in the front room. You should try to get some sleep."

"I *was* trying. Perhaps I'll read a bit. It seemed to put me to sleep earlier."

Officer Dailey exited with a chuckle.

The two journals on the nightstand beckoned to be picked up. Lindsey reached over and grabbed one. She snuggled under the bed covers and opened the cracked leather cover to check which journal she'd taken. It was Beverly Ludlum's. The illuminated numbers on the digital clock showed 1:07. Lindsey moaned. She really did need to sleep.

Slowly, she scanned what she had read earlier in the day. *Has it really been less than twenty-four hours?* Lindsey reached for the memo pad she always kept beside her at night just in case an idea worth remembering hit before she fell to sleep.

Look for marriage records for Quincy and Beverly Ludlum. She added the March 30 date that Anna had given her. Rubbing her burning eyes, she glanced at the clock again. It was 1:10. She closed the journal, clicked off the light, and settled down once again.

There was a tap at her doorway. "All clear, Lindsey. Good night."

Closing her eyes, Lindsey prayed for sleep, for peace, and for guidance. *Life should be quieter than this,* she mused. After all, weren't she and Marc living in a nearly empty nest? The boys only came home during college breaks. She fluffed up the pillow, rolled to her side, and examined the back of her eyelids.

✦ ✦

"Why didn't you tell me who you testified against in New Orleans?" Detective Harris demanded. He stood like a marine sergeant yelling at a young recruit as she entered the police station.

"Aren't we pleasant in the morning," she returned. "And the answer to your question is, you never asked."

"You photographed a drug transaction, and you didn't think it was relevant? You testified against the Cocaine King of New Orleans." He stepped back from the entryway to the conference room that had been their office last night to let her pass.

"Look, you might have the right to speak to those you work with in that tone," Lindsey replied, "but I am not your subordinate, nor am I under your authority. I'm here of my own free will, and I don't appreciate being talked to in such a tone."

"Harris," Captain Pitts bellowed from the doorway to the conference room.

"Yes, sir. Sorry, sir. Sorry, Mrs. Taylor. Excuse me." Detective Harris left the conference room and stomped down the hall.

Captain Pitts entered the room. "I apologize for the behavior of my men, Mrs. Taylor. I understand you recognized Mr. Tompkins in the photograph."

"Yes, I'm sorry."

The captain held up his hand. "Mr. Tompkins will be getting a private talk from me. Hopefully, he isn't addicted. If he is, I'll try to get him the help he needs, if he's willing."

Lindsey really didn't know how to analyze this man. He seemed gruff, yet he also seemed to care for his friends.

"I'd like to go home tonight if at all possible."

"I'm not sure that is a wise plan," Captain Pitts sighed.

Lindsey placed her hands on her hips. She didn't want to stay.

"Please, sit down." The police captain stepped up to the conference table and sat down in the head chair. "Detective Harris and I were discussing the matter before you came in. What he didn't know was your past run-in with the Melancon family in New Orleans."

"Obviously." Lindsey sat down. "What does that have to do with this?"

"Maybe nothing. But there's a rumor that a member of the Melancon family is the supplier for this area's drug traffic trade."

Lindsey's heart sank. Could Richard Melancon be the current

cause of all her problems? Hadn't she gotten away from him after his sentencing? Lindsey squeezed her eyes shut and tried to organize her thoughts.

"Captain, how would Richard Melancon even know I had the photograph of the drug transaction?"

Captain Pitts looked down and placed his folded hands on the table in front of him. Slowly he raised his bald pate. "There must be someone on the force who's being paid by the Melancon family." Regret mixed with shame, and anger lit his eyes.

"I see. What am I supposed to do? Stay here? Won't that just give the person another opportunity to tell Mr. Melancon where I am?" Lindsey stood up and marched over to the window. "I need to call my husband."

"I understand." The chair scraped the tile floor as the captain rose to leave.

Before he exited, Lindsey asked, "How much longer on this investigation into this drug case with the Melancon connection?"

"Could take a couple of months."

No way, she wanted to scream. She would not be put into protective custody for two months. Not if she could help it.

She picked up her cell phone and dialed.

"Are you coming home tonight?" Marc's voice seemed tight, straining to be upbeat and calm.

"They suspect Richard Melancon might be the cause of all the problems."

"What?" Marc held back his anger, but she could picture him standing there, his backbone stiff, his shoulders solid and inflexible. A moment of silence came over the phone. Then, in his most tender voice, the kind that made her want to leap into his arms, he asked, "Is it possible, Lins?"

"If the rumors of the Melancon family supplying the area drug trade are true, it's possible."

"Should I go to New Orleans and persuade him to lay off?"

Lindsey smiled. Marc would fly there and put any and all pressure he could on Melancon if she asked him to. "Let's pray. I don't know what to do. After the shooting yesterday, I don't think I am safe. But then again, was it meant for me?"

"I'm not taking that chance, Lindsey. I'm coming up there. I've cleared the calendar. I'll come to the police station. I don't care if the police think it's a risk or not."

"Honey, they're saying it could be months before the investigation is over. That's months in protective custody."

"We're not going to live apart again. I'll spend the time necessary to transfer my clients over to my staff. The rest can hire new attorneys."

"What about the mayor?"

"So can he. I don't care, Lins. We're not going to live apart for a long period of time."

"What about the kids' wedding?" Tears pooled in Lindsey's eyes. "Marc, you can't come up here. One of us needs to be there for the boys, my parents, everything."

Marc let out an exasperated breath. "Lins, with every part of my being, I don't want to be apart from you. I hate this. I hate being here and you being in the middle of this kind of pressure again. Let's pray. Hopefully, God will see it my way."

"Trust me, I'd rather be home than up here. I don't know how I can write with everything going on."

"I'm sure your editor will understand and extend your deadline. But then again, you'll be there all alone and have total peace. You should be able to write two novels, not just one."

"Ha, ha. I doubt it. What does my photographing a narc and a social drug user purchasing a small amount of cocaine have to do with Melancon? I'm sure they don't care who buys their drugs."

"Because I was trying to muscle my way into the drug trade in Lawrence," Detective Harris provided.

"Marc, I'll call you back. Detective Harris just came in."

"All right. Call me as soon as possible. I'm still going to join you for a few days. Perhaps we can figure this out together."

They said their good-byes and Lindsey turned to face the detective. "What proof do you have that Melancon is involved in the drug trade in Lawrence?"

JANUARY 24, 1912 ~ METHUEN, MASS.

"No, I insist you stay home, Jenna," Brad fumed.

She had never seen him this upset before. "I'm bored. I need to do something. I can't just sit here and wait for you to come home, or not. I don't like this, Brad. I don't like it one bit."

"If we're to build a future together, you must stay home. I can't afford to have you seen by anyone. I think you need to break off your relationships with Sylvia and Anna."

"Has someone stuffed your head full of worsted wool? They're the only friends I have."

"They're striking, and we can't be seen associating with strikers."

"I'm not being seen by anyone." Jenna crossed her arms and huffed. "You've even restricted my shopping at the market. You're picking up most of the food these days. I have nothing to do, Brad. I feel like your prisoner."

"Honey." He sidled up beside her. "I know it has to be difficult, but we agreed this was the only way."

"No, Brad. *We* did not agree. You decided. You had me fired. You decided we had to get married right away. You, you, you. When have I had a say in any of these decisions?"

"But, it's what's best."

"No, it's what is best for you. Not me."

"What are you saying?" His body became rigid, reminding her of a large loom bolted to the floor.

"I'm saying, I have no say in this marriage. You come and go as you please. I don't know from one minute to the next if you're going to spend the night here or be off to your uncle's, or who knows where. I can't even decide the menu."

"Don't you love me?"

"Of course I love you. But if you loved me, you'd let me be who I am—you wouldn't be ashamed of me. I'm not a socialite, and this plan of yours to make me into something I'm not in order to impress your uncle seems foolhardy at best."

"But . . ." Brad's plea trailed off. "Jenna, I love you. I thought we agreed this was best."

Jenna sighed. *Why does he have to be so controlling?* "Brad, you're treating me like a common mill worker, not your wife. You order me about without giving any thought or even asking a question as to how I feel. Don't you see? If you treat me as your servant, won't everyone in your family treat me the same way?"

"You're not—"

She cut him off. "I'm not your servant. Is that what you believe?"

"A woman's place is in the home."

"Until you think of me as more than a servant, our marriage is not a marriage." Jenna stepped away and looked out the front window of the cottage. "I think you should leave." She held back the tears. Her world was crumbling, and yet her world was nothing without Brad. How could everything in her life have shifted around in such a short period of time?

"No, this is my house. I'll stay if I wish."

"Fine." Jenna stormed to the bedroom, closed the door and locked it.

The doorknob twisted back and forth. "Open up, Jenna."

"No."

"Open the door, Jenna. Now!"

"I will not. You can't order me about like this, Brad." Jenna held her sides. She loved him, she'd never refused him anything. She had never complained to him like this before.

"Jenna, please." His voice softened.

Her heart ached. She wanted to open the door. She wanted to obey him. But he needed to understand how she felt and that what he was doing was wrong.

"Go home to your uncle's, Brad. Give us some time to think about everything that's been said."

He banged on the door with enough force to rattle its hinges. Jenna clutched her arms to her sides, turning away from the sound of his voice.

His footsteps departed, and the back door opened and closed. Jenna flung herself on the bed and cried.

Chapter Twenty-four

"I have no proof of Melancon's involvement," Detective Harris said. He slumped down in a seat near the middle section of the conference table.

Lindsey rubbed the back of her neck. "Okay, what makes you suspect Richard Melancon?"

"That's privileged information, and you don't need to know. If Melancon is after you, it could simply be because of the trial last year in New Orleans."

"Not likely. I was just one voice in a stream of evidence against him. My publicist is the one who took advantage of the trial to launch my book. Plus, Melancon and his entire organization are under a court order not to approach me." Lindsey opened her briefcase, removing her computer. "Is the Melancon family large enough that it has business up north?"

"There's a rumor he has a connection here in Lawrence, possibly family, but no one seems to know the specific connection," Detective Harris said.

"Has anyone done his genealogy to check?" Lindsey opened her laptop.

Detective Harris cleared his throat. "I'm certain that someone has looked into his family connections."

"I don't mean to be telling you your business. But, I won't live in protective custody for a long period of time. My oldest son is getting married, and my parents are moving down to Florida. I need to get on with my life."

The chair scraped the floor as the detective pushed it back from the table and stood up. "Excuse me." He left the room with strident steps. Lindsey flipped open her cell phone. Lindsey's anger surpassed her fears. She punched in the auto-dial for Marc.

"Hi, that was quick," Marc chuckled.

"Detective Harris left the room. Would you call your source at the FBI and ask if they've traced Richard Melancon's family back a couple generations?"

"Are you certain he's behind this?"

Lindsey rubbed the small scar above her left breast. "I don't know, but there might be a real connection."

"Great, I thought his attorneys and I came to an understanding." Marc said. "I'll get back to you as soon as possible. How far back?"

"I'm thinking cousins or second cousins. And more than likely from an aunt, since the name Melancon has not turned up around here."

"Gotcha. I love you, Lins. Stay safe. I'll call you back as soon as I have word."

Lindsey ignored the noises going on around her. The police station was too busy for a curious mind. She opened Jenna's journal and read about her first argument with Brad and her frustrations with his controlling nature. "Trouble in paradise." She opened up the timeline document and put in the notation. It was nearly a week after the strike had begun and about a month before her body was discovered.

She reached for Beverly Ludlum's journal. It bothered Lindsey that the journals were so similar. Could Jenna Waverly be Beverly Ludlum? She opened the journals and placed them side by side. The penmanship of the two was definitely not the same. Beverly's hand was less practiced, almost feeble, next to Jenna's. Surprising that Brad would be concerned about social class and yet marry a woman who seemingly had less training than Jenna.

Lindsey's hand froze over the journal. *Did Beverly push Jenna into the river? Did she kill her?* "That's far more than taking advantage of another's death," she muttered aloud.

She'd have to make a copy of this journal, every page of it.

Her cell phone rang. Ruth Emery's number popped up on the caller ID. "Hello Ruth, find anything interesting?"

"Yes, that's why I called."

"Wonderful. What did you find?"

"Remember the cottage that my grandparents purchased? Well, they bought it from Quincy Ludlum. Apparently Q. B. was a nickname."

Q. B. Quincy Bradley. "Interesting."

Ruth laughed. "If I read between the lines correctly, I suspect my grandmother thought Q. B. was responsible for Jenna's death. Oh, that's another thing. She's the one who identified Jenna's body the day after they found her. She hadn't seen Jenna since Anna Lopizzo's funeral. Because of the strike, she couldn't afford the travel to Methuen."

And Jenna wasn't allowed to go back to Lawrence, Lindsey thought. She picked up a pencil and started to drum it on the table.

Ruth's voice wavered. "Is what I'm hearing about you on the news true?"

Lindsey stopped her drumming. "What did the news say?"

"They've reported that someone has been stalking you and even tried to shoot you."

Lindsey groaned. "Someone tried to shoot me." *How'd the media hear about the stalking?* she wondered. She made a mental note to talk with Captain Pitts about his officers revealing too much information to the public.

"What on earth for?"

"I don't know."

"Be careful, Lindsey. The media's having a heyday with all this. Even Edgar and a few of the others have called me. Everyone is wondering if you're all right and if there is anything we can do for you."

"Pray. I want to go home."

"Of course. If you need a place to stay, Edgar has offered."

She thought it a bit odd that Edgar would relay a message through Ruth. Then again, he didn't know Lindsey's cell phone number. "Tell him thank you, but arrangements have been made."

"All right. Well, I really must get a move on. I have the entire family coming this weekend for a visit. Much to do and precious little time."

"Thanks for keeping me posted."

The mechanical hum of the disconnected signal reverberated in Lindsey's ear for a moment before she pulled the phone away and clicked it shut.

She went back to the two journals. Who from Beverly Ludlum's past knew who she was before she married Quincy Ludlum? And if Brad truly loved Jenna, why would he marry someone else so quickly?

She sniffed. The pungent smell of burnt coffee filled the air. An empty glass coffeepot stood on the hot element. Lindsey pushed herself up out of the chair, went over to the stainless steel coffee maker, and wearily went through the motions of making a fresh pot.

She went back to the table and wrote down her questions. She wanted to see Anna Ludlum Scott one more time. She had a couple more questions to fill out Quincy's genealogy.

Detective Harris entered the room, carrying a handful of papers. "I've pulled up some interesting information."

JANUARY 29, 1912 ~ METHUEN, MASS.

The past four days had crept by for Jenna. Brad had not returned. The first day, she went out and looked around the area for possible employment, but with the strike going on, no one was hiring. For the next couple of days, she cleaned, re-cleaned, and cleaned the house again, all the time checking to see if Brad had come home. She even thought she'd heard him last night, but it had been her overactive imagination. She had lost him.

She cried herself to sleep each night and ate precious little, making herself sick with worry. Again she pleaded with God to bring Brad home. Her eyes burned. She ambled to the bathroom and ran some cold water onto a face cloth. Holding the wet fabric to her eyes, she made her way into the kitchen and sat down at the table.

The back door thumped open. "Jenna?" Brad came up beside her. "You've already heard. I'm so sorry."

"Heard? Heard what?"

"Anna." Tears welled in Brad's eyes. "Your friend Anna Lopizzo was killed today."

A knot twisted in Jenna's stomach. "No, it can't be."

He held her close. The warmth of his breath on her neck gave her strength. She felt helpless to stand on her own.

"There was some gunfire during the strike, and a bullet bounced off the cobblestone sidewalk and hit Anna."

"No," Jenna cried. "Oh, Brad, please tell me it isn't so." She wrapped her arms around him.

"I'm sorry. I'm so sorry," Brad repeated.

They held each other and mourned the loss of their friend. Brad carried Jenna into the bedroom and lay down beside her. "I'm sorry about the other night too. I should have realized how hard living here alone would be for you. You have to believe me, Jenna. I'm not trying to control you. I just want to do what's right and have you accepted by my family."

Jenna wiped her eyes with Brad's handkerchief. "Why did you stay away so long?"

"I had some business out of town. I was sent out to find workers who would cross the picket lines. I wasn't sent out alone, so I couldn't come by and let you know. I'm sorry."

"Scabs? You were paid to hire scabs? Please tell me you didn't do that."

"Jenna, I had to. It's a part of my job."

Jenna rolled away from her husband and buried her head in her pillow. "You don't understand. This is not just about money, Brad. It's about providing for your family. All the things you've told me that are so important to you that we have to keep our marriage a secret. All those things are what the workers are after. You know as well as I do that Mr. Wood could afford to pay the workers more. He'll not go broke. Tell me, why does he have to be paid so much? An entire year's worth of work for an average worker pays less than one week of Mr. Wood's salary. That just doesn't seem fair. Why does he need so much for his family?"

"Jenna, honey, you don't understand. A man like Mr. Wood has higher expenses than someone like you or Sylvia."

"Or Anna?" her voice caught in her throat. She took in a deep breath and let it out slowly. "Anna died fighting for what is fair, Brad. Is that right? Is that fair? Do you think Mr. Wood will lose any sleep over Anna Lopizzo's death? I've been reading the papers. They aren't speaking very highly of Mr. Wood. Doesn't he see what's truly important?"

Brad sat up and swung his feet over the edge of the bed. "I know you're upset with Anna's death. I'm not going to take this personally."

Jenna squeezed her eyes shut. "Brad, I love you. But we do come from different worlds. We have to be able to talk about these differences. You have to be willing to at least listen to what I have to say. What's going to happen when we have children? How will we deal with discipline if what I think is right and proper behavior is different from what you think is right and proper?"

He turned to her and slowly reached for her hand. "My mother always did what my father commanded."

"Did she? Honestly think about it. Did your parents discuss things? Did your mother have a say in your father's business dealings?"

Silence stood between them like a great barrier. "Not until after the railroad investment went sour. But look where it's led them. They live alone on Martha's Vineyard, they have no real assets—"

"And are happy together," she added.

Brad's shoulders sagged, and he nodded his agreement.

A glimmer of hope surfaced as she saw Brad thinking over her words. She softened her tone. "Honey, I don't want to stand in the way of your business dealings, but I do want to discuss things with you. Is that so wrong?"

"No, I suppose not." He sat cross-legged on the bed. "I purchased this cottage for the two of us. The landlord gave me a wonderful price for it. I'm hoping we can purchase most of the homes on this street and rent them out to the workers. If the strike continues for a long period of time, there will be some choice real estate to pick up."

Jenna reached over and placed a hand on her husband's knee. "Brad, what have you done with your money that has helped others?"

"Huh?"

"You heard me."

He knit his eyebrows together. Jenna knew the entire concept was something he had never considered before.

"Honey, I believe that those who have more are responsible to give more. I'm not saying to give all that we have to other people, but if we choose wisely, we can help people, and isn't that what the Good Lord would want us to do?"

"But . . ." He pulled in a deep breath and let it out slowly.

Jenna reached over and held his hand.

"Brad?"

"You have a point." He rubbed the top of her hand with his thumb. "How do you think I can help the strikers without my uncle or Mr. Wood being the wiser?"

Jenna smiled.

Chapter Twenty-five

"Okay, here's what I was sent from the New Orleans investigation team concerning the relatives of Richard Melancon," Detective Harris said to Lindsey, reading from a yellow legal pad. "He was born in New Orleans, and his siblings are all still there. I then contacted the FBI and discovered that they had done an extensive search on his paternal grandparents but not his maternal grandparents. We're processing the information right now about the maternal side. As far as we can tell from the paternal, he has no one here in Lawrence."

He looked at Lindsey for the first time since entering the room. She explored his dark eyes and facial gestures, looking for any signs of frustration, anger, or resentment.

"I'm sorry again for assuming things I shouldn't have concerning you," he apologized. "You had a good suggestion about the relatives, and I hadn't paid that close of attention to it. I'd been tracking down known associates, but they are still in New Orleans or have gone deep underground because of pending arrest warrants."

Lindsey nodded and cast her gaze back to her laptop.

"My primary experience for the last two years has been the streets, and most of that has been spent undercover. It's not an excuse. I'm just stating the obvious. I know I come across harsh at times, and I'm sorry."

Lindsey nodded her acceptance. She glanced up at him and raised her right eyebrow.

"Okay, maybe harsh is an understatement. Rude, obnoxious . . . should I go on?"

"You're doing a good job."

Detective Harris cleared his throat. "We probably won't have anything definitive until later this afternoon. Is there something I can help you with?"

"I need to copy this entire journal. Is there a scanner I could have access to?"

"I'll ask around." He stepped back toward the door. "Can I get you anything else?"

"A diet cola, if it's no trouble."

"Not a problem."

Lindsey sat down and opened Beverly Ludlum's journal. *Who are you?* she asked, reading the opening line for the third time.

Beverly Ludlum. My new life begins today. Quincy came by, and we drove through the countryside. He was terribly upset about something, although he never did tell me what. I held him and passion overcame us.

Lindsey stopped reading and added to the timeline that Beverly and Quincy shared a passionate interlude with one another. Okay, Quincy and Brad are the same person. Jenna's pregnant at the time of her death. Beverly is pregnant at the time of their marriage in March. "So, did he eliminate one problem to fix another more socially acceptable situation he'd gotten himself into?"

Detective Harris walked in. "What situation?"

Lindsey's face flushed. "Quincy Ludlum had a couple of lovers."

Detective Harris's eyebrows rose. *"The* Quincy Ludlum? The man who spouted off about the moral decay of society on more than one occasion at town meetings?"

"Really? What else do you know about him?" Lindsey placed her first finger in the journal and closed it, then turned toward Detective Harris.

"Not too much. My father would complain a bit about the man and his overbearing ways. If I have the picture correctly, I'd say he would charge in and meet things with a great deal of bluster, but then if someone could prove their case, he would change his opinions. It's like he could think deeply—but not at first. He tended to react, then think."

"Interesting. Both women seemed to indicate that in their first encounter with him they were caught up with passion."

"Hmm. Who are the two women?"

"Well, that's the intriguing part. Both were his wives, eventually."

"He was married twice?" Detective Harris sat up in his chair.

"Yes, he married one gal in December of 1911, but she died in February of 1912."

"Ouch. What from?"

"She drowned."

Detective Harris slid a can of diet soda in front of her. "Unfortunately, the river has taken quite a few lives. I'm assuming she drowned in the river?"

"Yes." Lindsey pulled up the picture of the frozen river in 1918. "They claim it was an extremely cold year in 1912. Would you say this is a typical picture for winters back then?" She turned the computer and showed him the picture.

"Probably. There are always weak spots in the ice. You never can tell."

"Here's what I don't understand. Why didn't Quincy identify his wife when her body was found? Of course, it was a secret marriage, so he quite possibly didn't want to let anyone know," Lindsey answered her own question.

"Or he killed her?" Detective Harris sipped his coffee. "Crimes of passion, you know."

Lindsey had had similar thoughts on more than one occasion. *And if he's sleeping with another woman weeks before her death, he might make a likely candidate.*

"I'd like to talk to Anna Ludlum Scott again," she said aloud.

217

Fighting for Bread & Roses

A young officer came in with a flatbed scanner. He had short-cropped blond hair and blue eyes, and not quite a square chin. There was a small scar where a cleft would be. "Is there anything I can do for you, Mrs. Taylor?" he asked.

"Thank you, I'm sure I can manage."

Detective Harris stood up. "Officer Kendrick would be happy to scan what you need copied. I can take you to visit Mrs. Scott."

"Thank you," Lindsey said, surprised at his sudden graciousness. She turned to Officer Kendrick. "Are you familiar with a Macintosh?"

He smiled. "Yes. I'll get right on it, Mrs. Taylor."

"Thank you." Lindsey handed him the journal. "Save them according to the dates of their entries."

"Will do."

Lindsey recognized that glint in the young man's eye. Her computer was the latest model, and this young man clearly enjoyed working with new technology. She followed Detective Harris out of the room.

"We'll exit via the parking garage. We haven't seen any reporters this morning. Our sniper is long gone. We searched most of the buildings within his range yesterday but turned up nothing. We're still waiting for one superintendent to return from vacation to enter the few apartments where no one was home. We're working on search warrants as we speak."

"Thanks for cheering me up."

Detective Harris grinned. "Pleasure."

Though the man had his abrasive side, he did have a way of making a person relax in his presence. He opened the door to his unmarked, nondescript, four-door sedan. "Do you happen to know who Quincy Ludlum's uncle was?"

"Not a clue."

He stopped in his tracks. "Are you telling me, you didn't do his genealogy?"

"Touché. I suspect it's Phineas Archer, but I haven't done the genealogy yet. I'm working on it." Lindsey chuckled.

He wiggled his eyebrows and strutted around to the driver's door.

"Hopefully, Anna can help me out there. I know his parents lived on the Vineyard."

"Not bad."

Lindsey slipped into the passenger bucket seat. "I didn't see another Ludlum on the list of employees in the Wood mill."

"That darn maternal side gets ya every time." He sat down behind the driver's wheel.

"Now, hush. I didn't rub it in when you erred."

"True. My apologies. However, I did warn you that I'm not all that socially adept."

"One can learn," Lindsey hinted.

"I'm too old," Detective Harris roared. He turned out of the parking garage onto the main thoroughfare.

"Do you know who sat on the board of directors of the Wood Mill during the strike?" he asked.

"Yes, I have a list."

"One of them is bound to be Quincy Ludlum's uncle." He took a right onto a side street, then turned again.

"Wait," Lindsey shouted.

Detective Harris braked. The car behind him screeched to a halt, then another one. Horns blared. Detective Harris pulled the car toward the right, allowing traffic to pass by.

"Sorry, I didn't mean to make you stop dead in your tracks."

"What on earth is the matter?" he asked.

Lindsey glanced over. She so easily rattled this poor man's cage. "I'm sorry. I was just thinking."

Beyond Detective Harris, a car slowly crawled by. The nose of a pistol appeared in the window.

Lindsey screamed, "Get down." Reaching out for the detective, she tried to pull him out of the way.

The shot blasted through the air. Every microsecond ticked by with amazing clarity. Lindsey watched as her hand grasped at the detective's shirt front. She banged her head on his knee.

Glass shattered everywhere.

JANUARY 31, 1912 ~ LAWRENCE, MASS.

Jenna held onto Sylvia's hand. The streets were full. Every police officer and militiaman stood ready. The crowd gathering at Anna's house was scheduled to march from there to the church, then on to the cemetery.

"Can you believe they arrested Ettor and Giovannitti? We expected they'd be arrested, but not for Anna's death. It was the police, I tell you. I was there." Sylvia was more angry and defiant than Jenna had ever seen her.

"Did you see who shot her?" Jenna asked.

"No, but they've been attacking us, pushing us. I'm certain it was one of them," Sylvia sniffed.

Jenna held her tighter. Sylvia and Anna had known each other longer, but the pain of Anna's death was still as fresh as when Brad had told her the news. A sea of strikers dressed in black met at the undertaker's on Common Street. Troop A from the militia cantered down the street. The angry crowd quieted. Then the undertaker's wagon drove up to the front door and six men placed a black coffin inside. Everyone followed behind the wagon to the church, past the house where Anna had lived.

Sylvia's foot faltered on the cobblestone street.

Jenna held her up. "Hang on, I have you."

James Donovan stepped beside them and took Sylvia's other hand.

Jenna wished Brad were here to offer his support. She walked in numb response. She still couldn't believe that Anna was dead.

She glanced over her shoulder and prayed that no one would recognize her. With ten thousand mourners, who would notice? She'd tell Brad tonight when he returned. *If he returns,* she amended.

"Are you all right?" Sylvia asked.

"Fine." Jenna softened her voice. "I'll be all right. It seems so unreal, you know?"

"Yeah, I expect her to join us in line or something."

"Aye, 'tis a shame." James held his stride. "We best continue the fight now that blood has been shed."

They stood outside the church. No room remained to go inside. It seemed wrong that three of Anna's friends had to stand outside when strangers were taking up the front rows. And how many reporters filled the pews, Jenna didn't know. Brad had tried to tell her how wild the streets were, but if she hadn't seen it with her own eyes, she never would have believed it. Experiencing it now made her see how easily tempers could flare.

They waited for an hour, standing outside, praying a little and thinking a lot. Then Anna's casket was ushered back into the undertaker's wagon, and they worked their way to the cemetery. The crowd stilled as they plodded the final steps. A huge wreath covered the casket, and a flowered cross with the word *Annie* draped across it was placed at the head of the coffin. The priest said a few words, then one by one the mourners slowly walked up and silently gave their final respects.

Sylvia, James, and Jenna shuffled up together.

"God's blessings, my friend," Jenna said. Sylvia spoke in her native tongue. James wrapped his arm around her. Jenna held onto herself. *If only Brad were here. If only he would see what is truly important.*

Chapter Twenty-six

Lindsey held Detective Harris's head down. The coppery scent of fresh blood filled the air. Was it hers? Was it his? "Are you all right?"

No response.

Lindsey slid her hand to his temple and felt for his pulse. The slow but steady beat thumped under her fingers. "Thank you, Lord."

With her other hand she reached for the police radio and pushed the button. "Hello, can you hear me? Detective Harris has been shot. I don't know where we are."

She knew enough about police radios to let the button up to receive an incoming message.

"Who are you? Get off of this freq—" The voice paused. "Did you say Detective Harris has been shot?"

Pushing the button down once again, Lindsey spoke up. "Yes." Slowly she eased her head above the dashboard. The dark blue sedan was gone. Lindsey sat up. "I can't see a street sign, but we're near one of the bridges crossing the river. The black metal one," she added.

"We'll be right there."

Lindsey dropped the radio and checked Detective Harris. He had a wound on the side of his head just under the right ear. Rich crimson blood poured out. Lindsey looked for something to hold on the wound, something to slow down the bleeding. She tore off her cotton sleeve, folded it tightly, and applied it to the wound. "Please,

Lord, keep him alive." She hated the thought that he might die because of her. *Why didn't I simply call Anna or even Edgar?*

Sirens screamed in the background. "Hold on, Harris. They're almost here."

First the blue lights of several police cruisers revolved around the car. Then officers with weapons drawn came up. "How is he?"

"I don't know. He's unconscious, I think."

An officer in blue reached in and checked for a pulse. "He's alive. Where's that ambulance?" he demanded.

"On its way," a disembodied voice responded. Lindsey could feel the blur of emotions filling her body as it tried to shut down from too much stress. It was a defense mechanism, the counselor had told her. It was natural, but she would have to fight the response and not give in to it.

"Who did this?" the officer who arrived first on the scene asked.

"I don't know. It looked similar to the dark sedan that's been following me for the better part of a week," Lindsey informed him.

"Can you give us any description?"

"White male, possibly forties, dark hair. I didn't catch the make and model of the car. Sorry. It was a dark blue, four-door sedan."

"It's been following you for a week, and you don't know what kind it is?" The officer's anger was understandable.

"I'm sorry. I'm not very good with car makes and models, and each time I saw it, it was brief, and I was nervous."

The red lights of the ambulance approached, accompanied by two sharp blasts from its horn. Soon the traffic made room. Instantly, the EMTs took over the emergency care. They wasted no time and sped off with Detective Harris. Lindsey never saw whether he responded to them or not.

For the next several minutes, a small group of officers gathered around her, asking a variety of questions.

She shivered and rubbed her upper arms.

One officer placed her in the back seat of a squad car as the media arrived. Lindsey saw a television camera come out, and she was certain it had caught her being escorted into the police car. She lay down on the seat and tried not to pay any attention to what was going on around her. She needed to think. She tried to repaint the image in her mind of the man who shot Harris.

The shape of his face came into focus. It was more square than oval, and he had a high forehead. She replayed the slow-motion scene in her mind again and again. Suddenly, she realized he hadn't aimed at her but rather at Detective Harris. Again, she played it slowly in her mind. The barrel of the gun was focused on him, not her.

She sat up and reached for the door handle, but it wasn't there. She waved and tried to catch the attention of another officer. No one saw her. She couldn't reach for the radio because of the metal grille that separated the front seat from the back.

Her cell phone. If she used it, she would be sending a signal to whomever was after her. But if she didn't, someone could be waiting at the hospital to finish a job he hadn't completed.

She flipped it open and dialed the police station and asked for Captain Pitts.

"You're where?" he spoke harshly but never quite yelled. She heard some mumbling in the background.

"Captain," she tried to draw his attention back to her.

"Sorry, Mrs. Taylor, what were you saying?" he answered.

"I think Detective Harris was the target, not me. As I'm playing the scene over and over in my mind, I realize the gun was never really focused on me but rather on Detective Harris."

"I see. I'll alert the men. Thank you for calling. Someone should be letting you out of the car immediately."

A red-faced officer came over and opened the door of the squad car. "Sorry, Mrs. Taylor."

"Tell them to drive you to the station immediately," the captain ordered.

"Yes, sir, thank you." Lindsey closed the phone. "Captain Pitts said to take me to the station immediately."

"Yes, ma'am."

At the station, Lindsey found herself with the sketch artist working on a basic composite of the shooter's face. After an hour, Captain Pitts entered the room. "Mrs. Taylor, I thought you'd like to know that Detective Harris will be fine. The bullet just grazed the base of his skull under his right ear. Tell me, when you were shot at yesterday at the station, was Harris with you?"

"Yes. He escorted me out to the car. Once the shot was fired he was right beside me, holding me to the ground."

The captain nodded his balding head slowly. "Thanks. If I'm not mistaken, you were never the target, Mrs. Taylor. In light of what you saw today, and with the added information that he was there when the first shot occurred, I'd agree they were shooting at him, not you. On the other hand, that doesn't explain the tracking devices. So it's up to you whether you want to remain in protective custody or go out on your own."

"If you don't mind, I'd like to discuss that with my husband. Also, I'd like to visit with Detective Harris at the hospital, if that's possible."

"Sure, I'll arrange it." The captain slipped out of the room.

The police artist faced her. "You're taking this rather well," he offered.

Truthfully, her emotions were bouncing around all over the place—happy to not be the target, yet concerned for Detective Harris. She left the room with the artist and returned to the conference room where Officer Kendrick was scanning Anna's mother's journal. "How's it going?" she asked.

"Fine, two more pages and I'm done."

"You're fast." Lindsey started to gather her papers. It was time to go home; she'd had enough of this town.

"Thanks. This machine really hums."

Lindsey chuckled. "Yeah, I know."

"Makes scanning these kinds of documents a dream. By the way, I saved them as jpegs, as you asked, because of the penmanship. The text reader wouldn't be able to convert it without a lot of errors."

"I've been studying handwriting," Officer Kendrick continued. "I'm thinking there might have been an injury to her hand, or something. See these abrupt turns with the pen?"

Lindsey leaned over the screen and looked at where he was pointing. "Yes."

"Well, those could mean that effort was made trying to manipulate the pen in the manner she wanted it to go. Now, when she's writing the downward strokes, like these"—he pointed out the backward strokes of the lower case *c*'s, the left side of the *o*'s, and a few other letters—"see how even the strokes are? The pen is more fluid."

"Interesting. I'll have to ask her daughter if her mother had a hand injury at some point."

"It's just an observation. I'm not schooled enough in the art, but I find it fascinating." His blue eyes beamed.

"I can tell."

He lifted the scanner's cover, adjusted the journal to its final page, and proceeded to scan it.

"I appreciate all your help," Lindsey thanked him.

"You're welcome."

She continued to pack her belongings, waiting for the young officer to leave before she called Marc. As she suspected, he wanted her home as soon as possible. But there were still a few details. A one-on-one visit with Edgar Archer would be more productive. She wanted to see some reactions.

She placed a call to Edgar Archer and agreed to meet him and his wife in three hours. That left her enough time to visit with Anna Scott and return the journal.

As she drove up Anna's drive, something seemed out of place, but she couldn't pinpoint the problem.

"Lindsey, so nice to see you." Anna smiled and shuffled over to shake Lindsey's hand.

"I came to return your mother's journal. I scanned the pages so I wouldn't have to take it home with me." Lindsey handed the small black book over to Anna. The smell of fresh blueberries filled the air. *Muffins,* she guessed.

"Oh, you could have taken it. I was foolish to think you might lose it. Donald was quite concerned that I wouldn't see it again."

"You told him?" Lindsey cocked her head slightly to the right.

"Naturally, he had questions after your visit. He wasn't pleased, but what does it matter?"

Lindsey smiled. "It's safe now. I've barely had a moment to read it. I'm sorry."

"Please, come sit down and join me in a cup of tea."

"All right, but I can't stay too long. I have another appointment in a little over an hour."

Lindsey sat down in the same sitting room as a few days before. *Was it only a few days? It seems like ages, but it was really only yesterday, wasn't it?*

"Mother?" Donald Scott wandered in, carrying a laptop under his arm.

Lindsey narrowed her gaze to the silver machine. The underside had an identifying sticker. Her sticker.

"Mrs. Taylor," he stumbled over his words. "I didn't expect you."

"Obviously. Why did you steal my computer?" Lindsey demanded.

FEBRUARY 2, 1912 - METHUEN, MASS.

Jenna snuggled up to Brad. He'd spent the entire night. She couldn't wait until they could spend every night and wake up together. The early sunlight poured through the bedroom window. "Good morning," she whispered.

A broad smile spread across his face. He reached out and wrapped his arm around her. "Good morning, love." He kissed the tip of her nose.

The warmth of his love for her and hers for him calmed her. She'd been keeping a secret from him for a while. Today she would find out for certain if she was with child, Brad's child. Their child. One brought into this world from a deep love and passion for one another.

"What's going on in that pretty little head of yours?"

"Nothing." She had to keep it a secret for a bit longer. This could ruin his plans for when he would tell his uncle that they were married.

Brad stretched. "I need to go. We have an early morning meeting with Mr. Wood today."

"Is he bending at all?"

"Nope, and if he doesn't act soon, we're not going to be able to fill our spring orders." Brad sat up and reached for his trousers, which were draped over the chair beside the bed.

"Will you be coming home for dinner tonight?"

"I'll try. My uncle is going to be furious with me. He's certain I'm 'catting around,' as he puts it. I've spent too many nights here."

Jenna crossed her arms over her chest. "I don't think so."

Brad leaned back and kissed her on the cheek. "I agree with you. But as far as my uncle is concerned, I'm just a single man. He has no idea that we're married, that I've purchased this place and have plans to purchase other real estate. The real money is in real estate. I don't want to work for the mills any longer than I have to."

"Have you reconsidered my working?"

"Yes, and the answer is still no. I don't mind if you do some sewing jobs on the side, but I really prefer that you stay at home. I know it's hard on you, and I know it's harder still not being able to see Sylvia, especially after Anna's—I mean—we can't risk my uncle finding out before it's time. I wrote Father and used this address, so we should be hearing from him soon."

"I don't want to live with your parents on Martha's Vineyard. I'd never see you," Jenna pouted.

"Just for a little while. I'll try to figure something else out. But, honey, trust me with regard to the job. Right now isn't a good time anyway. Too many people are out of work, and if you were to cross the lines—"

"I have no intention of crossing those picket lines. The strikers are right. Mr. Wood needs to pay better. He needs to create safer working conditions. You don't know what it's like to see children pulled out of the machinery dead, or to watch someone lose a finger."

Brad sighed. "I know. And I do see your point. But there is another side to this. You can't ask him to solve all the problems at once."

"Isn't that where negotiations come in? Wood won't even discuss the matter with the strike committee."

"I know, I know. I've tried, but there's no convincing anyone at this point. Besides, I have no real authority. Maybe in a couple of weeks."

"Weeks? Those poor people will starve."

"Maybe, but I gave Sylvia's friend, James Donovan, some money to help with the soup kitchen."

"You did?"

Brad nodded his head and stood up to tuck his shirttails into his trousers. Jenna jumped up and hugged him. "I'm so proud of you."

"You made your point. I might be slow to listen, but I do listen to you, Jenna. It's hard. I've been doing things for myself and by myself for a long time."

Jenna giggled and reached out for her husband. "Not anymore."

Brad joined in the laughter and agreed. "Not anymore."

Chapter Twenty-seven

Donald Scott cleared his throat and stepped closer to Lindsey. "At first I was trying to protect it, then I realized what everyone thought, and I just kind of hid it."

"For Pete's sake, Donald, tell the woman the truth," Anna huffed.

Lindsey sat back in the chair, amazed at the two sides to these people. "You knew?"

"Not at first; but, yes, I discovered Donald's deception yesterday afternoon. Go on, tell the woman why you stole her computer."

"I didn't steal it, Mother. I intended to return it." Donald handed the computer back to Lindsey, took in a deep breath, and sat down by his mother. "There's some messy business in our family's past, and I wanted to see if you had discovered it."

"Why didn't you just ask me?" Lindsey took the computer, opened it, and discovered that the battery was run down. "Is everything still on here?"

"Yes. I haven't altered any of your files. You are very thorough in your research."

Did a person thank someone who had stolen their personal property for something as foolish as wondering if she had unlocked the family secret? "I take it that your mother wanting to know her mother's real name isn't the family secret."

"No, I wasn't aware of that deception."

"Do I dare ask what deception you are aware of?"

The man resembled a marble statue. "No, I prefer not to expose it."

Lindsey snickered. "You *prefer?* And just what do you think the police will say when they find out that someone running for political office stole my laptop?"

Donald Scott paled. He didn't say a word. His shoulders slumped; his body language was clear.

"As long as we're talking about preferences here," Lindsey shot back, *"I* prefer to know the truth. I've been followed, harassed, shot at, injured, and my personal belongings stolen. I want to know what's going on, family secrets or no family secrets."

"I understand your concern. But I'm afraid I simply cannot and will not tell you." Donald regained his stoic posture.

"Anna?" Lindsey questioned.

"I'm afraid I'll have to side with Donald on this one."

Donald stood up. He carried himself well for being in his retirement years. "Mrs. Taylor—that is your real name, correct?"

Lindsey acknowledged it with the nod of her head.

"I know you have no reason to believe me, but I was planning on shipping your computer back to you. There is a slight possibility you might one day learn the family secret while doing your research. If you do, I merely ask if you would be so kind as to let us know what you've uncovered. I give you my word that if what you uncover is accurate, I will confirm it. If it is off base but close, I'll help clarify the situation." Donald paced behind the sofa where Anna was sitting. "If, however, you do not come across the information, I'd prefer to leave it buried in the past. Most folks are gone now, but there are a few who still could be affected by this information." He stopped behind his mother and placed his hands on her shoulders. "I know I'm asking a lot, and deserving absolutely none of your kindness or consideration, but I am asking."

Lindsey sat stunned and silent. *What do you say to something like that? Does it even matter what their family secret is? If it has nothing to do with the story, why bother? Unless . . .*

"Was it criminal?" she asked in a quiet voice.

"Not on the part of my family," Donald said.

"And this happened during the strike?"

"Yes, some of it," Donald answered.

"Lindsey," Anna interjected. "I know this seems very awkward, to say the least. But as you know, Donald was unaware of my asking you to help me discover my mother's real name."

"That's the thing," Lindsey interrupted. "Your mother didn't say she changed her name. What she said was she took advantage of someone's death."

Anna dipped her head and looked into her lap. "Actually, she did say that Beverly wasn't her real name. But she didn't get as far as telling me what her real name was. And, yes, she also said she took advantage of someone else's death."

"I see." Lindsey needed to spend some time alone, where people weren't out to get her, or trying to take things away from her, or constantly following her.

Her cell phone rang and an unlisted number came up. "Excuse me," Lindsey said to her hosts. "Hello?"

"Mrs. Taylor, I'm an associate of Richard Melancon. He asked me to contact you and assure you that he has nothing to do with any of the problems you've been encountering in Lawrence." The voice had a distinct New Orleans Cajun twang to it.

"How'd you get my number?" she asked.

"When your husband made inquiries this morning, it seemed advantageous to assure you that no one in our association has been pursuing you. And I verified the information before placing this call."

"That doesn't answer my question."

"No, ma'am, it doesn't. Suffice it to say, it is not a number I will be using again."

Lindsey shook her head. "Thank you." She was tempted to ask him whether someone in their "association," as he put it, was after Detective Harris, but she knew he wouldn't answer the question.

"Be well, Mrs. Taylor." The phone line went dead.

Her two hosts stared at her. "Sorry. I'll see myself out, and if you don't mind, I'll take my laptop."

Donald Scott's face reddened. "I do apologize for any inconvenience."

Lindsey fumed as she walked out to her car. *How can that man think a simple apology bails him out of all responsibility?* After sliding behind the wheel, she stopped and prayed. She couldn't think straight when she was this angry, and she didn't need to waste any more time in Lawrence.

As she pulled out of the Scotts' driveway, she saw the same dark sedan that had been following her. It was parked across the street about a hundred feet away. She tightened her grasp of the steering wheel and revved the engine. *Maybe I should put the fear of the Lord into this guy.* The sedan's tires spun and churned up sand and gravel from the side of the road as the driver peeled away.

She stepped on the gas and sped down the street.

FEBRUARY 2, 1912 ~ METHUEN, MASS.

The kitchen door rattled in its hinges. Jenna peeked out the curtained window. A stranger held the doorknob in his hand and twisted it again. Jenna's heart raced. The police had come by a couple weeks ago about a prowler. She stepped back into the room.

The door crashed open.

Jenna screamed. She ran toward the bedroom and forced the door shut, hoping it would keep out the intruder.

"Come on, pretty, how's about some lovin' for me. I've seen you with Mr. Ludlum. I've watched you." His wicked laugh chilled Jenna's spine.

The locked doorknob rattled.

Jenna quickly surveyed the room, trying to find something to keep him out. She pushed the tall oak dresser toward the door, scraping the floor as she struggled to move it. Once it was in place she leaned against it.

A loud thump hit the door. Thankful the cottage had solid oak doors, she eased herself off the dresser. The bedroom windows came into focus as a possible means for escape. Should she try?

He said he'd seen her and Brad. Jenna shivered.

"Open up, my pretty." His words slapped like the leather belts of the loom against the pulleys. "I will have you," he threatened.

"I'd rather die," Jenna shouted.

"That's the plan, pretty. But I'll have you before you're gone."

His evil laughter caused her stomach to flip-flop.

"No sense wasting a perfectly good woman before a man has a little fun."

Jenna screamed for help.

"Cry all you want, pretty. I know Mr. Ludlum won't be returning this evening, and I have my orders."

Orders? Someone had sent him to kill her? *Who?*

He slammed against the door one more time. She thought she heard it crack, but it hadn't budged. Expletives filled the air from the other side of the door.

She looked back at the window. *He'll try to come in that way.* She pushed the dresser toward the window with every bit of strength she could muster. Once in place, she leaned against it to give it extra strength.

A few moments later, glass shattered behind the dresser. He'd have to unlock the window first, she reasoned.

If she ran out the front door, would she have time to escape? Taking in short, quick breaths she pondered the thought for just a moment, then went into action. She unlocked the bedroom door, ran to the kitchen door and opened it, then ran back to her bedroom where she hid in the closet, closing the door behind her as quietly as possible.

The dresser crashed to the floor. She heard the intruder curse again. She sat in darkness, silent, alone, afraid. Bunched into the corner, she prayed that God would rescue her and send Brad home immediately.

Loud footfalls ran through the cottage. Had he believed her deception? Tears filled her eyes. *Oh God, please help me.* Bright light appeared in the closet.

"You thought you could outsmart me?" His evil laugh pierced her heart.

"Please, leave me alone," she pleaded.

"I have my orders, and you've cost me plenty." He pulled her out of the closet by her right hand. Jenna felt her shoulder pop from the force.

Pain coursed through her body. "Help," she screamed louder than before. "Why are you doing this? I've done nothing to you."

He threw her down on the bed and pulled his belt from his trousers. She tried to get up. He forced her down with his own body. "Not yet, pretty."

He tied her right hand and wrist to the bedpost. Jenna fought, squirmed and pushed her body in any way possible. With her left hand she pulled the man's hair.

He laughed at her with contempt and cinched the belt. She could feel the bones in her hand breaking.

"Help," she screamed in his ear repeatedly. He stuffed her mouth with his handkerchief.

"Get off of her!" Brad hollered.

Chapter Twenty-eight

Lindsey's knuckles whitened from holding the steering wheel so tightly. The winding roads and the speed kept her vigilant. So far, she'd made out the first three digits of the license plate. Massachusetts. VK1. The last three still eluded her. The driver in front of her continued at ridiculous speeds. Should she continue to chase him?

A horn blasted in front of her. Lindsey lifted her foot from the gas pedal. As much as she wanted to catch the man, it wasn't worth risking other people's lives. She slowed the car and pulled into the small parking lot of a church.

She prayed, then called Marc to fill him in about the car chase and the Ludlum Scott family. She placed one last call to Abigail Adams. The librarian had been busy. She had tracked down the purchase of the Methuen property, and had determined when Quincy had purchased the present home he and his family owned. Apparently, he'd been fairly active in town meetings, serving as a selectman for a short time in the twenties. Primarily, he was well respected in the community.

Okay, so we have a conservative man who was politically active but seemed well liked by folks. What deep dark secret does his family not want exposed about him? Lindsey sighed. *That he killed his first wife?*

She placed a call to Ruth Emery and made arrangements to pay her one last visit.

Driving up to the old Victorian two-story home reminded Lindsey about the real reason for her visit to Lawrence, to track down the past and write an engaging novel about it.

Ruth greeted her at the front door. "I saw you pull up. Come on in. How are you? Is your life always this crazy?"

"Sometimes." Lindsey winked. "I was wondering if I could look over your grandmother's journal before I go home."

"Sure. I read it all. It's interesting, but I can't imagine there's much in there you'll find helpful."

Lindsey's cell phone rang, "Excuse me."

"Mrs. Taylor, I'm sorry to bother you again," the man with the Cajun drawl said, "but I just learned that someone did put a tracking device on your car. He's been ordered to cease immediately, but I was informed that you already had learned of the tracking device."

Devices, Lindsey wanted to amend. "For what purpose?"

"To put it bluntly, someone was trying to make a name for himself."

Lindsey wondered if she'd be dealing with people who wanted to impress Richard Melancon for the rest of her life.

"I apologize for not informing you sooner."

"Does he have a dark sedan?"

"Not to my knowledge. Hang on." She heard him cupping the phone with his hand.

Lindsey waited patiently. She didn't know if she liked having an association with the man against whom she had testified. It certainly wouldn't help her sleep at night—or maybe it would.

The gentleman cleared his throat. "Apparently he has a red Corvette."

Definitely not a stealth vehicle, Lindsey mused. "Thank you."

"You're welcome, and I promise not to bother you again."

I've heard that before. She held back her quip. "Good-bye."

"You okay?" Ruth Emery placed a hand on Lindsey's shoulder.

"Fine, just someone filling me in on who was tracking me."

"Tracking you? Oh my, the stalker the reporters were talking about. You definitely have to sit down and tell me what's been going on. I'll go fix us some hot cocoa. My grandmother's journal is in the living room on the coffee table. Go, sit down, and I'll bring out the cocoa in a couple of minutes."

Lindsey followed her hostess's instructions. The journal was not the same drab black leather as Jenna's or Beverly's. It was larger and had a feminine feel to the cloth binding. The musty scent of the pages was noticeably less distinct today than it had been a few days earlier. Lindsey began to read.

What am I hoping to find?

A link. Even though the handwriting appeared different in Jenna and Beverly's journals, the young police officer had said that Beverly could have had a hand injury. But Beverly's confession of having taken advantage of someone's death still didn't make sense.

She wanted to discover whether Ruth's take on Sylvia's feelings for Quincy was accurate, and how it felt for Sylvia to identify her friend's body. Quincy, a.k.a. Brad, should have identified his wife's body.

She turned a few more pages until she found one of the references that Ruth had noted. Sylvia had written: *I don't trust Quincy. I appreciate that he sold the cottage to us all those years ago, but it seemed like he did it out of duty. I don't know why after all these years I still don't trust him, but there he was tonight at dinner and sounding so pious.*

She wrote about the dinner party and all who attended. Naturally, Beverly had attended with Quincy. Her remarks for Beverly were kinder, commenting on her lovely gown and graceful manners. Lindsey read on.

"Beverly had taught Sylvia to read," Lindsey absent-mindedly commented.

"Yes. Apparently Beverly Ludlum and my grandmother, Sylvia, were very good friends. I recall her visiting once when I was little. She was a fine woman, very refined in how she presented herself, but she never seemed to look down her nose at anyone."

"Interesting. What else do you recall about Beverly?"

"Not much. Her daughter still lives at the Ludlum estate."

"Yes, I met her."

"Really? I didn't think she ventured out much these days. Oh well, she's a decent sort. Always friendly. Spent a lot of time with the arts. If I'm not mistaken, her husband was an artist. I don't recall what kind. My family never seemed to spend much time with theirs. Donald was ahead of me in school. Donald is Anna's son."

"I know." Lindsey sipped her hot cocoa to keep herself from revealing any of her personal feelings about the man.

"Heard he's running for office again. This will be the first time the cousins run opposing each other."

"Cousins?"

"Edgar Archer and Donald Scott are distant cousins. Edgar's great-grandfather was Quincy Ludlum's uncle."

Lindsey chuckled. "I meant to ask Anna about that."

"I imagine most folks don't know. They've always run at different times. Both have done well by the city. But the two families have never been close with each other."

Should be interesting to ask Edgar when I pay him a final visit. Lindsey glanced at her wristwatch and continued to thumb through Sylvia's journal.

She found the entry where Sylvia mentioned identifying Jenna's body. "Interesting," Lindsey mused. *The pieces are coming together.*

FEBRUARY 2, 1912 - METHUEN, MASS.

Jenna had never been so pleased to see Brad, and so terrified at the same time. She'd never seen a man so angry in all her life.

Blood dripped from his nose. "I'm so sorry, Jenna," his voice soothed. "I should have come home sooner." He unfastened the strap holding her to the bedpost.

Jenna cried. "It hurts."

"Don't look," he pleaded.

Jenna did. Her right hand contorted at an odd angle.

"I think it's broken," he supplied.

"It feels like it."

"I'm taking you to the hospital."

Jenna nodded.

"I'm so sorry, honey. I promise this will not happen again."

"How? He was ordered to kill me."

"What?"

Jenna went on to explain as Brad cradled her in his arms and carried her out to the car. "I can walk."

"Humor me." He kissed the top of her head. "I didn't get a good look at the guy, but I think I've seen him around."

"He's been watching us."

The small muscle over Brad's jaw twitched. "I'll take care of him."

She had no doubt of that. The drive to the hospital took a little time. The pain in her hand and shoulder were excruciating.

"Brad?"

"Huh?" He glanced over at her for a moment.

"I have some news. I hope you don't get too upset, but you need to know before we get to the hospital. We're going to have a baby."

"A baby?" His smile broadened. Then his eyebrows met at the center of his forehead. "Do you think . . . will the baby be okay?"

"I think so, but we need to tell the doctors."

"Of course, of course." He tossed his head from side to side. "A baby."

Jenna smiled through the pain. "Yes, our baby."

"You can't go back to the cottage, Jenna. It's not safe. We'll have to hide you somewhere else until we find the man who attacked you and put him behind bars."

"Brad, he knew you had to work late."

"What? How?" A moment passed. "My uncle." The same fury that Jenna had seen in Brad's eyes when he found her being attacked reared its ugly head. "I'll take care of it. You'll be safe, I promise you that."

Chapter Twenty-nine

"What did you find?" Ruth Emery set her mug of hot cocoa back on the coffee table.

"Your grandmother mentions the difficulty Beverly Ludlum had with her right hand."

"If memory serves," Ruth paused, "Mrs. Ludlum had arthritis in that hand."

"Actually your grandmother mentions an old injury. Let me read it to you." Lindsey scanned to find where to begin. "Beverly's been having trouble with her right hand again these days. It's hard to see a woman who had such beautiful penmanship write with such forced strokes."

The words of the police officer who had scanned Beverly's journal clicked into place. An injury had changed Jenna's beautiful handwriting into Beverly's awkward strokes. Someone else had died. It wasn't Jenna under that ice. But Sylvia had identified the body as Jenna. Why? So that the real Jenna could reappear as Beverly, married to her beloved Brad. A little late, perhaps, for the pregnancy, but married nevertheless. Lindsey nodded slowly. No doubt remained that Jenna Waverly was Beverly Ludlum. What else could explain the friendship between Sylvia, the former mill girl, and Beverly Ludlum, the wife of community leader Quincy Ludlum? But why keep the secret? It couldn't be just the social stigma, could it?

"I wonder if she wrote about how the hand was injured." Lindsey scrutinized the journal. Were the few remaining clues left in these pages? Or were they in Beverly's journal, which she hadn't yet had time to read beyond a few pages?

Ruth let out a nervous chuckle. "You really get intense when you're researching, don't you?"

Lindsey looked at herself. She was sitting on the edge of the sofa, hunched over the journal, examining and reexamining every entry, not to mention tapping her foot from the nervous excitement of putting together a possible clue from the past. "Afraid so," she admitted.

"If you'd like, I'll be more than happy to lend you my grandmother's journal. You can ship it back to me when you're through."

"Really?"

"Absolutely. I don't recall anything in there about how Mrs. Ludlum hurt her hand. I guess I simply skimmed over the parts that related to people I wasn't really interested in."

"I wonder if the hospitals have records of patients' care dating back that many years. It might be interesting to see if she'd been treated for anything."

"Historic hospital records? I've never heard of such a thing."

"There's always a first. But I doubt it. Who would have the room for all that paperwork, and where would they put it?" Lindsey commented, and placed her finger between the pages where she was currently reading.

"The hospital basements?" Ruth offered.

"Maybe. This was nearly a century ago, though. I'm sure some hospital administrator took care of the ancient records, but it's worth a call." Lindsey made a mental note to check. "If you really don't mind, I'd love to take this with me. After all that's happened, I'd like to get home."

Ruth nodded. "I understand. I can't imagine being away from Daniel for a couple of weeks. How does your husband handle it?"

"He's an understanding man. But the events of the past week have pushed him to the limits of his patience."

"Can't blame the poor man. The shooting made national headlines."

"I can't blame him at all." Lindsey slipped her finger out of the journal and closed it. "If you don't mind, then, I'll be on my way. I have two final visits I'd like to get in before I leave town."

"You're flying out tonight?" Ruth stood up.

Lindsey stood and cradled the journal in her arm. "If there's room on the last plane, I hope so. Otherwise, it'll be first thing in the morning."

"God bless you, and I hope you find what you're looking for in there."

"Thank you. You've been a tremendous help to me." Lindsey knew one of the credits for the novel would be to Ruth Emery and the buried treasure in her attic.

They said their good-byes and Lindsey debated whether to go on to Edgar Archer's or to the hospital for a visit with Detective Harris. She paused at the end of the driveway, undecided. Of course, a visit to the hospital could kill two birds at once. *Hospital it is.* She turned onto the road toward downtown.

Although the hospital dated back to 1875, Lindsey learned that the records of patients were kept for only thirty years before being destroyed.

The sound of various monitors recording patients' vital signs chirped and pinged as Lindsey traveled down the hallway toward Detective Harris's room. Two police officers stood guard outside his door.

"Identification please." The officer's rigid stance showed he meant business.

Lindsey pulled out her license and waited patiently for the officer to scrutinize the lousy picture. Then he examined the list of approved visitors. "Captain Pitts approved you, Mrs. Taylor. Go on in. He's been sleeping, but he wakes up every now and again, demanding to be released," the young officer chuckled.

She entered Detective Harris's room. "Hi."

"Hey, I think I owe you my life."

"Possibly." Lindsey took the vinyl chair to the left of his bed. "I had a couple of interesting calls that I thought you might like to be aware of."

"What's that?" He struggled to sit up.

"Stay down. I don't mind."

"All right." He flopped back down on the bed. "Tell me about these phone calls."

Lindsey filled him in about Richard Melancon's "associate" calling her. She also discovered that Captain Pitts had told the detective of her concern that he'd been the target—rather than her—in today's shooting.

"That sheds a different light on things. If they weren't aiming for you, that means someone was aiming for me."

"That's the same conclusion I came to. Which is why I wanted to share that tidbit with you, as well. I'm sorry if I blew your cover from that photograph."

"Don't be. I've been giving it a lot of thought. Someone at the station is probably on the take from Richard Melancon. It gives me an area to start looking into. Obviously, I'm no longer any good on the streets with regard to this case."

"Also, someone here was tracking me from Melancon's organization, which is interesting," Lindsey added.

Detective Harris rubbed the back of his neck. "Remind me, when did you first see that sedan following you?"

"After the break-in at the hotel, when I was heading up to my parents' to get away from the media." Lindsey thought back. "You know, I might have seen it before then. Oh, get this, the Melancon man drives a red Corvette."

Detective Harris bolted up. "A red Corvette?"

"You know the car?"

"I know one a little too close to this case." He tossed his legs over the side of the bed. "Can you grab my clothes from that closet for me? Thanks."

"Shouldn't you be resting?" Lindsey asked. "And who owns the red Corvette?"

FEBRUARY 2, 1912 - LAWRENCE, MASS.

Brad sat beside the hospital bed with his head bowed and his hands clasped. Jenna tried to lift her right arm. The pain, though dulled from medication, warned her to leave her arm where it was.

With tear-filled eyes, Brad glanced over. "I'm so sorry, honey. I promise this will never happen again."

"Brad, don't be silly. You had nothing to do with that attack."

He turned his head away. "You don't understand." His chest rose and fell with each breath he took. "I'll be back. You're safe now."

→ ←

Jenna glanced at the empty chair. "Where are you, Brad?" She felt so alone. All night she'd stayed in the hospital by herself. She had tried to read the Bible the nurse had given her. It fell open to Psalms and a verse about trusting God and not being afraid. "What can mortal man do to me?" she read.

A lot, Jenna thought. She wasn't sure which hurt more, her shoulder or her hand. The doctor had informed her he'd be releasing her this morning. Where would she go? Brad told her not to return to the cottage, and honestly she didn't want to. Her left hand flipped the pages of the Bible. It seemed like forever since she'd taken the time to read and meditate on God's word.

"Mrs. White?" A nurse approached, dressed in the traditional white dress, shoes, and stockings, with a white apron that appeared to be part of her uniform. "Your husband left a message and made arrangements for you to continue your rest in the convalescent home for a couple of days."

"A couple of days?"

"Yes, he asked me to give you this." She handed Jenna a small white envelope.

"Thank you." Jenna's left hand shook as she fingered the sealed envelope.

"Would you like me to open it for you?" the nurse kindly offered.

"Yes, please. Thank you." The nurse opened the letter and pulled it out just far enough for Jenna to finish the job, giving her all the privacy she needed.

When the nurse left the room, Jenna opened the letter and began to read:

> My dear Jenna,
>
> I apologize for not being with you last night or even this morning. There is a lot for me to do, so please bear with me. I've made arrangements for you to stay in a convalescent home. I know you'll be safe and well cared for there. They know you as Mrs. White. Please play along for your own safety. I don't want that man to find you. I'm closing in on his trail, and I think I know who he is and who is responsible. Trust me. This will not happen again. Pray for me as I try to work everything out for our future.
>
> I'll see you as soon as possible.
>
> Love forever,
> Brad

Jenna folded the letter, mindlessly rubbing her fingers over the seam again and again. Who would be after her and why? The only person she could think of was Brad's uncle . . . *Oh no, Lord. Please protect Brad.*

Chapter Thirty

"Waylan Tompkins?" Lindsey couldn't believe it. "There's your connection."

Detective Harris beamed. "I do believe you're right. However, I'll need to do some groundwork to prove it. Like following up on the man's ancestry."

"He's a friend of your Captain Pitts."

"I know."

Lindsey handed him the bundle of clothes from the closet. "Are you sure you're ready to leave?"

"They can't stop me from signing out."

Lindsey motioned behind her. "But *they* can."

The detective glanced over at the two officers keeping watch. "They'll obey my orders."

"Tompkins would account for one of the tracking devices—probably the more sophisticated one if he was working for Melancon. But who else was tracking me? And who owns the dark sedan that's been following me? He still is, by the way. I did manage to get the first three digits of his license plate number, though."

Lindsey turned her back and faced the hallway while the detective changed into his street clothes.

"Write it down and I'll have someone run the numbers," Detective Harris said. "It's the least I can do to thank you for the Melancon family connection."

She went through her purse and wrote down the numbers on a sheet from a small spiral notebook.

"Are you heading for the airport now?"

"I have one more person I have to follow up on." *To find out why Edgar Archer lied about who Quincy Ludlum was.*

"What's the connection with your story? You can turn around now, I'm dressed."

Lindsey turned and faced him. "According to Ruth Emery, Quincy Ludlum was Edgar Archer's great-grandfather's nephew."

"Could be, I wouldn't know. They're practically neighbors, but you wouldn't know it because of how the road bends around the properties. There's a small river just past the Ludlum place that prevents you from traveling straight over to the Archer estate."

"I never would have realized that, and I've driven to both places twice."

"You have to travel two different roads to get to either house. The Ludlum home is newer. The Archer place was built sometime in the eighteen hundreds."

Detective Harris lost his footing. Lindsey reached out and steadied him. "I think you should stay down."

"Maybe you're right. Tomorrow might be soon enough to track down the Tompkins lead."

Lindsey summoned the two guards, and one came in to help the detective back to the bed. "Get your rest and thanks for the help," she said.

"No problem," Detective Harris waved with the folded paper in his hand.

→ ←

After grabbing a quick burger at a drive-thru, Lindsey headed back to Edgar Archer's house once again. On the way, she realized she wasn't sure why she was going. She knew the connection between the Archers and the Ludlums, but what did it matter in the scheme of things?

She pulled over to the side of the road and took a moment to pray. The desire to see Edgar increased. She put the car into gear and continued to the estate. She noted the small river that separated the Ludlums' property from the Archers'. *What else keeps these families apart? Is it simply that Brad's uncle never accepted Jenna as a part of his family? And why did she change her name to Beverly?*

Inside the drive, she noticed a dark sedan. She caught a glimpse of the license plate; the first three digits were the same. *What is this car doing at Edgar Archer's? I can't believe it!* She hesitated, then placed a call to the hospital and notified Detective Harris about the sedan.

"Don't go in. I'll have the captain send someone over right away."

Lindsey pulled out of the drive and waited across the street. Within ten minutes, a set of revolving blue lights appeared up the road, and a cruiser entered the Archers' estate. Lindsey was surprised to see Captain Pitts at the wheel.

"Captain?" she said, pulling up behind the police car and getting out.

"Afternoon, Mrs. Taylor. This is the car?" He pointed to the dark sedan.

"I believe so. The first three digits on the plate are the same."

"Let's confirm that now. I'm not going to confront an old friend without knowing for certain." The captain stomped over to the back end of the car.

Lindsey walked along the passenger side of the vehicle and stopped. "Captain, this isn't the same car as the one used by the man who shot Detective Harris."

"How do you know?"

"The car is the wrong color. This one is dark green. The one that shot Detective Harris was dark blue. I'm certain of that."

Captain Pitts nodded.

Lindsey joined him at the rear of the car. "These are the same first three digits as the car that was following me. I wasn't able to get the last three."

"That's good enough. Come on. Let's go talk to Edgar."

The captain rang the doorbell and plastered a political smile on his face when Edgar opened it. "Harold, good to see you. Come on in. Mrs. Taylor, what brings you back?"

"A few more questions, if you don't mind." Lindsey smiled.

The captain no longer minced words. He stepped into the front parlor and shot from the hip. "Who owns the car, Edgar?"

"Uh," Edgar stuttered.

"You are aware that it is the same car that's been following Mrs. Taylor?"

Edgar paled. "Do I need to call my attorney?"

"Depends on what you've done. But stalking isn't looked on any too kindly. I'd appreciate it, friend to friend, if you'd be straight with me and Mrs. Taylor and not go hiding behind the coattails of an attorney."

"Let's go sit down."

Unlike the previous visit, Edgar led them to his study on the first floor. "Have a seat." He sat behind his desk, opened a crystal candy dish and silently offered a piece to his guests, then took one for himself. "I hired Bruce Hurd to follow Mrs. Taylor to see if she might have uncovered anything relevant to my family's history in the area. I never intended to have her feel insecure or like she was being stalked, as you put it. Obviously, Mr. Hurd isn't a very good private detective." The cellophane wrapper of the hard candy crinkled as he unwrapped it. "I do apologize, Mrs. Taylor, for any inconvenience that Mr. Hurd has caused you while under my employ."

Lindsey thought back on all the feelings of anguish and concern she felt over the past few days. "I don't understand why you hired him. Why not simply ask me what I had found? You've been less than honest with me. When you found those letters to Quincy Ludlum, you knew exactly who he was, didn't you?"

Edgar cleared his throat. "Yes. But I didn't say I didn't. Remember, my wife said she didn't, and that was a truthful statement."

"Why weren't you straight with me about him being your great-grandfather's nephew?" Lindsey asked. By not speaking the truth, he had conspired in the deception. *Just like a politician.*

"I have nothing to hide, Mrs. Taylor. Mr. Hurd told me that you have tracked down the Ludlum descendants, so I think I might as well give you my family's version of the story."

Lindsey wasn't about to tell him that she didn't know the story, just bits and pieces, and that most of that was guesswork.

"During the strike," he continued, "Quincy Ludlum lived with my great-grandfather, who was helping him get established in the business world. But Quincy seemed to have a problem understanding which people he should and should not associate with." Edgar pushed himself away from his desk, stood up, and began pacing back and forth.

"My great-grandfather, Phineas Archer, discovered Quincy had taken up with a worker from the mills and had set her up in a cottage. At first he didn't think much of it, young men being what they are and all. But then Quincy began to hint that he'd like to get married one day, and my great-grandfather couldn't understand why a man would have to marry a woman from a low social standing. Quincy didn't know that Phineas was fully aware of his behavior and had sent a man to get rid of Quincy's problem."

Captain Pitts interrupted. "Get rid of, as in, put a hit out on her?"

"Yes. It is something that my great-grandfather always regretted. But once the woman had been disposed of, there was little he could do to amend it, except for a gift of land that he gave to Quincy, the ten acres to the south of this property. Great-grandfather confessed this shortly before his death. He told my father. As you know, my grandfather died in World War II, a couple of years after my father was born. My father told me the story a few years before he died. Needless to say, it's something we've been trying to keep from the media." Edgar turned and looked at Lindsey. "Or from historical fiction writers with a desire to be accurate." He shrugged.

"I can't arrest a man for murder after he's dead." Captain Pitts shrugged. "Why all the secrecy?"

"Politics. Harold, you know as well as I the kind of mileage this information would get in the media." Edgar sat back down, this time taking a seat beside the captain.

"How would tracking me keep you informed of what information I had or didn't have?" Lindsey asked.

"Excuse me, just a moment." Edgar exited the room and returned a minute later with the man he'd hired to follow her. He had brown hair, and a receding hairline, as well as a sagging waistline.

"Hello, Mrs. Taylor. May I see your purse?" Lindsey handed him her purse. The middle-aged man rummaged through and pulled out a pen. "This transmits over just enough distance for me to have caught some of your conversations, including part of your interchange with Donald Scott earlier this morning. I was stunned to hear he stole your computer."

Captain Pitts faced her. "Did you report this?"

"Afraid I haven't had a chance. He returned it to me with nothing damaged. He too was looking to see if I had uncovered his family secret."

"Just how many skeletons do we have in this family closet?" Pitts asked.

"A couple more," Lindsey added. "Edgar, would you invite Donald and Anna Scott to join us? Let them know this meeting isn't optional." Lindsey had the pieces she needed.

"I'll make the call," Captain Pitts said. He stood up and walked over to Edgar's desk.

Edgar scrutinized Lindsey. "You know something else, don't you?"

"Perhaps."

FEBRUARY 4, 1912 ~ LAWRENCE, MASS.

"Jenna!" Brad marched into the room with his arms open wide. "I've missed you so much, honey. I'm so sorry this took so long."

"Where have you been, Brad?" His beard had several days' growth.

"I tracked down the man who attacked you."

"What?" Jenna pushed back from his embrace.

"Trust me. I've worked things out so he'll not be a problem to us again. Sit down and I'll explain."

Brad told how he'd suspected that his uncle had been behind the attack. "The man my uncle hired to get rid of you didn't mind taking my money and leaving town. My uncle now believes you are dead.

"Here's what I've worked out with my parents. I'm sending you to Martha's Vineyard. I'll be there in a week or two. I'll convince my uncle that I need to go home for a leave of absence, and with the strike there's not a lot to do anyway. He won't like it, but he'll let me go. I'm also going to let him know that I know he sent a man to kill you.

"Here's the hard part, Jenna. We need to change your name and get married again, with your new name, on the Vineyard. The lawyer told me it would take a couple weeks for your name to be legally changed and, since it is happening on the Vineyard, my uncle will be none the wiser. We'll return to Lawrence as husband and wife. My uncle never met you. He doesn't know what you look like, and I don't trust him. If he can be angry enough to send someone to get rid of you, then there is no telling what he can do."

"He should be arrested."

"Yes, but he'd have to know you didn't die if we pressed charges. And while I don't appreciate too much about the man, you weren't killed. Besides, I think he'd get off. He's too political and well connected to be convicted of any real crime."

Jenna knew it was true. "But I don't want to change my name. I like it."

"I like it too. But it's something we must do for you and for the life of our child. I can't risk losing you, Jenna. Changing your name is little sacrifice compared to that. The fact that I went home at Christmas time, and your being pregnant, will play well with the need for a quick wedding. My uncle will not question it, I hope."

Jenna's mind swirled. Admittedly, she had thought his uncle had been at the heart of their problem, and if he could send someone to get rid of her once, he could do it again. "All right. I'll do whatever you think is best."

Brad smiled. "That's my girl. My parents are anxious to meet you. They're very excited about the baby. I can't say I blame them. I'm pretty excited myself. How are your arm and hand?"

"The locations of the breaks in the wrist and hand have the doctor wondering if I'll be able to do fine, detailed work. I'll be able to use it, but things like needlepoint and penmanship will probably suffer."

"I can't tell you how hard it was to see you being attacked like that. I felt a rage I've never felt before. My uncle believes I'm upset over losing you, but it's him I'm furious with. My mother said she never would have believed her brother capable of such behavior, but she hasn't really spent any time with him in the past forty years."

"How old are you parents?"

"They're in their sixties. I was born later in their lives."

"I'm scared, Brad."

He wrapped her in a protective embrace. "Don't be. As soon as possible, I'll find a way to fully convince my uncle that you're dead. Just trust me, okay?"

Jenna nodded.

"What's my new name?"

Chapter Thirty-one

Lindsey composed her thoughts while the three men discussed the past week's activities. She still didn't know if she should press charges against Edgar or not. Currently, the thought of coming back to Lawrence for trial held no appeal.

Forty minutes later, Donald and Anna Scott came into Edgar's office.

"I believe everyone here knows everyone else, except for Mr. Hurd," Edgar said. "I hired him to follow Mrs. Taylor while she was in the area researching her book."

Anna Ludlum Scott sat with her back rigid, her white hair finely groomed, and the lines on her face showing her worries at hearing who Mr. Hurd was.

"Edgar, would you please excuse Mr. Hurd from this meeting?" Lindsey asked.

Edgar nodded, and Mr. Hurd left the room.

"Captain," Lindsey said, "I'll holler if my life is threatened. But I think what I'm about to share may need to stay private, at least until I write my novel." She winked.

Captain Pitts grinned with understanding and left the room.

The three remaining individuals stared at her. "Donald, you told me this morning that if I found out information that might be relevant to your family secret, you'd be honest with me, correct?"

"Yes," he admitted.

Lindsey took in a deep breath and began. "Edgar admitted that his great-grandfather hired someone to kill Quincy Ludlum's lover during the time of the strike." Lindsey watched Donald's reaction. The corners of his mouth barely twitched. "What Edgar and his great-grandfather didn't know was that Quincy's lover was his wife, Jenna Waverly, also known as Beverly Ludlum, his second wife."

"What? My great-grandfather died believing he was responsible for a woman's death, and she wasn't dead?" Edgar's temper rose.

"Quincy couldn't trust his uncle," Donald countered.

"But my great-grandfather gave him the land. Quincy knew the woman wasn't dead, yet he still took the land? He's no better than my great-grandfather."

Donald's face reddened. "I beg to differ with you, Edgar. Quincy was protecting his wife and his unborn child."

Anna looked down at her lap.

"The very least your grandfather could have done was let the dying man know his carnal sin had never happened." Edgar looked away in contempt.

Donald turned to address Lindsey. "Mrs. Taylor, as I said earlier, I wasn't aware of my grandmother's name change. What I did know was that Quincy was plagued with remorse after his uncle died. He regretted not telling his uncle the full truth. All these years, I thought it was only that he gained the land in an unethical manner. Yesterday, Mother explained about her mother's deathbed confession."

He rubbed his hands on his knees. "Mrs. Taylor, this is a deep family disgrace. Quincy trusted me not to tell anyone. I have the records of Quincy's payments to his uncle for the land. At first he accepted the property. It was a ninety-nine year lease. Then his own guilt over his deception wouldn't allow him to just keep the land, so he paid fair market value for the property at the time."

"I knew about the lease," Edgar admitted, "but I wasn't told that Quincy purchased the land. In fact, I have papers stipulating that I, or someone in the family, am to inherit the land again in 2012."

"Precisely why my grandfather saved the receipts and paperwork. He never trusted his uncle and feared something like this would happen to his descendants," Donald admitted.

"I'll need to see that paperwork."

"I'll send copies over to you tomorrow."

"Thank you." Edgar took in a deep breath.

Lindsey realized that Edgar had plans for that land, and they didn't include keeping the property in the hands of the Ludlum family.

Anna's eyes were filled with tears. "All those wasted years. So many lies, so little trust." She glanced up at Lindsey. "What else did you uncover about my mother's real past?"

Lindsey filled in what she knew about Jenna and the small cottage in Methuen.

"If Jenna Waverly didn't die in the river, who did?" Edgar asked.

"I found the answer to that in Sylvia's journal. Apparently, it was one of the mill workers who had been quite sick before the strike, and who had little to eat and died in her sleep. Sylvia knew about Brad's plans to change Jenna's name, so together they took advantage of the poor woman's death. They slipped her into the river, just north of the underwater gates. This allowed for someone to find the body in short order, and Sylvia could identify her as Jenna the following morning. If I'm not mistaken, her name was Donna Rose, but Sylvia doesn't spell it out. She drew a rose in the margin of the journal with the name Donna underneath it. It's purely speculative on my part but—" *and why hadn't anyone noticed Donna missing?*

Anna interrupted. "Mother did mention a Donna."

"I'll look into it further." Lindsey glanced around the room at the three individuals—all related and all unwilling to admit that both families had been wronged by each other.

"Are you going to expose this in your novel?" Donald asked.

"I haven't decided." That was the truth, but the story was too compelling to just walk away from.

Edgar stood up. "Obviously, none of us has the right to ask you not to use this material. However, if it is at all possible, would you be willing to change the names, protect those of us who are still living in this town and trying to run for political office?" He looked over to Donald, then back to Lindsey.

"I'll pray about it and give it some thought. But you're right; none of you has the right to ask. You've put me through horrible hours of anguish. You've worried my family. You've stolen my property. You've stolen my privacy. And you"—she looked squarely at Anna—"abused a trust."

Lindsey strode over to the door. "I'm sorry. I'm generally more gracious and considerate. I'll see where the story takes me, and I promise I will pray about it."

She wouldn't write the story just to get back at them, however tempting that might be, but she wouldn't ignore the story either. Changing the names for their protection would only seem the right thing to do. She met Captain Pitts pacing in the hall. "Hurd's left," he informed her.

"Good, I don't think I have the stomach to face him at the moment. Thank you for all your help, Captain." Lindsey continued to walk toward the front door.

"Mrs. Taylor, for what it's worth, Lawrence doesn't generally have these kinds of problems. I hope you'll want to come back and visit our fair city once again."

"At this point, I just want to drive down to Logan and catch a flight home to Miami. But I'll take your recommendation under consideration. Forgive me, I'd like to get on the road before rush hour."

"I understand, and again, I offer my apologies. If you decide to press charges, don't hesitate to contact me." Captain Pitts tipped his police cap. "Good-bye, Lindsey."

"I will, and thank you. God bless you. You certainly have your hands full." Lindsey exited the Archer estate and noticed that Mr. Hurd's sedan no longer took up space in the driveway. "Lord, get me home on the next available flight, please," she prayed. Slipping behind the steering wheel, she turned the key, fastened her seat belt, and prayed to miss rush hour.

Her cell phone rang. Jeff's name appeared on the small screen. A smile eased up her cheek. "Hi, son. What's up?"

"Lisa and I are. Where are you?"

"I'm heading to the airport to return home."

"Great, we'll meet you there. Who did you rent the car from?"

She told him, then asked, "You drove up from school?"

"Yup. When they started shooting at you, and you wouldn't let Dad come, Lisa and I borrowed her parents' RV and drove up. We'll take you home to Miami."

Lindsey chuckled. "Flying is a lot less time-consuming."

"Yeah, but the media will be watching for you. You're big news right now, Mom. I'm sure you don't realize half of what's been on the TV. This way, no one will know where you are for a couple of days, and the media will be onto the next big story."

"You're absolutely crazy."

"Yup, but I come by it honestly. See you in an hour or two. Love ya."

"Love you too." Lindsey pushed the end button, then punched in Marc's number. *Why hadn't he filled her in?*

FEBRUARY 10, 1912 ~ LAWRENCE, MASS.

Sylvia bit down on her inner cheek. It was a stupid idea to pass Donna off as Jenna, but Brad had made a convincing case. Brad allowed Sylvia and Donna to live in the cottage after he'd taken Jenna to the hospital. Sylvia liked the cottage, but Donna had been too sick, even with all of Sylvia's best efforts. Thankfully, Jenna was safe on the Vineyard, and this lie would protect her.

Though she might not trust Brad, she had to respect him for trying to keep Jenna safe. It seemed a bit far-fetched that someone was trying to kill Jenna, but why would Brad lie?

"This way, miss." A man dressed in a white lab coat led her down the gray painted cinder block corridor.

Sylvia straightened her shoulders. If she was going to convince the authorities that Jenna was dead, now was the time. What about Donna's family? Won't someone care? Won't someone want to know? Then Sylvia reminded herself that Donna had no one. Her family was dead or had scattered while she was still very young. Donna had grown up in the mills. She'd worked changing spools since she was seven, and in the past few years, she'd become skilled on the looms.

Brad was right; this was the only way to keep the person who was trying to kill Jenna permanently fooled.

The attendant snapped on the light. The naked bulbs hanging from the ceiling flickered, then shone brightly on the sparse room. There was a tall, narrow table but no chairs, a hospital bed on wheels, and a stretcher with a body on it, covered with a white sheet. Gooseflesh rose on Sylvia's arms. It had been hard enough to sneak Brad into the house and watch him wrap Donna's lifeless body in a sheet, then carry her silently out of the house in the middle of the night. She couldn't watch as he placed her body into the river. Sylvia knew that Donna was dead, but it still didn't feel right to just dump her there. Wouldn't it have been easier to simply call the police and tell them the woman who had died in her sleep was Jenna?

Brad had a reason against that. And thinking about it once again, Sylvia realized he was right. The police would have questioned the other girls, and you couldn't count on ten women keeping the story straight.

"Are you all right, miss?"

"Yes." Sylvia clutched her purse with both hands, hoping it would help calm her nerves.

The attendant motioned for her to come over to the stretcher, then slowly raised the white sheet off of the deceased person's head. "Is this your friend?"

Sylvia nodded. Her stomach revolted, and she covered her mouth with her hand.

The attendant covered Donna's face. "I'm sorry," he offered his condolences. "Are you all right? I have some salts if you need it."

"I'm fine," she lied. But what was one more lie in the grand scheme of things? And she hadn't quite lied to the attendant. Donna had been her friend too. *Stop justifying. You're lying. You know it, and God knows it.*

"God bless you, Donna. You've given your life for a friend, and you don't even know it," Sylvia whispered, then tried to regain her legs. "Lord, we're fighting for bread and roses. Please give Donna both in her mansion in heaven."

"Sylvia . . ." James Donovan came running down the hall. "I just heard the news. Who's gone?"

"Jenna," she answered. *And Donna,* she said to herself.

"I'm so sorry, my darlin'. What can I do for ya?"

"Hold me."

James wrapped his strong arm around her. "I love ya, lass. I have for years."

"Just keep holding me."

"Aye, it be my pleasure."

Sylvia chuckled, then sobered. "I'll need to tell you a secret, but we'll not be able to speak of it again, except in private."

"Aye, all in good time, me love, all in good time. I'll take you to the undertaker's and we'll make arrangements for Jenna."

"Thank you."

Chapter Thirty-two

Lindsey woke when the RV came to a halt. "Where are we?"

Jeff called back. "We're in New Jersey. We thought we'd stop for a late dinner. Are you hungry?"

"Famished." Lindsey smoothed the wrinkles from her clothing and exited the back room of the large RV. "Can you drive this, Lisa?"

"Only on the highways. I don't trust myself around corners or in narrow streets." She winked at Jeff.

"It's really not that difficult, Mom, once you get used to the size of it," Jeff added.

"If you don't mind, I prefer not to try my hand at the wheel." She clapped her hands together. "So, where did you stop to eat?" Lindsey glanced out the window, "Fast food?"

"No. On the other side is a sit-down restaurant with a nice variety of menu choices. Besides, there's something on the menu I think you'll enjoy."

Lisa giggled.

"What's going on?"

"You'll see." Jeff took ahold of her elbow and escorted her to the door. "Your dinner awaits."

Lindsey exited the RV, followed by Lisa with Jeff taking up the rear. The smell of grilled steak filled the air. "Yum, smells great."

"I thought you'd approve."

Lindsey knew the kids were up to something, but for the life of

her she couldn't figure it out. It felt wonderful to have slept without worrying about a single thing. The bed was comfortable, and the gentle rocking of the RV had helped her fall asleep. The only thing better would have been a nice Jacuzzi, but you can't have everything in a RV.

The plan that Marc and the kids arranged for her trip home made sense. She didn't like waiting three days to see Marc, but she'd also had enough of the media.

"I should call your father before we eat." Lindsey hesitated before entering the building. Its large wood frame and the thick smell of an open fire grill told Lindsey she'd be enjoying her meal.

"No problem," Jeff said as a large semi passed by. "But you might want to wait until we get inside. It's pretty noisy out here."

"You're probably right." Jeff held the door open. Lindsey smiled in appreciation. He'd learned his manners on how to treat a lady. A mother couldn't be more proud.

"Reservation for Taylor."

"Come this way, your party is here."

"Party?" Lindsey questioned, but followed the host. Her heart skipped when she saw Marc's handsome face. He stood up and opened his arms. She nearly leaped the length of the restaurant to be in his embrace. He held her tight. She held him tighter. "You're a nut, but I love you for doing this."

"I love you too." He kissed her lightly on the lips, then turned toward their son, "How was your trip?"

"A little tricky driving that rig through inner Boston, but we made it just fine."

"Good to see you, Lisa." Marc held Lindsey with his right arm and reached out to Lisa with his left and gave her a light kiss on the cheek. "Do thank your father for me."

"Daddy said he was happy to help, and we can have it for as long as we like."

"When did you start planning this?" Lindsey slipped out of her husband's embrace but continued to hold his hand.

"When someone shot at you. At first, I was just going to camp out up there until it was safe to pick you up from the safe house. But I needed to get the boys out of harm's way, just in case Melancon was a part of this. So I sent Jeff up to his future in-laws', and I picked up Justin. I'm sorry, honey, but no matter how much you protested, I was coming. I simply didn't tell you any more so you couldn't argue with me." Marc sat down on the chair beside Lindsey. Jeff held the chair out for Lisa. "So, we shifted our plans and decided to give you a much deserved vacation. I know how much you wanted to get right home, but the reporters immediately staked out the house."

Justin walked toward the table. "Hey, Mom, you finally made it." His smile, so much like his father's, lit up her heart.

Lindsey stood up and embraced her youngest son. "It's good to see you, Justin." She squeezed him and gave him a kiss on the cheek.

"I love you too, Mom. Do you think maybe you could stop getting into so much trouble?"

Lindsey chuckled. "I'll try."

"Yeah right," Justin quipped.

The table broke out in laughter. It was good to be with her family again. Then she noticed two empty chairs were still at the table. "Are we expecting more?"

"Possibly. Grandpa doesn't drive as fast as he used to," Justin chimed in.

"My parents or yours?" She turned to her husband for the answer.

"Yours, of course. They've been worried and calling me several times each day. They didn't bother to call you, because they didn't want you worrying that they were concerned. They figured you had enough going on."

Lindsey shook her head. "As scary as it got, I never quite lost myself to the fear. God gave me an incredible peace. He also gave me several verses to pray over when the stress level was high. One was Psalm 56. Verse four stood out especially: 'In God, whose word I praise, in God I trust; I will not be afraid. What can mortal man do to me?'"

She sat back and looked around the table at her family. "I was never in as much trouble as David when he wrote this psalm, and yet he had God's peace." She shook her head. "I think it was harder for all of you, not knowing. With me, I was in the center of it and keeping very busy finishing the research."

"Are you finished?" Marc asked.

"Yup, and I even figured out who the woman in the river was. In the process, I unearthed a couple of painful family secrets of two different politicians running for the same office."

Marc guffawed. "That's my Lins."

Lisa's eyes widened. "You do this all the time, don't you?"

Jeff and Justin looked at each other and shrugged their shoulders. Jeff turned to Lisa and answered her. "Honey, you'll get used to it. We couldn't get away with anything as kids, could we, Justin?"

"Nope. The woman has eyes in the back of her head." Justin reached for a breadstick. "I'm starved. When are we going to order?"

Marc signaled for a waiter. Everyone placed their orders, and Lindsey leaned closer to her husband. "Thank you. I needed this."

"So did we, honey. So did we."

"Where are we going?" Lindsey asked.

"Lisa has to be back at school in two days. So we thought we'd drop her off, then travel on down to Savannah," Jeff answered.

"Oh-h-h, I've always wanted to spend some time in the historic part of that city."

"We know," the voices around the table said in unison.

Lindsey laughed and fired off a silent prayer of thanks.